# BROWN, GHOST HUNTING DOG

## A COLLECTION OF TALES

# J.A. Campbell

For Jeff &
Ash
Watch out
for ghosts!
3-19-17

# Brown, Ghost Hunting Dog
A Collection of Tales

First Inkwolf Press Publication / December 2014

ISBN: 978-0692316122


Published by Inkwolf Press
P.O. Box 251
Severance, Colorado
80546-0251

www.inkwolfpress.com
www.writerjacampbell.com


PRODUCED IN THE UNITED STATES OF AMERICA

10 9 8 7 6 5 4 3 2 1

# Dedication

For Kira, my inspiration.
And for my Irish Sailor, who helps me take care of my
inspiration, and all the other things.

# Author's Note and Acknowledgements

All of these stories except for "Brown and the End of the Line" and "Elliott Heads Up Sheep Creek Without a Border Collie," have appeared previously in various anthologies. Also, I'm aware that Pluto wasn't discovered and named Pluto during the timeframe in which these stories occur. Who knows what the Plutonians call themselves, however. If you want to read more about Luke Tolbert, Scoot and De's adventures, check out Science Fiction Trails 11.

I want to thank David B. Riley for inviting me to submit a story to the Gunslingers and Ghost Stories anthology, which in turn gave me the idea for Brown and Elliott and their ghost hunting ways. I also want to thank him for jokingly asking me how the Brown vs. the Martians story was coming along...It came along just fine and I'm glad you enjoyed it. I wasn't actually intending to write a story about Martians, but those magic words triggered a really fun story idea.

Thank you to Sam Knight for editing almost every one of these stories and for all your wonderful comments. Thank you to my line editor Bridget Connors. Mistakes are, of course, mine. Thank you to Sean Hayden for the most excellent cover, and everything else you've done to help me with this project. Thank you to Shoshanah Holl and Kimberly Carmen for helping me come up with all the clever titles. The non-clever ones, well, those were all me.

Thank you readers, for without you, these stories wouldn't have been written.

The idea for Brown came about, as I said above, from an anthology invite. However, the story starts with a dog named Doc. Back in 2010, at the urging of a good author friend of mine, Devin O'Branagan, I wrote a short story about a vampire hunting dog. This story was so popular that I wrote more and self-published a small novella which, in turn, led me to meeting David B. Riley, which led to the anthology invite, and, you know...history was made. Just before the fated anthology invite, I'd discovered the weird western genre and was toying with the idea of an old west version of Doc, but I wasn't sure what I wanted to write, and when I got invited to write an old west ghost story, well, the result is in your hands. I do hope you enjoy reading these stories as much as I've enjoyed writing them.

# Table of Contents

# BROWN AND THE SALOON OF DOOM

*Miller, Colorado, 1900*

I sat on the front bench of our wagon, watching as the empty prairie gave way to a river valley. The dry dusty smell of the grasslands slowly changed to the wetter smells of the river and the sharp scent of pine. Mountains filled the sky ahead of us.

We traveled to Miller, Colorado. They had a ghost problem and I was the dog for the job. Of course, I'd never actually seen a ghost, but I'd been hunting them for over a year. My human said we were famous. People wrote to him and we went and fixed their problems. Sometimes we found the problems and the humans paid us to fix them. Sometimes we snuck away in the night. My human called those bad jobs.

"Only one river crossing, Brown, then we'll stop for the night."

I barked once and rested my muzzle on my paws.

"We'll be there tomorrow, and this time..." My human looked over his shoulder at me. "This time we'll make enough to settle down. I promise I'll get sheep."

I perked my ears forward and caught his gaze with my own.

11

He ruffled my ears. "Promise."

"I've heard you fine ladies and gentlemen have a ghost problem," my human said to the gathered crowd. He stood on the bench of our wagon. I sat next to him, sitting like a human, balanced on my hind end with my paws tucked under my chin.

A few of the children pointed at me and smiled. The adults looked scared. That wasn't uncommon. Humans were afraid of ghosts. I couldn't figure out why.

"Well, fear no longer! We are here to help. I learned to hunt ghosts at the finest universities back east and my fearless assistant Brown has never been defeated." He opened his arms wide.

I took a bow. A few people clapped.

"You sure you fight ghosts? This 'un is a mean 'un," someone in the crowd shouted.

"Of course, fine sir. Brown caught one herself just last week. It's that Border Collie Eye..."

I didn't remember that ghost, but I barked once in agreement anyway. That got a few more claps.

"If the individual who summoned me would step forward, I'd like to get to work right away. The sooner we dispatch the foul creature, the sooner you gentlefolks can get back to your lives."

The sheriff stepped forward and touched the brim of his hat. "That'd be me, Mr. Gyles."

My human's scent changed slightly to sour nervousness.

"Nice to meet you." My human jumped down from the bench and held out his hand to the sheriff.

"Luke Tolbert." The sheriff smelled of horses, gun oil, and dog. A star shone from his vest, and unlike Elliott, he had a wide brimmed hat on his head. Elliott's hat was round and didn't have much of a brim. His hair was darker and shorter than Elliott's. He had a kind smile when he looked at me.

"Let me grab my instruments and we'll take a look." Elliott grabbed his hunting bag.

I jumped off the seat and followed them down the street between rows of buildings. Unlike back home in the city, this street was quiet and mostly empty.

"Never seen a dog quite like yours. She really hunt ghosts?"

"Of course, Sheriff, and she works sheep. She's a Border Collie from the old country."

"Huh. Brown's not too original of a name for a brown and white dog."

Elliott shrugged.

I raised my hackles and growled when a local dog trotted over.

He was some sort of blue colored cattle dog. He wagged his tail but didn't invade my space.

"Hi. I heard that you're here 'bout our ghost."

"Yes."

"It's a bad 'un. Chased everyone outta the saloon every night last week." The dog looked around then whispered conspiratorially. "Even Willy, the town drunk. Had him swearing he'd give up the drink. Heard it from the Alley Cat."

I sniffed delicately. "Ghosts aren't dangerous. They just scare people."

The dog gave me a disbelieving look. He shook his whole body as if to rid himself of an itch. "If you say so. Got an old fish, says you're wrong."

I wrinkled my nose. "What would I want with an old fish?"

The cattle dog tilted his head. "City dog, ain't ya?"

I nodded.

"Well, you've been warned. Take care." He loped off before I could respond.

Elliott patted his leg and I hurried to his side. We stood outside a large two-level building. Several windows were broken and the strong reek of alcohol filled the air.

It stank and I sneezed.

Other scents drifted out of the building but I didn't know what they were. It almost smelled like the air after a strong spring rain—sharp, but instead of fresh the scent was musty. I sneezed again.

"You okay, Brown?"

I barked once and followed my human through the swinging doors.

"Holy Mother!"

I stopped and stared. My experiences with taverns and saloons were limited, but I knew they usually weren't this bad. The tables lay in pieces on the ground, more suited to fetch than anything else. Bottles littered the floor, most in pieces.

"What happened here?"

"The ghost."

I flattened my ears and whined. The weird after-rain musty smell was stronger in here.

My human sniffed. "Is that ozone? It smells like it, but also like a grave."

"You're the ghost hunter. You tell me," Tolbert drawled.

My human took a careful step inside. Glass crunched under his boot.

"Brown, stay out here. You don't want to cut yourself on the glass."

14

I flattened my ears and whined again, not wanting him to go in there alone, but I didn't want to cut my paws either. Elliott and Sheriff Tolbert stepped through the creaky doors.

"Are you the ghost hunter?"

I glanced up at a gray tabby cat that had perched itself on a rail above my head.

"Yes."

He sat and groomed himself for a moment before looking at me again. "Seems an odd profession for a dog. I've known cats who hunt ghosts, but never a dog."

"It's my Border Collie Eye."

"Oh?" The cat sounded bored. "And how does that work?"

I tried to think of an answer, because I didn't actually know. It had to be like working sheep though. "I catch them with my Eye. Then my human kills them." I tried to sound confident.

The cat sniffed. "How does your human kill something that's already dead?"

I tilted my head.

"You do know that ghosts are spirits right?"

"Spirits?"

"What is left over of the dead. Humans or animals that died badly. I think this ghost is an outlaw who was killed here last month. Sheriff Tolbert surprised him while he was drinking in the saloon. Rascal tried to get the drop on our Sheriff, but Tolbert was quicker." The cat stopped and groomed himself again, purring, obviously very pleased with his story.

"Are you the Sheriff's cat?"

The tabby sniffed. "Certainly not. I'm the Alley Cat."

"I see. Well, do you hunt ghosts?"

"Certainly not! I'm not an idiot."

15

I stared, not sure how to respond. The Alley Cat jumped off the railing and sauntered away.

"Best of luck! When the ghost kills you, I do hope you decide to move on. We don't need more ghosts around here."

I barked angrily, but the Alley Cat obviously wasn't concerned as he didn't even look at me. I lay down on the deck and sighed. Elliott said I knew how to hunt ghosts, but I didn't recall ever actually seeing one. If this Alley Cat knew more than I did, how was I supposed to do my job and help Elliott with the ghost?

"Don't let that old cat get you down." The cattle dog jumped up onto the porch.

I glanced at the saloon doors wishing my human would come back.

"I'm Scoot."

"Brown." I tried not to sound annoyed.

"Nice t'meet ya, Brown." We briefly sniffed noses then I went back to staring at the doors. He lay down next to me, apparently content to keep me company. I found I didn't mind.

"So the ghost mostly comes out in the evening?"

I perked up my ears when I heard my human's voice.

"Yep," the sheriff replied.

Glass crunched as they walked back toward us.

The musty-ozone smell grew stronger when Elliott and Sheriff Tolbert left the Saloon and stood on the porch next to us. I sniffed my human and sneezed. He was covered in the smell.

"Hi, Brown. Well, Sheriff. I'll go do a little research and tonight we'll hunt this ghost."

"Good day, Mr. Gyles." Tolbert shook my human's hand. "Come on, Scoot."

The cattle dog jumped off the stairs and followed Sheriff Tolbert down the dusty road.

16

"Well, Brown. Let's head back to the wagon."

I whined.

"Well, after lunch, and perhaps a bath. Sheriff Tolbert said we could stay at the inn, on the town. I intend to take advantage of that."

I thumped my tail on the ground at the mention of food. I wanted to tell him what the Alley Cat had told me but he never did understand when I tried to talk to him like I spoke to my fellow animals so I didn't try.

Elliott spent most of the day at the inn, 'relaxing after a long trip.' Then we made our way to the wagon, which, along with our horses, was at the livery. We climbed into the back and my human pulled down a book, the smelly old one he called his great-grand pappy's hunting Journal.

"I do wish these crazy old Scots knew how to write proper English," he muttered. "I can barely read this thing. His handwriting was very poor."

I lay at his feet while he muttered and grumbled over the book.

"It looks like we have a poltergeist. The restless and violent dead. Seems we either need a priest, and I believe we are fresh out, or some salt and an exorcism ritual. Or we need to burn the bones. One of those might work. What do you think, Brown?"

I whined, not at all happy with how uncertain he sounded.

"Let me see what I can learn. If I'm reading this right, great-grand pappy has the ritual in the back."

He went back to muttering to himself and flipping through pages.

"Well, Brown. I might have something here. Should impress the locals and might even stop a ghost if there really is one." He put his book down and dug around in one of the many chests in our wagon. "We need salt, frankincense, sage and some chalk to draw symbols. I should be able to draw this." He showed me a picture in his book. "Then chant the words, which hopefully don't require a Scottish brogue, and throw some salt water around and it should banish the ghost. Easy." He grinned.

I thumped my tail, hoping he was correct. He ruffled my ears.

"Okay, Brown, let's get to it." He put his supplies in his hunting bag, along with the book and his notes and we climbed out of the back of the wagon. I jumped around, happy to be able to stretch my legs.

The sheriff and Scoot walked down the street toward us, and feeling in a rare mood, I ran forward and sniffed noses with Scoot. The sheriff gave me a quick pat.

"Mr. Gyles."

"Sheriff."

"Thought about Brown's feet." He kicked the ground with his boots and smelled embarrassed. "Thought you might need her for your job, so I talked to some of the women, and they made up some moccasins for yer dog. Hard soles, glass shouldn't be a problem." He held up a small bundle.

Elliott smelled surprised. "That's very thoughtful. Let's try them on. Brown, come here."

"I'd laugh," Scoot said as my human put the moccasins on my feet and laced them up my legs. "Except, you're hunting the ghost, so I'll just be glad you won't cut your feet too."

I flattened my ears and picked my feet up high. "This feels very strange."

Scoot sniffed my feet and wagged his tail. "They look nice. They even put little bead crosses on them to keep you safe."

I looked. Scoot was right, small crosses decorated the top of each over my paw. They fit well and didn't chafe when I jumped around in them.

"I think I want a set." Scoot thumped his tail on the ground.

"Guess we're ready then," Elliott said.

"I cleared out the saloon early on account of the ghost. 'Course only the serious drinkers will even go in there. And I suspected you'd need some time to prepare."

"We have just the thing." My human patted the bag at his hip.

"Need any help?"

"No, thank you. We've got it covered."

"Alrighty, we'll let you get to it then." Tolbert tipped his hat and left. Scoot sniffed noses with me briefly than ran off.

"Let's go, Brown."

People stared as we walked confidently down the middle of the street toward the saloon. I put my tail up and raised my hackles as if I were facing down an unfriendly dog or a squirrel and hoped that the ghost wasn't as nasty as squirrels were. I flattened my ears at the thought.

The sun was almost down by the time we made it to the saloon. The bartender stood on the front porch and shook his head.

"God bless ya if ya can really banish this demon. God help ya, if ya can't. It's a bad 'un."

"Thank you, good sir." Elliott made a quick bow.

He stepped out of the way and I followed my human into the saloon. Alcohol smell almost covered the musty ozone smell and someone had cleaned up most of the glass.

19

I sniffed the air, and guessing that we'd want the room with the strongest musty ozone smell, I followed the scent up the stairs.

"Brown, do you smell the ghost?"

I barked once.

"Good." My human sounded a little nervous but he followed closely.

The saloon was open on the main floor with a few backrooms and the bar. The upstairs looked out over the main floor and had many rooms to sleep in. Elliott and I never stayed in saloons. He preferred respectable establishments or the wagon. I didn't care as long as Elliott was there.

The musty ozone smell was strongest from the corner room. It was a bit larger than the others I'd looked into and it was obvious no one had slept in there for a while. The bed was smashed much like the tables downstairs and I had to resist the urge to bring Elliott a stick. I stuck to the job and scratched at the floor where the smell was strongest. I thought I smelled old blood, too, but I wasn't sure. It was hard to tell with all the musty ozone in the air.

"This it, Brown?"

I barked.

"Good girl."

I thumped my tail and grinned at him.

"Okay, I'll get to work. Watch for the ghost."

I thumped the ground one more time and looked around for the ghost while Elliott drew on the floor and laid out his tools. I wasn't sure what I was looking for, and I got up and sniffed around the room. It didn't seem like anything was there, but suddenly the musty ozone smell got stronger. I sneezed.

"Brown?"

I looked around frantically but the smell seemed to come from everywhere. A slight wind ruffled across my back. My hackles rose and I growled, warning the ghost I was ready for it.

Elliott hastily finished his drawing and lit the incense. The spicy smells conflicted with the musty ozone and I tried not to sneeze again.

"Show yourself, Demon!" Elliott shouted.

The wind strengthened, whipping around the room and flapping the curtains. I noticed that the smoke from the incense didn't waver but everything else, including my ears, flapped in the strong wind. I looked around for the ghost so I could try and kill it.

A low howl built around us seeming to come from everywhere. I barked at my human, hoping he'd do something, except stare and smell scared. That got his attention. He focused on the book in his hand and started chanting. I didn't understand the words, but the low howl built to a high-pitched scream that made my teeth hurt. It drowned out his words until Elliott shouted to be heard.

The wind began to swirl like a dust devil in the middle of the room, just in front of Elliott's picture on the floor. I stared at it and crouched, as if it were a sheep.

The wind-devil slowly opened two eyes that stayed steady despite the spinning cyclone.

Elliott faltered in his chant and I barked, urging him to keep going.

The ghost's eyes floated around to look at me.

I growled.

It laughed and the remaining bits of glass in the windows shattered and fell to the ground.

I barked to tell it I wasn't afraid and it moved toward me. I gave it my best stare, catching its eyes with my own. I sensed the ghost's surprise as it tried to look away and couldn't.

I pushed it back, creeping forward slowly and never breaking eye contact. Elliott's chanting grew louder and more confident as the ghost gave to my will. The wind in the room died, though the wind-devil remained strong.

Every other noise went quiet except for Elliott's chant. The ghost strained against me, but I was stronger and held it still.

Elliott shouted his last words then everything went silent. The ghost's wind-devil stilled and seemed to disappear until all that remained was its eyes—locked to mine.

I wondered if I should let it go so it could vanish like the rest of its wind when something screamed so high pitched that my whole body ached. I wanted to run badly, but I had to hold the ghost.

"Brown!"

Something slammed into my side, sending me flying across the room and breaking my hold on the ghost. I slid through my human's drawings, scattered the incense, and yelped when I hit his feet and he fell on me.

I scrambled out from underneath him and jumped to my feet. The wind-devil had returned and, though it avoided my eyes, it laughed. Another wind-devil whirled next to the first one, glaring at me. I barked in alarm.

My human groaned and got to his feet just in time for the first ghost to slam into him, and send him flying back through the doors. The railing on the balcony caught him and kept him from crashing to the saloon floor below.

I growled at the ghosts, crouching and trying to catch them with my Eye. They avoided me though, and the first one tried to go after my human again. I snarled and leapt at the wind-devil. It screamed when my feet hit it and I fell through something that felt like cold, wet cow-pies, except it wasn't nearly as wonderful as when I rolled in them.

My ears hurt from ghost's scream and I hit the ground badly and fell. The ground was much closer when I'd jumped. I thought maybe the ghost had tried to lift me when I'd jumped through it, but I didn't know. The whirl had gone out of its wind and it was again just a pair of eyes, glaring at me.

I shook trying to get rid of the ozone smelling stuff cling to my fur. It landed around me with thick splats.

Elliott finally made it to his feet. He clutched his hand to his chest and stared, horrified, at the floating eyes. The other ghost screamed and flew toward me.

"Back, foul creature!" Elliott yelled and flung something at the ghost.

It screamed again and disappeared.

"Huh." Elliott tossed another handful of stuff on the angry eyes and they vanished. "Salt. Guess it really does work."

I whined and came over to Elliott. He patted my ears then stared at his hand.

"What is that all over you." He knelt and touched my fur again. "That's disgusting."

I shook, splattering Elliott.

"Brown..."

I flattened my ears in apology.

"Shh, that's okay, sweetheart. My brave, brave girl. I saw what you did. Your Eye really does work on ghosts." He hugged me, nasty goo and all." Then he stood and gathered his supplies. "Come on. I think we're done for tonight. Hopefully, for good."

I followed happily, glad to leave the ghosts behind.

"What's all over your dog?" Tolbert said when we left the building.

We stopped.

"Ev'nin, Sheriff." Elliott sounded exhausted. "You didn't tell me there were two of them."

"There's only one. What'd you do, call another one?" He sounded angry.

"Of course not."

23

Scoot wagged his tail and tried to sniff my nose, but I wasn't in the mood to be friendly and wrinkled my lips, growling softly. He backed off.

"Looks like you're girlfriend isn't your girlfriend anymore," the Alley Cat said from a high spot on the porch railing. "And whatever do you have in your fur?"

Scoot sat and thumped his tail on the ground. "It smells like the ghost."

I sighed and glanced up at Elliott. He was arguing with the sheriff.

"Look. They vanished."

"You're sure they are gone?"

Before my human could reply something crashed inside and I heard the second ghost's wail.

Sheriff Tolbert didn't say anything, simply crossed his arms and stared at Elliott.

"I'll try again tomorrow night. I need to get more supplies and wash Brown."

Something else shattered and we all winced.

"Damn ghost sounds like a Banshee."

"It could be," Elliott said. "Though hopefully no one is going to die."

"What?"

"Old legend of the Banshee is that it wails before someone will die. I think in this case it just hopes we will die."

"Best be right, Mr. Gyles. If you brought that here, and one of us dies, I'm holding you responsible." The sheriff turned and walked quickly away.

Scoot stood and shook. "Need any help tomorrow night?"

"No. Thank you. I'm a professional, and I work alone." Truthfully I didn't know how he could help, and I didn't want him to get hurt.

He looked hurt and ran off when the sheriff called him.

"Come on, Brown."

"Go home, Brown. Leave ghost hunting to the *real* professionals," the Alley Cat called as I left with my human. I didn't even bother to growl at him. Stupid cat anyway. What did he know.

"This stuff is nasty."

I suffered through the bath in silence. Elliott had to put salt in the water to get what he was calling ghost slime off of me. Then he had to bathe me again to get the salty water off. I hated baths. They weren't nearly as fun as splashing in rivers to cool down. I shook and shook once he was done with me. He cleaned up then we ate a quick meal in the dining room, then we went to our room. Instead of getting ready for bed Elliott stood by the door listening until the inn was silent, then he gathered his bag and gestured for me to join him. I followed him quietly down the stairs.

He hurried toward the livery and I wondered if this was one of our bad jobs. I didn't want to slip away in the night, though. We really had a ghost to hunt, a job to do, and I didn't want to leave without completing it. Elliott tossed his bag in the back of our wagon and climbed in behind it.

I caught Scoot's scent and whined. Elliott straightened and banged his head on a shelf.

"Going somewhere?" The sheriff said, stepping out of the shadows. I was surprised I hadn't noticed him there.

"No, sir," my human said hastily, smelling afraid. "Research. Couldn't sleep." He gestured at his books.

"You sure about that, Son? Looks to me like you're trying to run off."

"Why would I do that?" Elliott climbed out of the back of our wagon.

"Think you've done it a time or two before." He handed my human a piece of paper.

Scoot looked at me, but he didn't speak and I was still grumpy about the bath so I didn't try to talk to him either.

I whined when Elliott's scent changed to fear and pressed up against his leg. He ruffled my ears while he stared at the piece of paper.

"Did some looking earlier. Seems you're wanted in a few territories and states for fraud. A bit of a reward for catching you."

I tilted my head, listening to the sheriff. Fraud? I wondered what that meant, and who wanted us. Usually when someone wanted me, it was to give me pets or have me work sheep, but from the sheriff's tone it wasn't that.

"That dog even yours, son?"

Elliott straightened and glared at Tolbert. "Yes, sir." He buried his hand in my ruff.

"You sure about that?"

Elliott nodded. "I have her papers if you must see them. She's mine. So's the wagon and the horses."

"How'd you get her?"

"Brown chose me. We lived near a farm and one day a Scot showed up with a pregnant bitch straight from the old country. I'd help out on the farm now and again and was there when she had her puppies. Brown took a liking to me and spent a lot of time following me around, and she'd always find me after her work was done. The old Scot finally gave her to me in exchange for all the help I'd given him, papers and all. Apparently she's got a famous sire. Old Rope or something like that."

"Rope?"

"That's not quite right. Hemp I think. Yes, that's it. Old Hemp."

"Huh. Well, Son, I reckon there's more to that story, but okay. You really go to university to study ghost hunting?"

Elliott shuffled his feet on the ground.

"That's what I thought. Don't know no university that teaches ghosts."

"My great grandpa was a ghost hunter. Unfortunately he had terrible penmanship."

"Could be why we have two ghosts tearing up the saloon now, 'stead of just one?"

Elliott shrugged. "Perhaps. I am, however, educated and I scribed for a professor before I headed west."

"So you get rid of people's ghosts with your fancy words and learn'n."

"Yes."

"Seems most people think you're a fraud."

"Well, sir. Sometimes people think they have ghosts when they don't. This is the first real one I've come across."

"Seems to have won the battle."

"Yes, sir, but perhaps the war isn't over yet."

I heard something in Elliott's voice that I hadn't heard in a long time. Determination.

"You gonna run, or you gonna get rid of our ghosts?"

"I think there's one more battle in this war."

Tolbert nodded. "Then perhaps I've never seen this paper." He took it back from my human, crumpled it and shoved it in his pocket.

"Yes, sir."

"You need any help, Mr. Gyles?"

"Maybe tomorrow night, Sheriff. Tonight I need to do some research."

"Get some rest too. You still have a room at the inn."

"Thank you, sir."

"Ev'nin." He tipped his hat and left.

27

Scoot stared at me a little longer. "Are you sure you don't want help?"

"I don't know."

Scoot sniffed noses with me. "Okay then."

"Scoot!"

"Gotta go. Night, Brown." He ran off after the Sheriff.

"Good night, Scoot."

"Come on, Brown. Let's get some work done."

I climbed into the wagon and lay at Elliott's feet, dozing while he muttered over his books.

"Ahha!"

I jumped up, the sheep I'd been dreaming about scattering as I woke.

"I mispronounced this word here." He pointed at the book and I perked my ears forward and watched his hand. "I shouldn't have added the bit on the end. I think the original ritual will work if you can keep the ghosts off of me long enough. I just need to pronounce it correctly. I should translate this whole journal one of these days."

I barked once.

"Okay, Brown. I found something else. I can draw a symbol on the ground that should trap the ghosts. If you can push them with that Eye of yours, it'll catch them."

I barked in agreement.

"Excellent. We have a plan. Let's get some sleep."

I followed him out of the wagon. The sky began to lighten to the east as we walked down the streets and a few early risers began to stir by the time we made it to the inn. Elliott fell into bed without bothering to undress. I jumped up and pulled the comforter over him before curling up next to my human to watch for other vengeful spirits while he slept.

Sheriff Talbot waited for us when we approached the saloon that evening. Scoot was with him and the Alley Cat perched on the rail.

"Sheriff."

"Mr. Gyles."

They shook hands and I consented to sniff noses with Scoot.

"Hey, Brown, look what I got!" Scoot bounced around showing off boots that matched mine, down to the little bead crosses.

"Very fine. I do believe we'll set a trend."

He grinned at me. "So, how do we do this?"

"Well, I'm not sure how you'll do it, but I stare at them and freeze them with my Eye. I also jumped through one yesterday and it almost completely vanished."

Scoot nodded. "I don't have your Eye, but I sure can jump through them, herd them, annoy them, whatever it takes." He grinned at me.

"I'll set up for my ritual. Then I think the dogs have to hold the ghosts off of us until I finish the incantation. You're in charge of the saltwater in case things go wrong."

"Sounds fine. Don't summon a third one."

Elliott sighed and headed for the saloon doors.

"They didn't even bother to open today. Place is a mess. Two of 'em really tore it up."

We stopped just inside the doors and stared. The place was even worse than before and the musty-ozone smell was very strong. I even thought I saw some of the ghost slime.

29

"Wow."

"Yep. Even old Willy wouldn't come in."

"Willy?"

"Town drunk."

"Their presence was strongest up here." Elliott climbed the stairs.

I went ahead of him in case the ghosts came before we were ready.

"I think we should do the ritual up here."

The room we'd been in before was the worst. Nothing was in one piece. Even the walls had holes in them.

"Wonder if that ghost is the outlaw I shot up here a few weeks back. Didn't have any ghost problems until then."

"Could be. Who's the other one?"

Sheriff Tolbert shrugged. "Maybe the whore who caught a stray bullet?"

Elliott glanced at the sheriff and arched his eyebrows. I pushed my head under his hand to get his attention.

"Yes, Brown?"

I whined and scratched the floor where I could smell the old blood smell. I got the feeling if he drew his symbol over that patch, things would go better this time.

"Yep, that's about where they died. Smart dog."

"Maybe I should put the ghost trap symbol there."

I barked in agreement, wagging my tail happily. He'd understood.

"Thanks, Brown."

"She really that smart?"

"Yes. One bark means yes, two barks means no. She's never wrong." He knelt and drew on the floor with his chalk. "Sprinkle some saltwater on the circle. When the ghost goes over the line it will trap him."

"Don't we need two traps?"

30

"Can't hurt." Elliott drew another one and then set up the rest of the ritual.

The incense smell began to cover the musty ozone smell. Wind built though it didn't disturb the incense smoke. The banshee's howl lifted the hair on my ruff and hurt my ears. Scoot whined and I stood firm, trying to act like a real ghost-hunting dog. I growled a warning as the ghosts appeared in front of me.

"Sweet Mary," Sheriff Tolbert swore.

Elliott began chanting.

"Brown, what do we do?" Scoot barked urgently.

"Try and herd them over the traps."

The first ghost was wise to my Eye and wouldn't meet my gaze, but I caught the second one quickly. It struggled, but it fell silent and its wind-devil stilled. I crouched and pushed it backward, fighting to keep my hold on the ghost. My will was stronger and it fell back. A bright light flared when the ghost crossed the trap. I lost my hold on the ghost but the trap contained it. It beat against the edges of the trap but the light pushed it back.

"Brown!"

The original ghost threw things at Scoot. Scoot tried to dodge, but the ghost had him backed into a corner.

"Should I use the salt?" Tolbert shouted, standing firm against the windy attack, though his hat flew from his head.

Elliott shook his head and kept chanting. His voice rose in force and the original ghost howled.

I saw the piece of the dresser rise and knew if it hit Scoot it could kill him. I barked in alarm and leapt at the ghost, diving through it. The cold cow-pie feel made my skin crawl but I tumbled to the ground on the other side, off balance but unharmed. The ghost dropped the dresser and its eyes spun toward me. It still wouldn't meet my Eye but I had its attention.

31

"Scoot! Try and push it off of me." Now I was backed into a corner. I crouched, growling.

Scoot came in from the side, nipping at the base of the wind-devil. The ghost howled and the eyes spun toward Scoot. It tried to throw something at the cattle dog, but I dove in, nipping at the wind. It backed away and together we were able to push the ghost toward the trap, driving it before us. The ghost panicked, probably knowing what we intended. It hurled part of the bed at us. I dodged, but I heard Scoot yelp.

The ghost laughed and met my eyes, taunting me. I dropped my jaw in a grin when I caught it with my will. It still had some fight though, and tried to throw another piece of the room. I managed to dodge, and then Scoot was back at my side. He dove in and nipped at the wind-devil while I drove it backward with my Eye. It almost slipped from my control, but one final nip from Scoot shoved it into the trap. Blinding light shot up around it and contained the ghost. The wind in the room died.

I collapsed to the floor, exhausted.

Scoot lay next to me and we stared at the ghosts while Elliott finished the ritual.

He shouted the last few words.

The ghosts howled in rage.

"Now, throw the salt water on both of them!"

Sheriff Tolbert threw the water at the ghosts.

The light from the traps brightened until I couldn't look at them anymore. Their wails made my bones ache. Then suddenly the sound cut off and the light died. I opened my eyes a slit, just in time for one final flash of light. A clap of thunder exploded in the room and something cold and slimy hit me.

I whined and blinked my eyes clear of the light. Nothing was left of the ghosts except black outlines on the floor where Elliott had drawn the ghost traps. Slime coated everything.

Elliott sat on the floor, staring at the traps. The Sheriff had his gun out and a very startled expression on his face.

"Disgusting," Elliott finally said, wiping slime from his face.

Tolbert holstered his gun and looked around for his hat. He wiped his forehead with his sleeve, put his hat back on his head and offered Elliott a hand.

"I agree, Mr. Gyles. Scoot, you okay?"

Scoot limped over to the sheriff and thumped his tail on the ground.

"Suspect you'll be fine. Had worse from the cows." He scratched Scoot, despite the slime that coated the blue dog.

"Brown?"

I went to Elliott's side and he knelt and hugged me.

"You're the bravest dog ever, Brown."

Scoot barked.

"You too, Scoot. You're both very brave."

I grinned, pleased.

"Strange. That slime is all over everything but their boots. Who'd you say made them?"

Tolbert shrugged. "Some of the local women. One is a Native. Maybe she placed a native blessing on them. Maybe it's the crosses. Can't say as I'm going to complain. One less thing to clean up."

Elliott laughed. "Salt water gets the slime off."

"So, think they're gone this time?"

"I think that last explosion did them in. I'll stay one more night, if it's okay, just in case."

The sheriff nodded. "I suspect you could stay a week and no one would complain, if they're truly gone."

"Thank you, Sheriff. I don't want to overstay my welcome."

"Good job, son. Let's go clean up."

"Yes, sir."

"I can't believe we really did it, Brown," Elliott said later, as he scrubbed the last of the ghost slime from my fur.

I licked his cheek.

"You and Scoot sure did make a good team."

I barked once in agreement.

"Well, let's rest up and see if we got rid of the ghost. Maybe we really can hunt ghosts and help people instead of trick them out of their money."

I barked again, wagging my tail.

"Brown, my ghost-hunting Border Collie."

I danced around, overjoyed that Elliott was happy with me.

"Come on, I think I smell steak."

I licked my lips and followed him out into the dining room. Sheriff Tolbert and Scoot waited for us. They both looked freshly scrubbed too, though Scoot didn't seem very happy about it.

"I hate baths," he said when I joined him.

"I hate ghost slime more."

He huffed, but didn't argue. "Sheriff said we get steak, all of us."

I grinned and sure enough, when they brought out food, there were plates for us too. If I got steak every time I'd happily deal with the slime and the baths.

"So, Sheriff, ever consider giving up your career as a law man and hitting the road to hunt ghosts?"

"Can't say as it ever crossed my mind."

The humans laughed.

"Well, if you change your mind, I think we made a great team."

"Yes, Mr. Gyles, I do believe you're right. If I get tired of being the law, I'll look you up."

I glanced at Scoot once I finished my steak. "You did a great job, Scoot."

"You too, Brown. That Eye of yours is something else."

I grinned at him, then looked away, feeling shy.

He stood and licked me on the cheek. "If you come back through town, find me."

I thumped my tail and nodded. "Be happy too."

We sat on the saloon porch the following evening with the saloonkeeper and a few others waiting to see if the ghosts came back.

The Alley Cat jumped up on the railing and groomed himself. "Amazed you're still alive," he said once he was done.

I ignored him, in too good of a mood to fight with a cat.

"Well, I'm glad I won't have to deal with a dog ghost too. Good job."

"Almost as if I'm a professional ghost hunter." I growled at him.

The cat sniffed. "Never heard of dogs hunting ghosts before. That's a cat's job. Lucky you're alive is all I'm saying."

I barked angrily and the cat sniffed again.

"Oh, fine. Maybe Border Collies can hunt ghosts. You must have some feline in your pedigree."

I stared at him, trying to figure out how I'd be related to a cat. He sauntered off before I could come up with a good reply.

"Ah, don't let him get to you, Brown. Everyone knows all cats are good for is chasing mice."

I glanced at Scoot and grinned. He sat next to me and we resumed our vigil. Several hours past sunset the humans decided that the ghosts must be gone.

"Well, Sheriff, I'll take off first thing. Thanks for everything."

"Mr. Gyles, aren't you forgetting something?"

My human went still for a minute and I could sense his fear.

"What, sir?"

"This town owes you a bit of money. I figure double since you had to fight two ghosts."

"Oh, right!"

The Sheriff winked at him and handed him a pouch and a piece of paper. "Wrote you up a recommendation too. Sorry my penmanship isn't as nice as yours. Haven't had all that fancy learn'in back east and all that."

"Thank you, sir."

He nodded. "I hear a rumor there's a ghost haunting a train out in Kansas. Giving the railroad men fits."

"I think I may just be heading that way. I'll have to look into it when I pass through."

Tolbert smiled. "In that case, here's a letter of introduction to the local law. They'll help you out."

Elliott took the other letter and tucked them into his vest. "I can't thank you enough."

Sheriff Tolbert shrugged. "Figure we owe you a bit. Wasn't looking forward to having to build a new saloon and a man's gotta drink now and again."

Elliott laughed and they shook hands.

"Come on, Brown. We've ghosts to hunt."

I touched noses with Scoot and followed my human back to the inn. I couldn't wait to get to Kansas. They had a ghost problem and I was the dog for the job.

J.A. Campbell

# BROWN AND THE END OF THE LINE

*Kansas, 1900*

Tumbleweeds rolled across the prairie, and the sun beat down on us while the wind slithered through the tall grasses, bending them in half. I kept my nose in the wind, picturing the world through the scents it brought to me as we rode on our wagon. Elliot said that the sound of the wind in the grass reminded him of the ocean.

"Smelling anything good, Brown?" Elliott reached over and scratched my ears.

If only he could smell the world the way I did. It would make hunting ghosts easier too. I could detect their distinctive scent better than he could. They smelled like the air after a hard rain, but old and dingy. Elliott called the scent musty-ozone.

Barking once, I sniffed more. The scent of many humans living close together reached me and I stood on the bench, wagging my tail.

"Almost there?"

I barked again.

"Good." Elliott slapped his hand over his small round hat when the wind tried to rip it off his head. Again. "I'm ready to be out of this weather."

We followed the barest hint of wagon ruts; traveling from Miller, Colorado to a small railroad outpost a few

39

days outside of Dodge City, Kansas. The railroad had a ghost problem, and I was the dog for the job.

Elliott was excited about Dodge City and hoped we would be able to make a stop there. He'd spent the last few days telling me all sorts of interesting stories about the famous people of Dodge, but he didn't know any about famous dogs. That was okay though. I'd ask the locals if we got to go. It was a relatively quiet city now, but once it had been very exciting.

"Look at that, Brown." Elliott scratched my ears again and pointed when the small town came into view.

I could hear the hiss of steam over the steady sound of the wind and saw a train pulling away from the station. It sounded its whistle, but I was far enough away that it didn't hurt my ears. A few buildings surrounded a main street and I smelled cows. There were probably many farms around here too. Maybe we could find sheep. I thumped my tail on the bench at the thought.

"Get up." Elliott clucked to the horses.

I jumped down off the wagon and raced ahead a short distance before circling back. I'd rested long enough and I wanted to run before we got into town and I had to stay with Elliott.

The sun was low in the sky behind us by the time we reached the town. Jumping back on the bench, I grinned, content after a long run. Elliott directed the horses straight to the railroad station. I leapt off again when Elliott stopped the wagon outside of the building. Someone shouted inside. Elliott patted his leg and I stayed next to him while we climbed the stairs up to the platform.

"I can't take it anymore. I quit!" A man stormed out of the office, slamming the door. He didn't even glance at me or Elliott as he brushed past us on the stairs and stomped off down the street.

Smelling the barest hint of musty-ozone as he hurried past, I whined.

"It's okay, Brown. He's not mad at you," Elliott said, misunderstanding my concern.

Huffing in annoyance, I followed Elliott inside the office. If only humans could communicate properly.

"I told you, there's no such thing as ghosts!" A man sitting behind a desk and staring intently at something on it shouted when the door shut behind us.

"Um, well, I'd beg to differ since that's why we're here, but I don't believe we've met."

The man looked up, smelling surprised. He pushed glasses up his nose with a gesture that seemed to be an old habit, like when Elliott took off his hat and ran his hand through his hair when he was nervous.

"Well, I'm sorry to have snapped at you, sir. Having a problem with some of my men."

"I saw."

He narrowed his eyes. "You said you're here on account of a ghost?"

I could hear the anger in his voice and I put myself in front of Elliott.

"Yes, sir. Sheriff Tolbert from Miller, Colorado sent me. I have a letter."

The man behind the desk stared at Elliott hard for a moment before holding out his hand. His scent was hopeful even though he still looked angry.

My human took the letter out of his vest pocket and handed it over. The other man settled back and studied it for a time before grunting. "Says you got rid of their saloon ghost?"

"That's right, sir. My name is Elliott Gyles. This is Brown."

"Huh, well, I'm Clement Dalton. Welcome to the Outpost."

41

"Mr. Dalton."

"My pap was Mr. Dalton. I'm just Clem. Really think you can take care of this ghost?"

"I thought you said there was no such thing as ghosts."

Clem stared at Elliott for a minute before bursting out laughing. "Come on, let me buy you a drink and I'll tell you about it."

"Let me get this straight. It's rattling the cars, blowing wind around inside and knocking things over, especially in the dining car, and it makes things appear on the track."

"Yes," Clem said.

Resting my chin on Elliott's knee, I listened to Clem's story. This ghost sounded just as bad as the one in the Saloon.

"Does it appear in one spot, or does it affect only one train?"

"It's happened on several different trains, though it does seem to be localized to one spot on the way to Dodge."

"Do you know of anything bad that happened out there?"

Clem laughed and took another drink. "You name it, Elliott. This is Dodge City we're talking about. Train robberies, murder, theft, famous bandits, infamous ones, hell, the Marshals were almost bigger rogues than the outlaws."

"I see your point. I'll need to experience the ghost myself to trap it."

"Understood. I also understand that your dog helps you. I'll make sure no one gives you any problems about her. You can keep your stock in the livery and I'll get you a room for the night. Best be up early though. Train leaves as soon as it's loaded. Usually not too long after sunup."

"Understood."

Elliott and I were up before the sun. Breakfast was some leftover meat scraps that tasted marvelous, though I could tell the innkeeper wasn't happy about having me in the dining room. However, Clem had insisted and since the railroad owned the town, they'd done what he said. I made sure to be on my best behavior. Once we were finished, Elliott packed his hunting bag and some clothing and we headed to the platform.

Men hurried around, shouting above the noises from the train. A few seemed to be urging people to get back onto the cars. I thought they might be passengers by the way they were nicely dressed, and not coated with soot. Clem stood on the platform and shouted orders at everyone. Following Elliott, I tried to stay out of the way and by his side.

"Ahh. Elliott." Clem said when he saw us. He gestured us forward. "This is Hal, the conductor. Hal, Mr. Gyles and his dog, Brown."

"Nice to meet you." A taller, lanky man wearing a uniform with shiny buttons held out his hand.

"Hello."

The conductor glanced down at me. "Is she house trained?"

I put up my paw as if to shake.

He laughed. "Should I take that as a yes?"

"Yes." Elliott sounded offended but I forgave Hal when he shook my paw.

43

"I've told the stewards that she's allowed and even though we officially don't believe in ghosts, they know why you're here. You shouldn't be bothered," Hal said.

"Thank you."

"Elliott, make sure you get off in Dodge City. The conductors will know to let you and Brown on the train headed back this way as soon as you are ready. If you can't get the ghost on the first trip, you can get it on the second," Clem said.

Elliott smiled broadly at the mention of Dodge City.

"Now, if you'll follow me, I'll show you to your room. We're about ready to leave," Hal said.

We followed the conductor into one of the train cars. The aisles were narrow and smelled of soot and lots of people and the barest hint of ghost. My hackles rose and I growled.

"What's that, Brown?" Elliott turned to glance at me.

I flattened my ears and whined.

"She doesn't like the train?" Hal guessed.

"No." Elliott glanced around, but no one else was near. "I suspect she smells the ghost. Has this train been haunted?"

Hal nodded after also looking around.

"Easy, Brown."

I huffed, but quieted, following close behind Elliott. The conductor showed us to a small room that smelled reasonably clean by human standards and told us to settle in.

Elliott slid the door shut after the conductor left. "Well, Brown. Our second real ghost. What do you think?"

Using my indoor bark, I woofed softly and thumped my tail, dropping my jaw in a doggy grin. I was glad to have a job.

"We have a while before we get to the haunted spot. I'm going to do some research."

I sighed and jumped up on the bed, making myself comfortable. Research was boring.

Dozing while Elliott read, I dreamed of the last ghost we'd fought and how I'd teamed up with Scoot, the sheriff's cattle dog.

Finally, Elliott woke me for dinner. I followed him through the train until we reached the car with the yummy smells. My stomach grumbled and I licked drool from my lips. The stewards brought me a plate along with Elliott and I happily dug in until someone screamed.

I jumped up, looking around, certain the ghost was early.

"There's a dog in the car!" A woman shrieked. She smelled of flowers and wore a dark colored dress. Her hair had flowers in it, but not the ones she smelled like and she wore it piled on her head like a lot of the ladies I'd seen back east. It was brown like my fur, but otherwise was as uninteresting to me as the rest of her.

I looked around, wondering how another dog had gotten aboard before realizing she was talking about me. The finger pointed in my direction was a big clue. Wagging my tail once, I went back to my dinner. The ghost wasn't here yet, and I was hungry.

I heard some shushing noises coming from the table and ignored them along with the woman's hysterics until she said something about fleas.

"I can feel them already, fleas, crawling all over me. Of all the things, a dog on the train!" Her breathing was high and rapid. I'd seen a woman pass out after breathing like that, and hoped this woman would do that too so she'd be quiet. As if I were some city mongrel. Fleas…the nerve. Stifling a growl, I went back to my dinner.

Elliott scratched my shoulder and he seemed to be trying to ignore her as well.

"Sir." An older man who looked like a priest walked up to our table.

Elliott turned toward him. I finished my dinner before resting my chin on Elliott's knee. "Yes?"

"Perhaps you would consider removing your dog from the car? It's disturbing the lady."

I could smell Elliott's anger and his voice was quiet when he answered, like the time I'd chased the sheep out into the road and they'd escaped into town. I flattened my ears.

"Father, perhaps you'd consider removing the lady from the car. She's disturbing everyone."

The priest smelled amused, but his voice stayed even and he frowned when he replied.

"Dogs aren't allowed on the train."

"This one is, and she doesn't have fleas."

One of the railroad men, the one who'd brought my dinner, hurried up just then. "Please, Father. This dog has permission and is allowed everywhere," he said.

"I see. Sorry to bother you then." He tipped his hat and returned to the table with the annoying woman. They spoke quietly and I heard her huff, but apparently the matter was settled.

Elliott lingered in the car longer than normal, drinking something and staring out of the window. I sat up on my hind legs, then stood, so I could see out, careful not to put my paws on anything in case that made someone else mad. Not seeing anything but grass I sank back down and rested my chin on Elliott's knee again while he scratched my ears.

"This ghost is going to be interesting to trap," Elliott said once no one was close enough to hear. "We're moving and putting out one of the traps like I drew at the saloon won't be as easy. Apparently motion disturbs it or something. Great-Grand Pappy had a solution but the drawing is more difficult. I'll have to draw it in our room so we don't scare anyone, but that shouldn't be a problem."

Perking my ears forward, I licked his hand to let him know I was listening.

"Come on, Brown. Let's go get ready."

By getting ready, I knew he meant I had to keep an eye out for ghosts while he drew on the floor with his chalk.

We took a walk back to the stock car so I could stretch my legs before returning to our room. I jumped up on the bed while Elliott moved the rug from the floor so he could draw on the wood. Then I settled in to watch while he muttered to himself, turned the book this way and that and scratched lines on the floor with his chalk. Dozing, I jerked my eyes open when I heard Elliott's satisfied, "Done."

"Well, Brown, what do you think?"

I sat up and stared at the drawing. Tilting my head, I tried to decide if I saw anything wrong with it. I tilted my head the other way and decided it looked fine, though I truly didn't know what I was supposed to be looking for. Woofing quietly once, I settled back onto the bed.

Elliott laughed. "Okay. I'll take that to mean it looks okay. Now I need some incense." He reached into his bag. "Yes, this, and salt. Hmm..." He went back to staring at his great-grand pappy's hunting journal and muttering.

Wondering when the ghost would return, I settled my muzzle on my paws and watched Elliott work. He moved a few things around then sat back again.

"There. I think we have it."

A muffled exclamation caught my attention and I glanced at the door, wondering who was there. Elliott didn't hear. He still glanced between his drawing and the book until the door slammed open. Then he dropped the book and spun around, smelling startled. I barked, alarmed.

"What are you doing?" The priest from the dining car grabbed Elliott's arm and jerked him out of the car. Elliott dropped his book and I darted out before they could lock me in the room.

"Nothing!"

"Doesn't look like nothing to me," another man said. This one had a shiny star on his chest, like Sheriff Tolbert wore. "Looks like devil worship."

"Arrest him!" The priest shouted over Elliott's protest.

I growled as the sheriff leveled his gun at me.

"Call off your dog, mister," the sheriff said.

Growling more loudly, I crouched to the floor and glared at him.

"Brown, easy. It's all a misunderstanding."

I continued to glare, but I quieted my growl.

"She won't hurt you, and I'm not worshiping the devil."

The sheriff slowly holstered his gun and grabbed Elliott's arm. "We'll just see about that."

"Ask the conductor. I'm trying to stop the ghost. We got one in Miller, Colorado. Wire Sheriff Tolbert." Elliott smelled afraid and sounded desperate.

I stifled another growl.

"Time enough for that. Let's go." The sheriff shoved Elliott in the back, making him stumble down the narrow hallway. The priest followed and I stayed behind them, not letting Elliott out of my sight but staying far enough away that they wouldn't be able to grab me. A few passengers stared as we marched past, but no one said anything. Though I was more concerned about Elliott, I didn't forget the reason we were on the train and I kept my nose alert for ghost smells.

"Sirs, please, I'm here to hunt the ghost. I must get back to my room. It could be here any minute." Elliott stopped and turned toward the sheriff and the priest.

"Son, there's no such thing as ghosts."

I couldn't understand why the sheriff called Elliott son. He wasn't that much older than my human. The priest on the other hand looked very old, with thin white hair and lines on his face like humans got when they were older.

"Yes..." Elliott's reply was drowned out by a sharp screech that would have set me to barking if I'd still been on my feet, but the train lurched at the same time and I went sprawling, hitting the back of the priest's legs and knocking him into the sheriff.

Elliott stumbled into the wall but stayed on his feet. He stared at the fallen men in shock and I had to bark to get is attention.

Run! I would have shouted at him if I could.

"Of course." He seemed to know what my bark meant and sprinted past the fallen men before they could regain their feet.

Running close behind him, I got a strange feeling and, even though I knew I shouldn't, I darted forward and grabbed Elliott's ankle with my teeth and sent him sprawling.

"Ow! Brown, what are you doing?"

Gunshots rang out behind us and an eerie howl rattled my teeth. Something white shot by overhead. It seemed brighter than the lights in the hallway and it rattled the glass as it raced past.

"Good girl, Brown. I should know better than to question you."

Women screamed up ahead.

"Go, get the ghost. See if you can push it back to our room."

I jumped over Elliott's back and I heard him get to his feet and start running as I chased after the ghost. It had made it to the dining car where a few people were enjoying an evening snack. Well, they had been enjoying it, but I smelled musty-ozone everywhere and the walls dripped with ghost slime. One woman was having hysterics and I could smell the ghost all over her and she looked wet with slime, too.

Despite all the slime, the ghost was not in the dining car anymore. I barked, seeing if it would come when I called. No luck, but screams from the next room down let me know the ghost was still there, and if I hurried...

I barked at the bright white thing hovering in the middle of the room. It turned to look at me, but didn't spin like the wind-devil shaped ghosts from the saloon. Instead it seemed more like a bed sheet flapping on a clothesline, but it had eyes and a slit-like mouth that slowly opened, voicing that same eerie howl. My hackles rose and my teeth ached at the sound, but I forced myself to meet the ghost's eyes and stare. Its howl cut off abruptly and the flapping motion quieted. The ghost struggled but I'd done this before and I was confident that I could control the ghost and push it back toward Elliott. I crept into the room, dodging obstacles I didn't even bother to identify, all my concentration on the ghost. It turned as I did, eyes locked to mine as I maneuvered so that I could push it out the door and into the dining car.

Once I was lined up with the door I pushed the ghost, creeping forward. It struggled harder, perhaps reacting to my moving it, but it couldn't get away as I pushed it like I moved a flock of sheep into a holding pen. The dining area was a mess but I managed to navigate around the fallen chairs. The nice, juicy steak lying on the ground didn't even tempt me, though a little drool leaked from my jaws when the scent overpowered the ghost smell for a moment. People screamed but I ignored them, pushing the ghost into the hallway and toward the room I shared with Elliott.

Shouting distracted me, and I felt the ghost slip. A ripple went through it and I tightened my focus, concentrating as hard as I could until it quieted again. I pushed until I reached our door, but I wasn't sure how to get around the corner. There was no room for me to get behind the ghost.

"See! There!"

Elliott's shout distracted me and the ghost howled as it tried to escape.

"Holy Jesus!" I heard the sheriff exclaim.

The priest began to pray.

The ghost dove at me and I wished I had my special boots on. They protected my feet from sharp things and had extra protection against ghosts. Elliott hadn't had time to put them on yet. Dodging, I yelped when the ghost passed through me. It was cold and my fur got slimed but I wasn't dead so I spun and launched myself at the ghost, snarling.

It seemed startled, eyes going a little wider and I plowed through it, shoving it backward a little and toward the room.

A couple of shots rang out, deafening me, and I barked in alarm. I thought I heard Elliott shouting something over the ringing in my ears but I wasn't sure. The ghost turned and flew into our room. Chasing after, I skidded to a halt

51

just short of the ghost trap drawing. I didn't want to smudge it. The ghost howled, flapping around inside the trap and the priest and the sheriff, both covered in slime, stared, mouths agape.

"I have to banish it," Elliott said.

The priest seemed to jerk before he tore his attention from the ghost and looked at Elliott. "You can banish that demon?"

"Yes, that's what I've been trying to tell you. I hunt ghosts."

Wincing when the ghost howled again, I looked for Elliott's book. He'd need it and I remembered him dropping it.

"Very well, get on with it then."

I found his book near the priest and pushed it with my nose.

"Good girl, Brown. Good girl." Elliott picked up the book and flipped through it.

I sat and stared at the ghost, daring it to try and escape, while Elliott found the right page.

"Mother of God," a new voice said.

"Hal, we caught the ghost," Elliott said to the conductor. "I'm going to banish him now."

"Pleased to hear it, Mr. Gyles." He sounded a little out of breath, like he'd run a long way.

Elliott nodded and began reading from his book. The ghost howled. The humans covered their ears, except Elliott. Whining in pain, I crouched down but continued to watch, just in case. Elliott reached the end and shouted the last words over the ghost's scream. He picked up the salt and tossed it at the ghost. I thought my teeth were going to rattle out of my muzzle at the noise and I had to shut my eyes as the ghost light grew too bright. Suddenly, I heard a loud pop and ghost slime splattered me. The howl stopped and I opened my eyes.

The humans all stared at the empty ghost trap, covered in dripping slime and looking a little shocked.

I went over to Elliott and pushed against his leg. He rubbed my ears.

"Good dog."

Thumping my tail on the ground, I grinned up at him.

"Well..." The priest shook his head, glanced at the sheriff and then they both walked out.

"Salt water gets the slime off," Elliott called after them.

Hal laughed. "Guess you showed them. They give you any problems?"

Elliott nodded. "Tried to arrest me."

The conductor shook his head. "This is a mess. Let me get you a new room. Salt water you say?"

"Yes."

Suddenly I remembered the steak I'd passed in the dining car. Woofing happily I ran back out into the hallway and toward the dining hall. Once food made it to the floor, it was mine. I didn't even think it had slime on it.

"Brown!"

Elliott chased after but he didn't call me back.

To my dismay the annoying, flower scented lady was in the dining area when I arrived, and she'd picked up my steak! I huffed in annoyance and she gasped when she saw me. We stared at each other, her eyes wide, mine narrowed. That was my steak.

"Whatever is all over you?" At least she wasn't screaming.

"Ghost slime," Elliott said coming up behind me.

"Ghost slime?"

"Yes, we banished the ghost that's been plaguing the train." Elliott sounded wary.

"I see."

"You don't sound surprised."

53

She actually smiled. "I'm the owner's daughter, I was investigating the so called claims."

Elliott frowned.

"I nearly slept through the whole thing, though getting thrown to the floor when the train stopped did wake me. Why is she staring at me like that?"

"Brown?"

I looked at the steak on the plate and licked drool from my lips.

"I think she's decided that's her steak."

"You're certain she doesn't have fleas?"

"Yes."

The lady set the plate on the ground and backed away. I darted forward and grabbed the steak before she could change her mind and took it back to Elliott's side. There was no slime on the floor except where it dripped from us so I set my steak down and tore into it, wagging my tail happily. Maybe I'd forgive her for thinking I had fleas.

Hal laughed when he joined us and said something to the lady, but I was concentrating fully on my steak. If I got paid with steak every time I hunted a ghost, I hoped we found many more.

"So, Mr. Gyles. How do you feel about steamboats?"

"Never been on one."

"I've got a friend in St. Louis who has a ghost problem. I think you and Brown could help them."

If they had a ghost problem, I was the dog for the job. Especially if they had steak.

# BROWN GOES FULL STEAM AHEAD

*St. Louis, Missouri, 1900*

I watched the rail men unload our wagon and horses. The horses snorted and shook their heads once they were on solid ground, looking grateful to be off the train.

"Sure was nice of the railroad to give us a lift," Elliott, my human, said. "Well, Brown. I guess we should find a livery and the docks." He looked toward the city. "This is the furthest east we've been in a long time." He sounded a little uneasy.

We used to hunt ghosts for people in the east. Sometimes they got mad at us and we had to slip away in the night. We called those, 'Bad Jobs'. Now we hunted real ghosts and people liked us a lot more. We'd just defeated a ghost on a train, and the railroad men knew of a ghost on a steam ship in St. Louis. So here we were. They had a ghost, and I was the dog for the job.

We used to live in the east, near a sheep farm on the edge of a big town, but it had been quite a while since I'd been in a city. The clangs and bangs of people unloading freight, the neighs of horses, and shouts of humans, not to mention the smells of hundreds of people and animals and waste was a little overwhelming.

Elliott went to collect our wagon and horses. I stayed on the platform and watched. Steam hissed and the train

55

whistle blew. I was far enough away that the noise was merely uncomfortable instead of painful. I sniffed the bench I sat on, and scented cat, but no dogs. Nothing was fresh.

"Brown, let's go!"

I jumped down and darted around a few rail workers, leaping up onto the wagon bench to stay out of the way. It was easier to ride the wagon than run through city streets, though I was anxious for a good run after such a long time in the train. Elliott told me we'd traveled across the entire state of Missouri and part of Kansas to get here. If we'd gone by wagon it would have taken us weeks. But I would have been able to run. Though the treats and attention from the ladies in the passenger car where we rode had been nice. After Elliott had assured them that I didn't have fleas… I flattened my ears at the thought. As if I were some street mongrel. The nerve! But they'd given me steak, so I forgave them.

The wagon bumped down the rutted street, going around the main part of the city. I stared, watching the hustle, flattening my ears at the racket.

Elliott scratched me. "The rail workers told me there was a good livery just down the street."

I sniffed the air. The horse smell was stronger ahead of us and I barked once in agreement.

"They gave me a letter of introduction to the captain. His name is James Arnault. I gather he doesn't like the train much, but he and Clem know each other. And if he doesn't want our help, well, I'm sure we'll find something soon."

I tilted my head and perked my ears, dropping my jaw in a doggy grin.

Elliott laughed. "Yes, maybe even some sheep."

I thumped my tail on the bench.

"Ahh, here we are." Elliott stopped the wagon in front of a barn that smelled of horse and sweet hay. "Stay here."

My human hopped off the bench and went into the barn. I heard him talking with someone inside, and then they came out together. The other man smelled of iron and burnt hoof and horse and he had a friendly smile. They shook hands and Elliott climbed up on the wagon. "We'll bring them around back so we can store the wagon here. Then we can go find our steamship. The farrier said she's in port."

I wondered what traveling on a steamship would be like. I remembered seeing one when we took the ferry across the river on our way out west.

It didn't take long to get the horses unhitched and the wagon secured. Elliott grabbed a couple of bags from the back and we went on our way.

We skirted around the city, dodging a few wagons and a bunch of people on foot until we reached the road that ran along the shore. We stopped for a moment and stared at the vast river. The far bank seemed miles away. I hadn't seen that much water in a long time. The smell of fishy water overwhelmed everything.

"Come on, Brown." Elliott patted his leg and I trotted up next to him.

The docks weren't quite as busy as the train yard had been, but we could see the steamship resting at its dock.

"Well, Brown, that's our ship. The Ruby."

From here the ship didn't seem very big but as we went further out on the docks I had to look up and up to see the top. The ship looked fancy and I could hear music playing somewhere inside. The ship smelled of oil and food. I sniffed, certain I smelled steak. I wagged my tail and whined. I was hungry.

Elliott scratched my ears and we stopped by the ramp that let people walk from the dock to the ship. I jumped when a whistle shrieked nearby.

"Hello?" Elliott shouted. "Hello the ship?"

I perked my ears forward when I heard something clank. Someone swore then a door banged open and a man stepped out. He straightened his coat and put his hat back on his head.

"Pardon me. I thought all the passengers were on board." He was younger than Elliott and looked fancy in his uniform.

"Oh, I'm not a passenger. My name is Elliott Gyles and this is Brown. Clement Dalton sent me. I've a letter for Captain Arnault."

"What did the railroad send you for?" He sounded suspicious.

"Clem said the Ruby had a problem with a ghost. I'm here to help."

The boy looked around, eyes wide. "Shh. We're keeping that quiet. Business is slow enough as it is without people knowing about her."

"Her?"

"The ghost. She's a real bitch." The kid looked around again. "Anyway. I reckon if you can help us the Captain will be interested in talking to you. Come on."

We followed until the boy stopped and stared at me. "We don't allow dogs."

"She helps hunt ghosts."

He frowned. "Well, we'll have to ask the Captain. I'll go get him."

"Perhaps you'll hand him this letter. It's an introduction."

"Sure." He took the letter and we waited on the ramp while he went back into the steamship.

Elliott knelt next to me and scratched my ears. "Maybe they'll let us on if we give you a bath. You smell like you've been on the road for a while."

I flattened my ears and sniffed him before wrinkling my lips. As if he smelled any different.

Elliott laughed. "You have a point, Brown. We both need to clean up."

I woofed in agreement, though I thought we smelled better now than we did after a bath, but humans smelled differently than dogs. I wondered if there would be any cats on board. Though if they didn't allow dogs, I'd be surprised if they allowed cats.

It seemed to take forever before the boy returned with an older man wearing a uniform with a lot more shiny pieces on it. I guessed he was the captain.

"Mr. Gyles, I'm Captain Arnault. Clem says you and your dog managed to banish their ghost?" He held up the letter that Elliott had brought.

"Yes, sir."

"Have to have the dog to fight ghosts?"

"Yes, sir."

"Hmm. Well, we don't allow dogs." He held up his hand before Elliott could protest. "But if we can come up with a good explanation, maybe we can make an exception. Can't tell the passengers you're here to fight the ghost. Hmm... Dog do any tricks?"

"Brown knows a few, but she's a working dog. If you had sheep, she'd be able to herd them."

Arnault laughed. "Don't think the passengers would appreciate me bringing sheep on board. Well, maybe you can spend a half an hour a night entertaining passengers. I'll even pay you for your trouble, and give you room and board for you and your dog, same as I do other performers. You banish this ghost for me and I'll pay you a whole lot more."

59

"Thank you, sir. I'd be happy to help. When will the ship be back to St. Louis? I have my horses and wagon at the livery and I need to make arrangements."

I stopped listening to the humans while they made arrangements. A white and black bird hopped down the rail, tilting its head this way and that as it got closer.

I stared at the bird and it ruffled its feathers.

"No need to be rude," it squawked.

"Sorry." I sat down and looked away for a moment. I'd never had a bird talk to me before. "What do you want?"

"What makes you think I want something?" The bird stretched out a wing and plucked at its feathers.

"Usually birds want something when they get close."

"Ahh. I just heard you talking about the ghost. This is my ship and I've met the ghost before. Foul temper. You're going to get rid of it?"

"Yes. I hunt ghosts. What does the ghost do? And how is this your ship? I thought it was the Captain's?"

The bird squawked laughter. "He thinks it's his, but really it's mine. I've sailed on it longer than he has after all."

I tilted my head, trying to understand how a bird could own a ship, but finally I gave up. If the bird wanted the ship, who was I to argue?

"As for the ghost. Well, mostly it scares the patrons by making weird sounds at night, chasing ladies and stealing their hair brushes or messing up performances. It's quite entertaining." The bird preened.

"Damn seagull," the captain said. He stalked forward and waved his hat at the bird.

The seagull squawked and flapped away, yelling curses that would have turned the captain's ears red if he could have understood them.

"Bird thinks he owns the place. Always around. Maybe he's friends with that damn ghost. Anyway. Think you can do it?"

"Yes, sir."

"Well, you're hired. We sail in an hour."

"I only need to make arrangements with the livery."

The captain and Elliott shook hands.

I quickly grew used to the shrieking whistle and the rumble of the steam engines that vibrated my paws constantly. We stood in the front of the ship while it rumbled down the Mississippi. Occasionally water would splash my nose and the scents that filled the air kept me busy with all the stories they told. I was almost disappointed when Elliott told me it was time for our performance. The sun was low in the sky and the people who worked on the boat said the ghost, they referred to it as a she, usually came out during the performances or at night when the passengers would stroll on the decks. We were supposed to be the first act during dinner. I walked next to Elliott, enjoying the weird feeling of the carpet under my paws as we entered the main hall. I'd heard Elliott exclaiming about how beautiful and elegant everything was. Mostly, I just wanted to discover how beautiful and elegant the food was. I licked my lips and wagged my tail, glancing up at Elliott hopefully. He scratched my ears.

"We'll eat as soon as we are done performing. Then we'll hunt."

I dropped my jaw in a grin and held my head high as we walked through the dining hall where guests gathered.

Some pointed, others exclaimed and a few explained that we were performers. I wagged my tail.

I jumped up onto a stool on the stage and Elliott stood next to me while we were introduced. The audience clapped and I sat up balanced on my hind end with my front paws tucked under my chin. That got a few claps. Next I did the basics, shake, roll over, the sort of boring things that still seemed to entertain the crowd. I knew we would have to get creative though so when I noticed Elliott frowning, as if trying to think of what to do next I stood up on my back legs and walked around. People laughed.

"She doesn't know she's a dog, folks," the announcer said, getting more laughter.

A cool breeze blew across the stage, smelling vaguely of musty-ozone. I dropped back to the ground and sniffed the wind. A few of the patrons exclaimed about the cold breeze.

"It's just a draft, folks," the announcer said.

"Brown, what do you smell?" Elliott whispered.

My hackles rose as the musty-ozone smell got stronger. The wind gusted, blowing out a few lamps, and then was gone, the humid heat of summer shocking after the cold.

I woofed and shook. Then I jumped back up onto the stool and sat on my hind end again.

The audience clapped and we were done. I wanted food, and then I wanted to hunt that ghost.

We left the dining room and followed one of the servers back to the kitchen. The food they set on the ground for me tasted every bit as good as it smelled and I licked the plate clean, grinning when I was done. Elliott wasn't quite finished so I looked at one of the cooks hopefully. He snuck me a few more scraps, winking. I grinned and returned to Elliott's side once he finished his food.

"Let's go get our things, Brown."

"Sir." One of the cooks stopped us.

"Yes?"

"You're here to look for that ghost?"

"Yes. What can you tell me about it?"

The cook looked around, smelling nervous, and he lowered his voice. "We're not supposed to talk about her. Bad for business and all that but I'm guessing no one told you."

"Told me what?"

"Well, we think it's the ghost of a performer that hung herself a few years back. Not sure on the whole story. I wasn't here back then so I've only heard rumors, but they said she and the Captain got into it over wages or some such. She lost the argument and hung herself in retaliation. We think that's why the ghost bothers the stage the most. Well, and she had long hair, so stealing the ladies' brushes makes sense too."

"Where did she hang herself?"

The cook shook his head. "The stage. Was quite the finale to the cruise."

"I imagine so. Thank you for the information and the excellent food."

The cook smiled in pleasure. "You're welcome."

I wagged my tail and barked happily.

"You too, Brown," the cook said.

"Well, we'd better get to it. The quicker we can defeat this ghost, the better."

"Yes, sir. Good luck."

I stayed close to Elliott while we went back to our room, alert for the ghost, but it, or she, didn't make an appearance.

"Let's put your boots on."

I sat and let him put on the leather boots that protected my feet from broken glass. They had little bead crosses sewn onto them to help protect against demons. Then he pulled out his hunting journal that his great-grand pappy had written and read a few pages.

"It says here that sometimes a ghost will be tied to a place by an object they owned when they were alive. If you destroy that object you can destroy the ghost. I doubt there is anything left if it was that actress though. So we'll try and trap her like the other ghosts."

I wagged my tail and followed Elliott back out into the hallways. The gas lamps stayed steady and no cold breezes came out of nowhere, so I was fairly certain we were alone. We spent several hours wandering the halls of the steamship before we went outside for some fresh air. It was night now and the cool breeze felt good after the hot day. I put my nose into the wind.

"Brown, let's go up to the top. I want to see the stars."

I grinned and followed him up to the top deck. A few couples were out enjoying the nice night, but almost everyone was still inside.

The seagull fluttered down to the rail next to me. "Did you find the ghost yet?"

"I think so."

"Did you banish it yet?"

"No, not yet."

"Good." The gull squawked.

"Good?"

"Well, it'll be much more boring without it to scare the people."

I huffed and tried to ignore the bird.

"They had a priest here to exorcise it. Did they tell you that?" The bird tilted its head and hopped sideways along the rail.

"No."

"Yeah. Did all sorts of funny incantations or whatever they're called. They even managed to summon the ghost, but she escaped." The bird sounded pleased.

"How'd she escape?"

The bird tilted its head the other direction. "I don't know."

"Is there anything of hers on the ship?" I tried to ask casually, as if it didn't matter, but I think my intense stare gave my interest away.

The bird hopped back and squawked again. "Maybe."

Elliott turned around and the gull shrieked and flapped away. My human stared after the bird for a moment before gesturing toward the stairs. "Let's go back inside and see what we can find."

Nothing else happened while we wandered the ship and after dinner and the entertainments were done we went back to the stage. The captain found us there.

"Well?"

"What can you tell me about the ghost, Captain Arnault?"

"It's a ghost." He shrugged.

"Do you have any idea whose ghost it is?"

The captain sighed and sank into a chair. "The rumor is that it's Betty's. She sang on the ship for years and eventually she wanted a raise. She deserved one, but the railroads stole most of our business and we were having a hard enough time making ends meet as it was so I told her no, and I told her why. She didn't like that and a few weeks later she hung herself, though I'm not completely sure it was related to not getting a raise. She was troubled, and before hiring on with me she'd been running from something. I heard an argument, but I never did find out who she argued with and then she was gone. Betty had a marvelous voice." He sounded sad.

"Well, I'd say we should try to summon her and trap her in one of our traps we build. Then we can banish her."

"You've done this before?"

"Yes, several times."

"Need anything from me?" Captain Arnault stood.

My human hesitated, and then shook his head. "No. Thank you. Could you lock the doors though, so no one can disturb us?"

"Of course. I'll leave the serving door open so you can get out."

"Thank you."

The captain locked the doors. As the last lock clicked shut and he left the room, I felt something watching me.

My hackles rose and I growled, looking around and trying to find what was watching me.

"Is it the ghost?"

I sniffed and caught a whiff of musty ozone. I barked once.

"Try to keep it off of me while I draw this." He drew his designs on the floor while I looked all around for the ghost.

Slowly the musty ozone smell grew stronger until I sneezed, but I couldn't find the ghost. The air chilled until my breath steamed like the ship's pipes. Still the ghost remained hidden.

Elliott lit his incense and began to chant.

The ghost howled and something flickered at the edge of my vision. I spun in time to see a white form race around the edges of the room. All of the gaslights went out until the only light came from windows high up toward the ceiling. Elliott's chant faltered for a moment, but he picked it up again.

The ghost screamed and flew at us, a creepy glowing form in the darkness. I barked angrily and glared at the ghost, using my Border Collie eye to try and stare it down.

The ghost rushed to a halt and hovered nearby. I stepped forward and it floated backward. I crept slowly, pushing, feeling the ghost struggle against my mind. I pushed it until it floated over the trap. Light flared, blinding me for a moment and I looked away. The ghost screamed in rage.

Elliott shouted over its wails.

As soon as I could see I looked at the trap. The glowing wisp of ghost was inside writhing around like a snake. Elliott was almost done with the chant that would banish it forever when it vanished. The lights came back and Elliott faltered again, frowning.

I barked in alarm.

He finished the chant, but nothing happened since the ghost was already gone.

"What happened, Brown?"

I huffed in annoyance, wishing he understood more than body language so I could communicate better.

He took his round hat off his head and spun it in his hands while he stared at the drawing on the stage. "The trap is perfectly drawn."

"What happened?" Captain Arnault came back into the dining room. "One of the servers said they heard the ghost screaming."

Elliott scratched his head then put his hat back on and folded his arms across his chest. "We had it in the trap, and then it just vanished. I'm pretty sure it shouldn't be able to do that."

The captain looked at the trap Elliott had drawn and smelled nervous. "That's not devil stuff is it?"

"No. Quite the opposite. My great-grand pappy was a strong, God-fearing man. He learned these techniques from priests in the old country and passed them on to me."

"Ahh, well then."

I'd never heard that story before, but if it made the captain feel better then I guess it was a good story.

Elliott paced around the circle again, staring at it. Then he stopped and spun, facing Captain Arnault. "Do you have anything of Betty's still?"

Finally, he asked the right question. I woofed quietly but they ignored me.

"No."

"Are you sure?"

"Quite sure. She didn't have much."

I barked twice and stared at Captain Arnault. He took a step back. "What's wrong with your dog?"

"Brown seems to think you're wrong."

I barked once.

"How the devil would a dog know anything?"

I wrinkled my lips but didn't growl at him.

"Are you sure you don't have anything of hers?"

The captain sighed and pulled out a cigar. He didn't light it, but he stuck it in his mouth as if it helped him to think. "Well, now that I think about it. I believe one of the girls kept her purple scarf. It was one she wore on stage on cooler nights. Haven't seen it in years, but it might be in a trunk. Yes, it just might. I know the trunk too. Wait here." He hurried away.

Elliott studied his book while we waited for Arnault to come back. It took a while, but he finally returned with a scarf in his hand.

"This is it. I looked to make sure and it's the only thing I can identify as hers." He held it out to Elliott.

As Elliott reached out to take the scarf, the ghost screamed, glass shattered and a gust of wind ripped the scarf from the Captain's hand. I barked in alarm and raced after the ghost as it flew from the room, scarf fluttering behind it.

I ran as fast as I dared inside, keeping the ghost in sight, but I had to slow to turn corners and it didn't. The ghost got further away and I lost sight of it around another corner, but screams from the passengers told me where to go. I raced down the carpeted hallways, trying not to bounce into any of the people as I ran. The ghost went into an empty part of the ship and I lost it for a minute but then I caught a hint of the musty ozone smell and chased after it. I barely managed to keep my feet when it went down into the ship and I had to take steps so steep they were almost a ladder. I landed on one unfortunate, soot-covered man, but I was off of him and gone before he could do more than shout.

The oil and grease smells overwhelmed the ghost scent and I couldn't hear any screams over the hissing of steam so I slowed and looked around. Everything was dirty and black down here and when it didn't smell like oil it smelled like burning wood. I panted in the heat and searched for a trace of the ghost.

"Hey, get that dog!"

I barked in alarm and ran away from the person chasing me. Something fluttered at the edge of my vision and I turned a corner. The ghost was right in front of me! It shrieked and sped away. I chased it and the man chased me.

"Hey, shut that door!" The man shouted and another worker slammed the door, right in front of the ghost.

It vanished, but the purple scarf stuck to the door, coated in slime from the ghost. I skidded to a halt and barely managed to avoid getting in the nasty goo myself. I stood on my back legs and pulled the purple scarf off of the door with my boot-covered paw. Then I stood over it, growling protectively whenever one of the men tried to get close.

"Hey, go get that guy who owns the dog. Or the captain. Don't want to get bit," one of them yelled to another.

It didn't take very long before both Elliott and the Captain joined me. They both breathed heavily as if they'd run too.

I grinned and pawed the scarf.

"Good job, Brown." Elliott bent over and picked up the scarf with two fingers. "That's nasty."

"What is that?" The Captain asked.

"It's ghost slime."

"Why'd it leave the scarf?"

"I guess it couldn't take the scarf through the door. Come on, let's go finish this."

They had to carry me out of the boiler room because I couldn't quite make it safely back up the stairs, but otherwise we made it back to the dining room without incident, though I did feel like we were watched the whole way, and not just by the passengers that crew still tried to calm.

The wind picked up again in the dining room, trying to rip the scarf from Elliott's hand, but they were prepared this time and as soon as he reached the trap he placed the scarf in the middle. The ghost screamed and more glass shattered. I winced, whining in pain from the noise.

Elliott relit his incense and began his chant. This time the Captain held a lantern over the incense smoke and when the ghost tried to put out the lights, that one stayed lit. The ghost howled and raged, glowing in the faint light from the single lantern. It flew at us but didn't let me catch it with my Eye this time. It dodged as I tried to catch it, but it didn't see what I was doing. It dodged one more time and then it was between me and the trap. I barked and leapt, shoving the ghost forward over the trap with my body. Light flared and threw me away. I yelped when I landed on my side, but the ghost was again caught, and this time it didn't escape. It wailed and twisted but Elliott shouted the last of his incantation and the ghost exploded, sending slime flying in all directions. I ducked under a table and avoided the worst of the splatter but Elliott and the captain were coated.

"Is it dead?" Captain Arnault asked.

Elliott wiped away a little slime from his face and smiled. "Yes, Captain." He snapped his book shut and put it into his hunting bag. The book never seemed to get slimed, and my boots were clean as well. I slunk out from under the table, a little sore from my landing, but otherwise okay. All that was left of the trap was a blackened ring on the stage. The scarf was gone.

"This stuff is everywhere." The captain sounded disgusted.

Elliott laughed. "It comes off in salt water."

"She won't come back?"

"I hope not."

"Well, Mr. Gyles, you've more than earned your pay. However can I thank you?"

"Well, sir. Food and lodging until we return to St. Louis and the pay you promised is all I need. Perhaps a good word if you hear of someone in need of my services."

"Mr. Gyles, it's a deal." He clapped Elliott on the back and left the stage, dodging piles of goo as he did.

My human laughed and I grinned.

"Brown, another job well done, my brave girl. Are you hurt?"

I shook my head, body language I'd learned from him.

"Well, I don't think we'll find any sheep on this steamship, but I bet when we return to St. Louis I'll be able to find a farm or two."

I thumped my tail happily.

"Come on, let's clean up. You smell like a ghost."

I pointed my nose in his direction and very deliberately sneezed.

"I guess I'm not much better."

I trotted next to Elliott as we left the dining room. I couldn't wait to tell that obnoxious seagull how we'd defeated the ghost.

# BROWN AND THE SAND DRAGON

*Golton, Arizona, 1900*

"Look Mommy, fireflies!" Christy danced around trying to catch the glowing bugs. "They're a lot faster than at our old home."

"Christy, there aren't any fireflies in the desert," her mom called from the house.

She laughed and jumped, but the little bugs slipped through her chubby fingers. "They want me to follow!"

"Christy, come back inside."

"They glow." Christy giggled and chased as the flashing bugs clumped into a swarm and darted off into the night. She wished she had a jar to put them in. She knew she could catch the bugs if she just ran a little further.

"Christy!"

She ignored her mom's worried shout and chased the bugs into a small clump of scraggily trees. The ground was still warm under her feet but the chill air brought a flush to her cheeks as she ran.

Christy laughed and danced and chased the beautiful bugs into a canyon. She knew she wasn't supposed to be this far from home, but her mommy would forgive her when she brought back a beautiful bug.

"Christy!"

She thought she heard her mommy's shout, but it was so far away. How far had she run? Christy stopped and looked around. The bugs had vanished and it was very dark and she had no idea where she was. Tears sprang to her eyes.

"Mommy!" she called, and then stopped and stared as the glow reappeared. It was much larger and it rose slowly from the ground, lighting the sides of the canyon.

The light grew in intensity, casting shadows of giant wings upon the canyon wall. Glowing slits appeared in the sky, slowly opening to round orbs that bobbed and weaved toward her.

A dark shape resolved into a giant head complete with gleaming yellow teeth. The creature seemed to smile at Christy.

She stared for a moment and then screamed. "Momm..." Her cry cut short as the swarm reappeared and flew around her. She felt her body go numb and she collapsed to the still warm ground.

"Well, Brown, here we are. Golton, Arizona."

I looked around at the dusty, dry landscape and thought my brown coat blended in well. Though my eyes told me there were no sheep, my nose suggested there might be cows and I smelled water. Enough to make me think there was a river close by.

We had traveled forever across the desert to get here and I was sure the horses would be glad for a break. I disliked rattlesnakes and scorpions and this environment was stranger than any I'd been in before. I missed the soft green grass of home, but the sun-baked dirt presented its own interests. I sniffed a bug, which flew away.

"We came a long way. I hope they have a proper livery and inn."

I leapt back up onto the bench when Elliott clucked to the horses, and slapped the reins to start the wagon. It was close to noon and normally we would have stopped to rest for several hours but we were very close.

There wasn't much to the town. A double row of buildings with a dirt road between, but there was a ghost here that needed killing and I was the dog for the job.

A couple of kids ran up to our wagon, laughing and running with us for a time while the horses plodded to the stables. A man smelling of hot metal and horse came out to greet us when we arrived.

"Don't get too many gentlemen 'round here," he drawled. "Where ya headed?"

"I'm here about a ghost."

The man frowned and scratched his head. "Devil is more like. You must be Mr. Gyles."

"Yes, sir."

"I'm Butch, the farrier. Your horses look tired, let's get this wagon round back and we can give 'em a rest."

"Thank you, sir. Could you also see to their feet?"

"Certainly."

I jumped down while the humans sorted out the wagon and horses. I hoped to find a local dog or, much as I didn't like them, a cat. That was usually the best way to get information about ghosts.

Naturally I found a cat first. In fact, I could smell that dogs lived here, but the scents were all older. I stared up at the gray tabby perched on a shop bench and she stared back at me, tail puffed and hackles up. I thumped my tail on the ground to show her I wanted to be friendly, raising a puff of dust.

She stared for a moment longer then groomed a paw. I took that as an invitation.

"I'm Brown."

She sniffed. "Yes, you are quite dirty."

I stifled an annoyed growl and tried again. "I'm here to hunt the ghost."

The tabby stopped grooming and stared at me, eyes wide. "It's not a ghost. It's a devil. Took most of the children, a bunch of the cowboys, and all of the farm dogs. All the town dogs had to go out to the ranch to work. You're really going to hunt it?"

I stared. This cat wasn't anything like most other cats. They were always condescending, even in bad situations. This cat just seemed afraid, and a little in awe. That worried me.

"Well, they called us about a ghost."

The tabby's tail twitched and she looked very alarmed. "You'll need every blessing you can get to fight this devil."

The cat's strange behavior scared me and I whined.

She licked her shoulder then looked behind me, spun and ran off. I stared after the cat while listening to my human walk up to me.

"What's going on, Brown?"

I whined again and wished he understood how to listen properly. Humans were so limited in their ability to communicate.

"Well." He scratched my ears. "We have a room at the inn. Let's get lunch and then we can meet with the mine owner, Mr. Markie. Guess he and the ranch owner, Mr. Taggart have been having trouble and their local hero is off on some other adventure. That's why they called us. I get the impression it's not exactly a ghost we're after though."

I flattened my ears and hoped the creature we had to fight wasn't worse than squirrels.

"You did call me here for a ghost," Elliott said to the two men seated across from him. One, Taggart, smelled of cows and horse and dog. Markie smelled more of horse and dirt and hot metal, but not quite the same as the farrier.

"Weren't sure you'd come if we told you the truth. We need someone who's faced demons before. We'll pay well," Markie said.

Elliott leaned back in his chair and I rested my head on his knee. He scratched my ears and stared at the men for a moment. "We've never faced a demon. Only ghosts. Are you sure you shouldn't have called a priest?"

"Our preacher's new to the area. Educated man from back east. He's not up to fighting a demon." Taggart frowned at Elliott. "You sayin' you can't do it?"

"I, sir, am an educated man from back east. I can and have vanquished many ghosts. I suspect your priest is similarly qualified, though perhaps not as experienced. I've never fought a demon."

The two men shared a look then Markie dropped a bag on the table. It thunked as if it were heavy. "Enough silver in here to pay a railman's wage for a year. Suspect it'll keep your horses and dog fed for longer."

"Yes, if Brown and I survive to spend it." Elliott sounded annoyed. "Perhaps I should see what we're up against, before I say yes or no. Can this demon be viewed without getting killed in the process?"

"Yes," Taggart said. "I won't say it's safe, but one of my men knows the way. Native named Nata. Good man."

"Excellent. How soon can we be ready to go?"

"Soon as you saddle a horse." Taggart stood.

"Ah, mine are cart horses and not used to the saddle."

Markie nodded. "Take mine. Got business in town anyway. We'll bring one up from Taggart's ranch for you to borrow while you're here. Don't imagine you want to hitch up your wagon every time you need to go someplace."

"Thank you, sir." Elliott pushed back his chair and Markie stood to shake his hand.

"We do appreciate your coming here, and the hardship of the journey. Know it took some time to get here." He handed Elliott a smaller bag. "For your trouble so far. We hope you can help us, but if not, we understand."

"Thank you. I should get a few things from my wagon, and then we can be off."

"We'll be here with the horses." Taggart touched the brim of his hat.

I followed my human out of the saloon and back toward the wagon.

"I don't know about this, Brown. Sounds like bad business."

At least we weren't going to sneak away in the night. We used to do that a lot. Now we had real ghosts to fight, a real job to do. It was the best kind of life. Well, except for working sheep.

Elliott grabbed his hunting bag and went back to the saloon. Taggart gestured to a horse and Elliott mounted. I followed as they rode out of the small town.

"That dog of yours any good on cattle? I could use a good farm dog while you're off killing our demon."

Elliott laughed. "She's great with sheep. I'm sure she'd love cows, but she helps me hunt."

"Really? Not a hunting dog."

"No, she's a Border Collie from the old country. She uses her Eye on ghosts. She can hold them still or herd them into traps so I can banish them."

"Huh. How'd you train her to do that?"

78

"She's a natural."

"She's not going to have puppies any time soon, is she?"

I could feel Taggart's eyes on me while they talked about me and I looked up and grinned at him.

"No."

"Shame. Pay a lot for a dog like that if she works as good as you say."

"Border Collies are the best. She's not for sale."

Taggart laughed. "Didn't figure she was, son. Good dog like that's worth more than all the silver in Markie's mine. 'Specially if she fights ghosts. We're almost there. Ranch is just over the rise. I'll have Nata take you the rest of the way. Best be back by sunset though."

"That won't give us much time."

"You won't need much to see what you're up against." Taggart kicked his horse into a canter and Elliott followed. I raced alongside, reveling in the run. It was hot but not unbearably so and the pads of my feet had toughed against the heat in the last month. We rode around a bend in the canyons and a valley opened up before us. A river ran in the distance and cows grazed along its banks.

"Nice place."

"Yep, been in my family for ages. Best grazing in the area, on account of the river. We've fought tooth and nail to hold it." I could hear the pride in Taggart's voice and I barked happily.

I raced up ahead and waited by the barn for the horses to catch up. By the time they arrived I'd already made friends with the person who'd been cleaning the barn and he'd brought me a bowl of water.

"Ahh, Nata. I see you've already met Brown. This is Mr. Gyles, the other half of the ghost hunting team. Would you take them out to see our demon?"

"Yes, sir." He scratched my ears. "Let me get my horse."

Before too long we were on our way.

"So, Nata, please tell me about this demon."

Our guide was quiet for a minute.

"It's plagued us for months. We don't know where it came from, but a strange man came to town. White guy from the west coast. Said he was going to look for gold. We told him it was mostly silver in these parts, but he wanted gold. He bought supplies and vanished into the canyons. Shortly after, this demon appeared. We haven't seen the prospector since. Everyone in the area has tried to kill it, but arrows, guns, and everything we've tried don't hurt it. Many died fighting it. It lures our children away, and traps those who get to close. Of course no one's gotten close recently."

"Except you?"

Nata shrugged. "If you're careful you can see it. Doesn't mean you can get close."

"What does it look like?"

"Probably best if you see it for yourself."

They fell silent after that and we rode until the shadows got long.

"We should stop here and tie the horses. They make too much noise. We're not far now. Stay quiet, Brown," Nata said.

I nodded my understanding and Nata stared at me for a minute, as if surprised, before leading the way through scrub brush and canyons. Before too long he led us through a narrow crack in the rock walls and gestured for us to crouch down behind some scrub and rocks. We looked out into a small box canyon. Most of the details were lost because of the long shadows, but there didn't seem to be much in it except some brush and what looked like a giant round rock in the center. It glowed faintly and I could hear something that sounded like a large animal breathing.

Nata put a finger to his lips and picked up a rock. He threw it hard and then ducked. It bounced against the far wall, clacking as it fell. The rock in the center of the clearing shuddered, and then something that looked like a giant head shot upward and darted toward the sound. Giant wings stretched from its back, uncovering a glowing center, much like a flying bug from back home. It stood on four, bent, massive legs and lunged toward the sound. When it didn't find anything its head bobbed and swayed around the clearing, neck twisting like a snake. It hissed and looked straight at us, eyes glowing the same burnished gold as its stomach.

I almost peed on the ground when its gaze fell on us. I was so frightened I couldn't move, couldn't think. Elliott reached out and touched my ruff and suddenly I could move again. I pressed up against him, trembling.

The demon searched the clearing far longer than I would have, and I hoped it couldn't smell us. It had a nose, but it didn't seem to be using it or I'm sure it would have smelled our fear. Finally it settled, folding its wings across its back and muting some of the glow from its belly. It stared out of the box canyon and opened its jaw. Long teeth glinted in the fading light. The creature breathed out and a swarm of tiny dancing lights left its mouth.

I tilted my head, wondering what those were. They swirled around like a dust devil for a moment then left the canyon.

Nata tugged on Elliott's shoulder and we crept away from the demon. I hated turning my back on it, and I couldn't keep my hackles down until we were back at the horses.

"Is it safe to talk?" Elliott asked quietly.

Nata nodded.

"That's not a demon, or a ghost! It's the bastard child of a lizard and a firefly. What the hell!"

"Shhh. I said it was okay to talk. Not to shout."

"Sorry. Quite right." Elliott took off his hat and scratched his head. "Let's get back to the ranch before it gets dark."

They mounted their horses and set a brisk pace back to the ranch. It was dark by the time we got there and I was grateful for dinner and a spot by the fireplace while Mrs. Taggart fed Elliott and Nata.

"I'm not even sure what to say. It's a bloody dragon. Ahh, pardon my language." Elliott bowed slightly toward Mrs. Taggart.

"It's okay, lad. I live with ruffians."

Nata frowned. "How did it get here? My tribe has been in the area for years and we've never seen anything like that."

Elliott shook his head. "I have no idea. I'm not sure I can do anything against it, but I have books in my wagon and they might have some information. I understand you want this beast gone quickly, but until I have an idea of what to do, I can't help."

"So, will you help us?" Mr. Taggart walked into the kitchen followed by Mr. Markie.

"I'll see if I can find something that may help. I make no promises. I've never heard of anything like that, let alone fought it. With ghosts there are rituals and traps and other things you can do to fight them. This is beyond my experience."

"That's fair enough, Mr. Gyles. Why don't you stay in the guest room tonight and we'll get you back to town tomorrow. Once you have something, we'll proceed. I've men who will face it, if there's a hope of killing it. Don't be afraid to ask for men or supplies."

"Thank you, Mr. Taggart."

Mr. Taggart ruffled my ears as he walked past and we followed him down the hallway to a dark room.

"Please, make yourself comfortable."

"Again, thank you."

He left us, and Elliott sat on the bed and covered his face with his hands. I put my head on his knee and he scratched my ears.

"Oh, Brown. How do we get into these situations?"

I whined.

"Can we fight this?"

I didn't answer.

"That's reassuring."

I licked his cheek and thumped my tail on the ground.

"Well, let's get some rest. We have a busy day tomorrow."

By busy I knew he meant boring. He'd sit and stare at his books all day and I'd have nothing to do.

"Your dog looks bored."

I lifted my head from my paws and thumped my tail against the wood floor of the wagon. I'd given up wandering around once we got back to town and was trying to sleep away my boredom.

"Yes, Mr. Taggart. She's used to being out and running around all the time."

"Mind if I take her out to the ranch? Need some help with the cows and a lot of our dogs have gone missing."

Elliott frowned. "I don't want anything to happen to her."

"It was the creature that took 'em. She knows better, I'd reckon."

"Brown, want to go work some cows?"

I perked my ears forward and met his eyes. Was he serious?

"You can go if you want too."

I sprang to my feet and leapt out of the wagon, wagging my tail happily and dancing around like a puppy.

"She really that smart? Never met a Border Collie before. Ranch dogs are smart, but she seems like she knows exactly what you want."

"Brown's the smartest dog I've ever met."

"Well, we'll see how she works. Maybe I'll have to see if I can get one or two out here."

I pushed my head under his hand and he scratched my ears.

"Okay, Brown. Go with Mr. Taggart and be careful."

I barked once to show my understanding then followed as Mr. Taggart walked away from the wagon.

The trip back to the ranch didn't take too long and instead of going to the house, Mr. Taggart rode around to the pasture and I followed. Several other men on horses milled about with a few dogs. They looked like town dogs, used to lounging away the day instead of working on the ranch.

The dogs stared at me as I trotted up. I kept my distance and watched Mr. Taggart for orders.

One of the dogs, a shaggy thing, came forward, waving his tail. I wrinkled my lips.

"Gosh, sorry. I just wanted to say hi." He went back to the other dogs and they stared at me. I tried to ignore them. I didn't want to play. I just wanted to work.

"Okay men. Let's go round up the cows. See if you can't keep your dogs under control."

"Ain't our dogs, sir. That's the problem."

Mr. Taggart laughed. "Well, maybe Brown can whip 'em into shape. She's got experience on sheep. Brown, go with Nata."

I looked around and found our guide from the other night and trotted to his side, wagging my tail.

"I'll be damned. She does understand."

Nata grinned. "Thanks, Boss."

"Don't thank me. You get the hard job. Go get 'em out of the canyons. We'll meet you with the other cows in a few hours. Hopefully the demon hasn't got to them too."

"Yes, sir." Nata mounted his horse and I followed when he rode off, dismayed to see another dog following. He wasn't any breed I could identify and had a large scar across his dust colored muzzle. His nose and paws and the tip of his long tail were black.

I didn't try to talk to him, and he left me alone. That was how I liked it. We trotted on either side of Nata's horse and headed for the ridgeline.

"Okay, dogs. Watch for snakes and get them cows." Nata pointed into the mouth of a canyon. The other dog barked once so I did too and followed him in. Nata went a short way into the mouth of the canyon and waited.

I put my nose into the air and looked for the cows. I thought this would be like clearing sheep from a pen, only bigger, so I ran up one side of the canyon and circled around the back. The other dog seemed to think this was a good idea because he followed. We trotted back toward the entrance, the other dog going down the middle, me along the side. He found the first cow. A small one grazing on some scrub. I watched as he dove at the cow's feet. It turned and ran. I snorted. His technique worked, but lacked finesse.

I got the next cow we came to. It moved off with a good dose of my Eye.

The other dog watched, seeming to consider my technique. He crouched and stared at the next cow like me. It worked and pretty soon we had the canyon cleared. The cows had gathered around Nata and his horse and I trotted

85

out to join them. The other dog barked a warning and I froze. One of the cows broke and tried to come back at us. I got in its face, giving it plenty of Eye. It ignored me but I held my ground, knowing I could stop it. Finally, at the last moment I dove forward and gave it a solid bite on the nose. The cow threw up its head and ran back toward the herd.

Once Nata moved further away the cows stayed with him.

"Good job, dogs. On to the next one."

Me and the other dog, who I finally spoke too when we stopped for a meal, spent the rest of the day in blissful labor, clearing the canyons of cows and bringing them out to a growing herd. Nata and a few other cowboys kept an eye on the cattle while we worked. Nata was the other dog's person and he was the only other experienced working dog. Nata called him Ch'al, apparently because he used to hop around like a frog as a puppy. He was friendly enough, though reserved. He didn't think much of the other dogs either and sighed repeatedly while he watched them race around the growing herd of cows, wasting energy.

"They'll be exhausted in an hour. They just don't learn."

I snorted and lay down, watching the herd in case one of the cows broke away. We went back to work after our quick break, pushing the herd back toward the ranch. The other dogs started complaining about being tired halfway back. Ch'al and I trotted along, ignoring the other dogs until one darted in at the cows. I barked in alarm, but Ch'al was more practical. He tore after the misbehaving mutt and clamped down on his leg before he could reach the cows. The dog yelped in pain and spun on Ch'al.

The cows mooed nervously but I kept them going in a straight line while Ch'al chased off the offending dog. It ran away out past the cowboys yelling curses.

Ch'al and I shared a look and kept on trotting back to the barn. I thought I might even like him. We were both grinning when we pushed the cattle into the corral awhile later. The other dogs had all dropped back and were dragging themselves to the shade in the barn. I felt good and I spun in a happy circle once the cows were put up and Nata called us off.

"Good job, dogs."

Ch'al and I barked once together then headed for the shade. One of the town dogs tried to growl us off the water bowl but I put up my hackles and wrinkled my lips. He backed off and we drank our fill before finding a good spot in the shade.

We spent the next several days rounding up cows. The food was excellent and the work was good, but I missed Elliott.

"Hey, Brown. That your person?" Ch'al gestured with his nose as we brought another group of cows up to the ranch.

I saw someone leaning against a corral panel watching us. The round hat, slightly hunched posture and height were all right and I almost barked happily. I wanted to run to him but we had to get the cows up first. He'd understand.

"Yes! I'll introduce you once we're done."

This group of cows resisted the corral but I was determined to see Elliott and even though one turned and tried to fight I promptly bit its nose and pushed it into the corral. As soon as the gate was shut I tore away, running as fast as I could and skidding to a halt in front of Elliott. He was grinning.

"Having a good time, Brown?"

I yipped and danced around, then couldn't take it anymore and crouched. He knew what I wanted and held

J.A. Campbell

out his arms. I leapt and he caught me. I licked his face while he laughed.

"That's one fine dog, Mr. Gyles. You sure she isn't for sale?"

"Yes, Mr. Taggart. I'm sure. I wouldn't trade her for all of Mr. Markie's silver mine."

I wagged my tail and jumped to the ground. "Come on, say hi, Ch'al."

He walked up more sedately and I wagged my tail and ran back and forth between him and Elliott.

"Who's your friend?" Elliott crouched down on one knee and held out his hand.

"Oh, that's Nata's dog. Only dog out here worth a damn besides Brown," Mr. Taggart said.

Ch'al sniffed Elliott's hand and wagged his tail. Elliott scratched his ears. "Nice to meet you. What's his name?"

"Something Navajo that means frog. Can't pronounce it. We call him Frog."

Ch'al sat and thumped his tail on the ground. Elliott gave him a good scratching.

"Well, Mr. Taggart. We might have something."

"Excellent. Join us inside for dinner and you can tell us about it." Mr. Taggart dismounted and led his horse away.

"Well, Brown. Did you have fun?"

I barked happily and followed Elliott into the house where a cool bowl of water and a heaping plate of meat waited for me and Ch'al. We were the only dogs that got to eat in the house.

"I see why you like it here. You're never going to want to come home. Cows and plates full of meat."

I pushed up against his leg to reassure him I'd always go wherever he went. He scratched my ears.

"Go eat. I was joking."

I perked my ears and grinned.

"So, I've never read of a dragon that looks like this, and I couldn't find anything that suggests anyone else has either. However I did find something about magical constructs. This creature might be one of those."

"What?"

"Well, something a human creates and somehow imbues with magic making it sort of alive. Usually there is some sort of object of power that keeps it animated. If we find that, we can destroy the creature."

"Well, Mr. Gyles, I'm fairly certain you're speaking English, but I don't follow."

Elliott sighed. "It's not something I know much about, but apparently magic is real and some people know how to use it. Someone with magical knowledge created this dragon. And if it is what I think it is, we should be able to defeat it. We just have to find the object of power and take it away from the creature."

"Huh. Sounds reasonable. I suppose." Mr. Taggart sounded anything but convinced.

"We need to observe the creature to see if we can find out what the object is. Then we can make a plan."

"Nata, the cows are all in. Can you assist Mr. Gyles?"

"Yes, Boss."

"Excellent. Everyone get some rest, and you can set out first thing in the morning."

I followed Elliott back to the spare room and pressed up against his leg while he slept. I'd missed him, and while I'd enjoyed working cows, I never wanted to be away from him for that long again.

We set out in the morning and Ch'al and I raced ahead for a time before settling down and keeping pace with the horses. Finally the humans dismounted and we followed Nata quietly through the scrub and around the canyons until we were crouched, staring at the dragon. It currently had its nose tucked under a wing and it looked as if it were sleeping. The glow was less noticeable during the day and it wouldn't have been hard to mistake the dragon for a rock.

We watched forever and it did nothing, except once when a rabbit came into the clearing. The dragon snatched up the rabbit and ate it before tucking its head under its wings and going back to sleep, or whatever it was that dragons did. I had a feeling this thing was worse than squirrels. Squirrels didn't eat rabbits.

I got bored and fell asleep. Elliott shook me awake later. The sun was lower and the shadows long when I followed the humans and Ch'al back to the horses. They rode in silence for a while.

"Did we learn anything?"

"The dragon eats rabbits," Elliott said. They both laughed. "Nata, we're going to be at this for a while. Why don't you teach me how to get here on my own? Then I won't keep you from your other job. I promise I won't try to do anything without help."

"Okay. Your dog probably already knows the way, but I'll teach you the signs."

They talked until we were back at the ranch then we turned in for the night. The next day was the same, only we went without Nata. I was really tempted to stay on the ranch but I couldn't let Elliott go into danger alone even though it seemed like he was perfectly safe. The dragon was actually very boring and I couldn't see how it could be dangerous until the third evening.

It was late and we were about to leave when the dragon breathed its small lights out into the night. We waited and before too long a small desert cat chased them back into the clearing, pouncing, trying to catch them. Once the dragon saw the little cat, the small lights stopped dancing and spun around the cat. It yowled in fear and even though it was a cat, I wanted to help it. I wouldn't wish what happened on anything but a squirrel.

The frightened yowl was cut off and the cat fell limp with strands of something the lights created wrapped around it. The dragon then picked up the small cat and carried it out of sight, long tail sweeping over the sagebrush and flattening it.

The desert cat was nowhere to be seen when the dragon returned and settled into its normal spot.

Elliott smelled afraid and he hurried away from the canyon. I stayed right with him. He was quiet until we were back at the ranch. Then he told everything to Nata and Mr. Taggart.

"That'd be how it caught the children then. Kids love things that glow and flash."

"How many children did it get?"

Mr. Taggart shrugged. "Not sure. Enough."

"Could they still be alive? It didn't look like it killed the cat."

Nata and Mr. Taggart shared a long look. "We don't know. Some of them have been gone months. Some not as long. We can't imagine they're still alive, but we have a little hope."

"We have to rescue everyone we can. Have you tried capturing the dragon yet?"

"Took a couple of men out but the horses wouldn't go near it. Suspect we could try again. Might be the best way to get that power object you're on about. If you can't find it, maybe we should rope the thing and try that way."

Elliott nodded. "Do you think you'll be able to get horses to go near it this time?"

Mr. Taggart shrugged. "Got a handful of retired cow horses that'll do anything. Hadn't thought about using 'em before, but I'll have 'em brought round. They're the most likely to cooperate."

"Okay. Give me one more day, then we'll try that."

"You know how to use a rope?"

Elliott laughed. "Sorry, no. I could sheer sheep in a tight spot but I'm a stranger to cattle and ropes and such."

"Suspect you'll have a more dangerous job getting the object anyway."

Elliott was quiet for a moment before nodding. "I'd like to get some rest. Then we'll see what we can find tomorrow."

"Night, Mr. Gyles."

"Good night, sir."

We watched the dragon for an hour before Elliott threw the first rock. The dragon reacted the same as when Nata threw a rock. It reared up and struck at the wall. I wasn't completely sure what we were looking for but I thought Elliott might know so I watched him carefully. After a while I decided he didn't know either and sighed.

I was dozing when a familiar scent made my nose twitch and jerked me out of a dream about working cows with Ch'al. I opened my eyes and sniffed, sneezed, and jumped to my feet. Musty-ozone. A ghost! This I could fight.

"Shh... Brown."

I whined as quietly as I could and looked around for the ghost. I had to tell him what it was, but I didn't know how.

The dragon stirred but I didn't pay it any attention. I looked back at Elliott and there was a man standing behind him. I barked in alarm.

Elliott saw where I was looking and spun around, and then turned back to me.

"Brown, be quiet!"

I stared at the ghost. It was a tall man with dark skin like Nata's. He wore strange pants and what looked like a blanket for a shirt. His hair was long and he wore feathers and beads in it. I could almost see the rock wall behind him through his body. He had to be the ghost, but I'd never seen one that actually looked like a man before. I growled.

"Brown!" Elliott obviously couldn't see the ghost.

"Be quiet, dog," the ghost spoke.

I wasn't sure how to react to that either.

A shadow blotted out the sun and Elliott gasped. I turned and realized my mistake as the dragon's head loomed over us, staring directly at my human. Fear made me feel weak, but my desire to protect Elliott was stronger and I leapt at the dragon's head, barking as loudly as I could.

It snapped at me. I bounced off of one of if its huge fangs and fell to the ground. The dragon breathed out its little lights and I ran underneath the creature to escape. It was big and fast but I was faster. It tried to sweep me away with its tail. I jumped over the tail and snapped at its back leg. I got a mouthful. It tasted like sand.

The dragon roared in anger and spun around. I barked and snapped, trying to drive the thing off of Elliott. It was working. The dragon stepped back and I hoped Elliott would run.

"Brown!" His panicked cry was cut off and I turned to see him fall to the ground. The firefly lights frantically dancing around him.

I ran back to him. The dragon took advantage of my distraction and lunged past me, grabbing Elliott with one large clawed foot.

I lost my mind, attacking anything that glowed. The little lights turned to sand in my mouth and bits of the dragon fell to dust as well but I couldn't get it to stop. It ignored me once it had Elliott. It took him to the back of the canyon and I followed, barking my rage the whole time.

There was a small cleft in the rock wall and the dragon went through it. I tried to follow but something prevented me from entering. I tried again and bounced off of a wall I couldn't see. I threw myself against it again. I had to get to Elliott!

"Dog! You can't get in. Not yet."

That damn ghost again. I spun around, teeth bared, growling. I threw myself at the ghost, hoping to tear it apart. It vanished and reappeared behind me. I spun and jumped again.

"Dog! We must hide. If you want to save the human we have to escape."

I snarled. "What is this we. I'm going to destroy you."

"That would be unwise."

I stopped, startled. It had understood me. Humans were limited and couldn't understand animals unless they learned our body language. This ghost, apparently, could.

"Yes, I can understand you. Let's hide before the creature returns. I will tell you what you want to know."

I snarled.

"Or you can stay and be captured." The ghost turned and walked away, back toward our hiding spot.

I didn't want to follow but I could hear the dragon returning. Claws scraped across stone and the dragon's light filled the cave. I ran.

Shame made me curl up next to a rock and bury my nose under my tail when I got to safety. It was my fault Elliott was captured. I was a bad, bad dog. I whimpered and thought about letting the dragon catch me too, so at least we could be together.

The musty ozone smell returned and I looked up, baring my teeth. "This is your fault."

"I'm sorry, dog. I've never had an animal react like that before. I get along with all the creatures of the earth."

I snarled. "I hunt ghosts."

The man looked surprised. "Truly?"

"Yes."

"I'm not sure I've ever met a dog that even knows what I am. Peace, dog."

"My name is Brown."

"And you may call me, Old Man."

"What kind of name is that?" I buried my nose under my tail again.

"It is not a true name, but my true name has been lost to time, and I no longer need it."

"Well, Old Man, my human is gone and as soon as I am ready I'm going to kill you."

The ghost smiled. "Peace, Brown. I will help, if you'll let me."

The ghost's voice was deep and gravely. It soothed me and I found myself wanting to like him, despite his being a ghost. I resisted the urge and didn't answer.

The ghost sighed. "I was a shaman for the Navajo a long time ago. I lived a good life and was honored in death. For many years I was at peace. Then, not long ago as the living measure time, something disturbed me. A white man found my resting place and took something from me to power his creature. He wanted it to protect a small amount of gold he found. The man's greed killed him, but the creature remains. You can destroy it by taking the necklace it wears."

I peaked out from under my tail. "Yes?"

"It is tied on with a string and would break easily if pulled."

"Then why don't you take it back yourself?"

"I can't interact with the physical world, Brown. Humans never see me unless they are very in tune with the spirit world. Animals are far more perceptive, though I admit I've never met a dog like you."

I sighed. "How am I going to get the necklace off of the dragon?"

"You are fast."

I rested my head on my paws and stared at the strange ghost. "I've only heard ghosts laugh before. Why are you different? The ghosts I've met are angry and need to be destroyed."

He shrugged. "Perhaps it is because I was at peace. I am not a remnant. I was pulled back by the greed of another. I didn't remain out of vengeance or some other evil desire."

I huffed and got to my feet, and stalked out into the clearing.

"Brown, what are you doing?"

"I'm going to get that necklace."

"You'll get killed."

"You're the one who told me what I had to do." I barked at the dragon.

One glowing eye opened a slit. Then the other one opened.

I barked again and boldly met its eyes, wondering if my Eye would have any effect on it.

The dragon rose up, exposing its glowing belly. It towered over me, but I was too angry to be afraid. Now that I was looking, I could see the necklace around its neck. Some of the stones were green and some a brownish yellow. A black feather hung down from the center.

I stared but my Eye had no effect. With ghosts I could feel the struggle of my mind against theirs. It was almost as if the dragon had no mind. It reared back as if to strike.

I barked and darted forward. The dragon caught me with its front foot and tossed me into a wall. I hit it, feeling something snap. I yelped and sank to the ground. Elliott needed me. I forced myself to my feet and tried again. This time the dragon snapped at me. My Eye had no effect. I danced back, having a hard time moving because my side hurt. I ignored the pain. Saving Elliott was more important.

"Brown! You need help."

I tried again, lunging at the creature's neck. It reared up and lashed at me with its tail. I leapt over it, stumbling when I landed. The dragon struck and I just barely got out of its way. Maybe the ghost was right, but how could I get help?

I darted back, snarling and snapping and then hid behind a rock. Maybe Ch'al would come, but how could I leave? I looked back to where the dragon restlessly prowled its canyon then toward the place where Elliott had tied his horse.

"Brown, if you go back alone, the humans will understand that something is wrong. Perhaps you can convince them to come back and distract the dragon long enough for you to remove the necklace."

"And if I get it, then I will be able to save Elliott?"

"Yes."

I whined. I couldn't leave him.

"Brown, you will both die if you don't go get help."

I spun around in a circle and sat. Then I turned and did the hardest thing I'd ever done. I left.

The run back to the ranch took forever, but the pain in my side was nothing to the pain I felt at leaving Elliott behind.

I was exhausted by the time I got back, and I wasn't used to ever feeling tired. I collapsed in the shade, resting briefly before finding the water they kept out in the barn. One of the town dogs taunted me but I ignored him. I was looking for Ch'al.

Mr. Taggart saw me first.

"Brown, did it get Elliott?"

A question I could answer. I barked once sadly and nodded.

"Damn."

I barked and spun around, trying to get him to understand, but it was clear he didn't.

"Don't know what we'll do now." He scratched my ears.

I whined and looked at the barn.

"Need some water?" He followed me over, but I ignored the water dish and went and sat by a stall with a horse in it.

"Guess we should go find the poor kid's horse."

Nata rode up just then with Ch'al.

"It took Elliott!" I couldn't bring myself to tell the other dog that it was my fault. "But I know how to defeat the dragon. I need the humans to come distract the dragon for me."

Ch'al tilted his head then nodded. He grabbed Nata's pant leg with his teeth and gently pulled. Then he ran in the direction of the dragon for a few steps then came back and tugged on Nata's pants again.

"Boss, I think the dogs want us to go along."

"Well, we gotta go get the horse anyway." Mr. Taggart looked sad.

It didn't take long for Mr. Taggart and Nata to be ready. I wanted more men, but two would have to do.

"How do you defeat the dragon?" Ch'al asked as we ran.

"An old guy who looks kind of like Nata, told me I had to take a necklace it's wearing. Then we can defeat it."

"An old guy?"

"You'll see. He was a ghost. But he wasn't a nasty one like most ghosts."

"Most ghosts?"

"I hunt ghosts. Didn't I tell you that?"

Ch'al snorted. "I thought you herded sheep."

"Well, I do that too. Come on, we have to save Elliott." I ran faster even though I was more tired than I'd ever been before and my side hurt.

We left the humans behind and paused to rest by Elliott's horse. As soon as Mr. Taggart and Nata caught up we took off again.

"Hey, come back!"

We ignored Nata and kept going. I heard hoof beats and knew the humans followed.

Ch'al slowed where we normally spied on the dragon but I kept going, determined to defeat this thing. Ch'al followed and I dove straight at the creature's face.

It didn't seem to be expecting me and I was almost on top of it before it threw its head into the air and spread its wings. I lunged at the necklace but it rose too quickly and struck at me. I jumped out of the way.

The humans charged into the canyon on horseback. The horses snorted nervously but didn't balk.

I jumped at the thing's neck again and hoped Mr. Taggart and Nata could figure out what I was after.

One of them fired their gun. I winced and the dragon didn't react. I jumped again and missed.

"Hey, Boss, I think Brown's got something."

"Get yer rope, see if we can't hold it still for her."

"Right, Boss."

Ch'al went after the dragon's heels, avoiding its lashing tail while I continued to jump for its neck.

The horses dodged around and the humans shouted, trying to keep the dragon occupied.

Nata's rope landed around the dragon's neck. "Ha! Got it!" His horse backed up and whinnied nervously as the dragon turned toward them.

Taggart threw his rope and snagged the beast. Then they backed in opposite directions trying to hold its head down. The dragon roared in rage and tried to jerk itself upward. The horses and humans pulled back. I jumped, just barely missing the necklace.

It jerked back again, this time using its forelegs to shove itself up from the ground. Nata yelled and his horse fell. I leapt at the same time and snagged the feather with my teeth. I clamped down, determined not to let go. I hung from the thrashing dragon's neck, and then the necklace broke and I fell to the ground.

The dragon froze. Then it exploded. Sand and glowing motes showered the clearing. I yelped as sand almost buried me and struggled out of the pile, shaking, still clutching the feather in my mouth.

I spit it out and ran for the cave. The ghost had said I'd be able to save Elliott and I hoped he was right. I didn't slow as I came to the cave entrance and unlike last time, I easily entered and ran into the darkness. I could see well enough to avoid the walls and smell well enough to find Elliott. He was pressed up against the wall and I jumped, paws landing on his chest. I felt something sticky under my paws and tore at it with my teeth. It too tasted like sand and fell away easily. Elliott crumpled to the ground and I barked again and again and licked his face.

He groaned and pushed me away. "Brown, I'm sleeping."

I tugged on his sleeve and barked again. He pushed me away and sat up. He rubbed his eyes and looked around, but probably couldn't see.

"Brown, where am I?"

I tugged his arm again and he staggered to his feet. He put his free arm out in front of him, but I led him safely from the cave. He stood blinking in the sunlight. Then he straightened and looked around.

"Where's the dragon? What happened?"

I leaned against his leg and crouched, ashamed that I'd gotten him captured.

He knelt and hugged me. "Shh, Brown. It's okay. Is that Taggart?" He stood and I followed. Nata and his horse were on their feet and Ch'al trotted up, wagging his tail.

"Brown, that was amazing!"

I dropped my jaw in a doggy smile, but I couldn't hold his gaze. "It was my fault he got caught. I barked at the ghost and the dragon got my human." My ears drooped and I sighed.

Ch'al nudged my shoulder with his nose.

"Elliott, you're alive," Mr. Taggart said.

"It appears so. Thanks to you guys. What happened?"

"When Brown came back alone, we knew the dragon had taken you. We came back to get the horse, but the damn dogs wouldn't stop. When we got here she kept trying to get at something on the dragon's neck and we thought she'd found the object of power. Nata and I managed to lasso the thing long enough for her to get it. Damn thing just came apart once she pulled it off of him."

"Into a giant pile of sand?"

"Yes. How'd that thing get you?"

"Brown tried to protect me from a ghost she saw. Unfortunately she got the dragon's attention too."

101

He'd seen the ghost? I whined in shame.

"Shh, Brown. You saved me. It's okay. I would have barked at the ghost too, if I were you."

I tilted my head and perked my ears forward at that silly thought.

He scratched my ears.

"Well, Mr. Gyles, if you're still alive, I bet others are too. Nata, find some stuff to make a torch. We'll go in."

"Yes, Boss."

I sat pressed against his leg while Nata and Mr. Taggart made fire for light and went into the cave. I'd already seen a few animals stagger out and I hoped the humans were okay too.

Ch'al stayed outside with us.

"Good job, Brown. Ch'al, we meet again," the ghost said, appearing from wherever ghosts were when they weren't here.

The other dog whined and thumped his tail.

"You know the ghost?" I stared at Ch'al, surprised.

"Didn't know he was a ghost. He's an elder of Nata's tribe. That explains why Nata's never seen him."

I looked at the ghost. He stood near the pile of sand. I got up and found his necklace. I carefully picked it up and held it so he could take it.

The ghost stared at me, then he knelt and took it. The necklace was a narrow band of leather with yellow and green rocks. The feather was undamaged despite my rough treatment. His hands seemed more solid, though I could still see through the rest of him.

"I want you to wear this, Brown. The amber matches your eyes and it will help keep you safe in your dangerous job." He put it around my neck. Somehow it fit. Then he scratched my ears and stood.

I wagged my tail and glanced back at my human. Elliott was watching us with a very surprised expression on his face.

"You have an amazing dog, Mr. Gyles. And you are quite perceptive for a white man."

Elliott took a deep breath. "Thank you, sir."

He could see the ghost!

"I wasn't sure if I saw you earlier, and the dragon had my attention. How'd it get here?"

"Greed. I must return to my rest. I'd suggest you sort through this pile of sand. One man's greed might benefit you. Brown, Ch'al, thank you." The ghost faded from view.

Elliott came over to me and scratched my ears. "My beautiful, brave dog. Good girl. Now, let's see what he meant."

I barked happily. He wasn't mad at me. All was right in my world. I sniffed the pile of sand left by the dragon, and then Ch'al and I dug until we reached the bottom. A yellow rock sat there and Elliott picked it up. It sparkled in the sunlight.

"What'd you find, Mr. Gyles?" Mr. Taggart came out of the cave.

"Not sure, but it looks like gold to me."

"Hell, both those dogs are covered in gold dust."

"Are the children alive?"

"Yes. Nata is helping them. We'll ride back to town to get help."

Elliott held out the rock to Mr. Taggart.

"Keep it. I'm sure there's more here. I'll tell Markie. He'll know what to do."

My human's eyes went wide. "Sir, this is enough gold to buy a ranch."

"Couple of ranches and pay hands to work it for you if you've a mind. Plus we still owe you a bag of silver. Come on."

Elliott followed silently.

"I wonder if this means I get sheep," I said to Ch'al.

"If you do, can I come visit?"

I grinned and wagged my tail. "Any time."

# BROWN AND THE LOST DUTCHMAN MINE

*Arizona Desert, 1900*

"Damn wheel." Elliott kicked the ground before sighing.

I trotted along beside him, panting in the heat as we wound our way through the desert canyons.

"We're almost to shelter, Brown...I hope." He muttered the last bit, but my keen ears heard the desperation in his voice.

Our two horses followed us, one tied to the other, loaded with food and what water we could carry. A day's walk back, and not far from our destination, one of the wheels on our wagon had cracked, and we had already used the spare. Not far from civilization by wagon and not far by foot were two very different things, at least according to Elliott.

I preferred to walk most of the time anyway. The horses didn't seem to mind the lighter load either, and though both smelled of sweat, neither balked at the travel. We were on our way back to Colorado after working for a ranch in Golton. We had made enough money to start our own sheep farm. Now we just had to get there. This rocky, hot terrain was hard on the wagon and the horses.

"We need to find a place to rest, Brown. I bet there are some overhangs in these rocks."

105

Sniffing, I thought I smelled water, and I angled toward it.

Glancing around while I followed my nose, I looked at one rocky hill that stood out from the rest of the rocks in the rough terrain. Tall and narrow, it reached way up into the sky. We needed to go around its base and head north and west to get to civilization.

"Just a little farther, Brown." Elliott sounded exhausted.

Whining, I bumped into his leg. He needed to stop and drink.

"What is it, Brown?"

I nudged the container of water at his hip with my nose.

"Are you thirsty?"

Woofing twice for no, I nudged it again.

"What then?" He took the container off his belt and drank.

Woofing once for yes, I continued on, glad he had figured out what I wanted.

"Oh. Thanks, Brown. This sun is awful." He wiped his brow and replaced the container at his hip. "There has to be some shade."

Putting my nose to the air, I sniffed and sniffed. Finally, uncertain if I was right, I trotted off toward something that smelled cooler than the hot air around us. It was near the water smell at the very least.

After a moment the horses perked up and nickered, obviously smelling the water too.

Elliott, catching on, followed me for a ways until we reached an overhang in a canyon wall across, from the rock spire. Close by, desert scrub hid a small pool of water that seemed to seep out of the side of the canyon wall. The horses dipped their noses into the shallow water and after a moment, I did the same. It tasted fresh and sweet, and I drank my fill while Elliott stood with the horses. Once they were done he led them to the shade.

Taking one last drink, I jumped back when something rustled on a nearby rock. Worried about snakes, I looked around until I met the eyes of a lizard. It was colored like the rock and very hard to see until it lazily blinked its eyes at me.

Growling a warning, I backed away. Lizards weren't high on my list of animals I wanted to be around at the moment, but at least it wasn't a rattlesnake.

"I'm wounded," the lizard said, flipping its tail around. "It hates me and it doesn't even know my name."

Ignoring the lizard, I dashed to Elliott's side under the overhang.

"I don't suppose you two are going anywhere," he said to the horses. He tied the lead rope over the pack. The horses nickered when he unloaded grain for them and food for us before he collapsed to the cooler rock. I lay down next to him, panting. The shade and cool rock felt good, and before long I drifted to sleep.

I woke when I heard Elliott moving around. I perked my ears and watched as he explored the back of the overhang.

"Interesting," he said to himself as he disappeared from view behind a rock.

Not about to let him get to far away, I scrambled to my feet, pausing when I felt something clinging to my back.

"Hey, you're disrupting my nap!"

Tossing my head at the weight on my ruff, I tried to dislodge what I thought was the lizard from earlier.

"Woohoo, ride'm cowboy."

"Get off!" I snarled.

"No, you're warm."

"So is the rock."

"You're furry. The rock is hard. It's an easy decision."

That made me pause. The lizard was comparing me to a rock? "I don't have time for this." I went to the back of the small shelter and scraped the lizard off on an overhang. Going around the corner I found myself in a cool, dark cave. Ignoring the lizard's angry protests, I looked around in the dim light that filtered in from outside. I could see reasonably well, but Elliott looked around and peered into the darkness as if he couldn't.

Walking around him, I brushed against his leg.

"What?" Elliott jumped and twisted around. "Oh, Brown, you startled me. Silly dog." He ruffled my ears and then I stepped away further into the cave. Something lying on the floor had caught my interest. Smelling old leather and gun oil and metal, I lowered my nose and sniffed the object. It was a gun.

Whining, I pawed at it and glanced up at Elliott.

He knelt next to me and picked it up. "It looks like it has been here a while, Brown, but the metal isn't rusty at all. It's shiny in fact." Elliott tilted the gun until it caught the faint light. "I'm not sure what material it is made out of, but it's not a normal gun."

Hesitantly, he rotated the cylinder. "It only has one round left. I wonder whose it was."

Going deeper into the cave, I found something else. Woofing quietly, I sniffed the dried up body on the ground. It also smelled of old leather and gun oil and I thought the gun probably belonged to the body. Investigating further, I smelled the hints of fear and... I growled and my hackles rose. A scent filled my nose, sharp, like just after a spring rain, but old and musty. Elliott called it musty ozone. I called it ghost scent.

"What is it, Brown?" He came over to me and stared. I heard a quick snap and smelt sulfur as Elliott lit a match. He cupped the light in his hand and shone it over the body.

"Wonder how he died. I guess this gun was probably his. Easy, Brown. It's just a body."

I heard a quiet scamper and glanced over as the lizard joined me.

"Body got you worried, dog?"

"No, lizard."

"Good. It's dead. There's other things in this cave that aren't, but should be." The lizard scampered closer to the body. "It's not friendly."

Continuing to growl, I looked further into the tunnel. I wasn't growling at the body and I wanted Elliott to know it.

"Wait, do you smell something else?" Elliott asked.

Woofing once for yes, I wagged my tale and then went back to staring into the darkness of the cave, and ignoring the lizard.

Elliott leaned forward and took the belt from the corpse "Sorry, good sir. I hope you don't mind me borrowing your belt." He fastened it around his own waist and holstered the gun before crossing himself. "Rest in peace, good sir. Come on, Brown. Let's get out of here."

Before we could turn to leave the tunnel, wind howled around us, damp and chill, blasting us with the musty ozone scent and sending Elliott's hat flying.

Whining, I looked wildly around for the ghost. I had to protect Elliott.

"And me without my hunting bag," Elliott said, voice tight.

"It'ssss mine." The voice hissed around us, echoing and bouncing off the cave walls.

Barking in alarm, I spun around, trying to find it, trying to find something I could fight.

"Oh no," the lizard said and leapt onto my ruff. "Run!"

"Brown, run!" Elliott sprinted back down the cave. I followed, for the moment not caring that I had an unwanted passenger.

"Noooo! Death to all who trespass." The voice rose from a quiet hiss to a piercing scream, hurting my ears and chilling me to the bone.

A spray of dirt jetted up in front of Elliott, forcing him to stop and back away. It was hard to see in the dim light, especially with the spray of dirt between us and the exit. A face pushed out of the dirt, nose and mouth and brim of a hat distinct, all the other details were a blur.

Trying to catch the ghost's eye, I stared at it, but even barking didn't get it to look at me enough for me to capture it.

"Thought you'd take it, did you? Think again!"

The wall rushed toward us. I grabbed Elliott's sleeve and pulled. Stumbling blindly, he grabbed my ruff and let me guide him deeper into the cave, away from the menacing wall of dirt. It was so dark I could barely see, and I relied on my nose to guide me. I followed a faint scent of oil and other human things, hoping if we went far enough the ghost would leave us alone.

Its wind whipped at us, tearing at my ears and almost deafening me with its roar. Seemingly herding us, I saw no choice but to run before it, even though being herded by a ghost rankled.

Finally, the cave opened up into a larger space. I could tell by the way the sound echoed and the wind lessened. Stopping abruptly, I sent Elliott stumbling to the ground and, since he was still holding onto me, I yelped and tumbled on top of him. The lizard cried out in protest but its weight vanished from my back.

"Sorry, Brown."

"Die..." The ghost's voice trailed off and the wind faded away until we were left in silence, and darkness. Even I couldn't see.

For a moment, I couldn't hear anything, but finally my ears adapted and I made out the sound of a more normal breeze whispering through the rock. It tickled my ruff and brought the dry desert scent of open lands. At least the air wasn't bad. Other scents filtered to my nose. Elliott— smelling fearful, dry dust, iron, chemicals, and...I sniffed again...oil. It reminded me of a lamp Elliott occasionally read by.

Tugging on Elliott's sleeve, I led him to the smell. Woofing softly, I nudged the lamp with my nose.

Kneeling, Elliott felt around. "What?" He said when his hand brushed the lamp.

"Oh, Brown, good girl." Liquid sloshed. "There's still a little oil. Now if only I can figure out how to get it lit."

After much grumbling and cursing, Elliott coaxed a small flame into the globe. "There's not much left, but you may have saved our lives, Brown."

Wagging my tail, I nudged Elliott's hand happily.

"Let's see what we have here." He held the lamp up and scanned the area. "Can't see much, but we're in a cavern. Which way did we come from?"

Nose to the floor, I followed our scent back the way we had come.

"It's not safe here." The lizard's voice was quiet as it scampered out of the darkness to my feet.

"Really?" A low rumble stopped my sarcastic reply and my hackles rose as laughter echoed around us. The lizard scampered up my leg and this time I stood still while he did. As much as I didn't like him, I wasn't going to leave him to the ghost either.

"Die..." The voice hissed, barely louder than the building rumble.

My instincts told me to run, and, grabbing Elliott's sleeve, I did, away from the tunnel to freedom.

"Brown?"

Apparently he hadn't felt or heard the vibrations yet. Still gripping his sleeve, I ran as fast as possible across the cavern until the ground felt more stable. Then I slowed, but kept going as the laughter grew in volume, echoing around us. I could smell Elliott's fear, but he trusted me enough to follow.

"Die." The voice hissed again just as the far roof collapsed in a roar of rock and billowing dust.

"Brown, run!"

We sprinted away, finding another tunnel out of the cavern purely by luck. I could feel that this rock was stable so I slowed, sneezing the dust out of my nose.

Elliott coughed. "I hope this leads somewhere sunny." He held up his lamp. "What's that?"

Peering at the wall, he brought the lamp closer. "Gold. I wonder if the ghost was a miner?"

"He was," the lizard told me. "The body you found was the last person to try and claim the mine from him. I remember the cowboy talking about his gun being special, hoping to defeat the ghost so he could have the mine for himself."

"Apparently it didn't work." Despite myself I wanted more information about the ghost.

"Not permanently, but it certainly injures the ghost." The lizard burrowed further into my ruff, clinging to my neck.

Woofing softly, I trotted down the tunnel. I could still smell fresh air but it was faint and the press of the earth around me made me uncomfortable.

"Good girl, Brown. We certainly don't need a gold mine at the moment. What we need is a way to fight the ghost and to escape."

I woofed in agreement.

"Okay, what do we have?" He talked while we followed the cave. "We're in part of the mine. This rock has been worked, but the floor is pretty dusty. I could probably draw a circle in the dust, but it won't be a very good one. I think I have the banishing incantation memorized. Hmm...we might be able to find a mineral deposit that will be close enough to salt down here."

I nudged his gun with my nose, hoping the lizard was right.

"I'm not sure I can shoot a ghost, Brown."

Huffing, I kept walking. Before long we came to an intersection.

"Okay, now which way do we go?" Elliott leaned against the wall, sounding depressed.

Sniffing the air, I looked down one path and then the other. One had much fresher air and I wanted to go that way, but something drew me to the other direction and I sat and stared for a while, uncertain. Fresh air probably meant a way out, but there was something down the danker tunnel that called to me.

"What is it, girl?"

Wagging my tail uncertainly, I wished I could tell him that there was something down there. The ghost smell was stronger but there was something else too. Old and dried out that had perhaps once been alive. It was important, so I started down that tunnel. After a moment, Elliott followed. The lizard remained silent.

Before long we found another intersection. This tunnel had old metal tracks on the ground.

Elliott paused and shone his light on them. "I bet that way goes deeper into the mine because it starts to go down, and that way might lead out, if there wasn't a cave-in or something. We're running low on oil. I hope we can get out."

113

Though the scent I wanted to follow was further in the mine, I followed when Elliott turned to follow the rails. I knew if we ran out of oil we were in big trouble.

The wind picked up again and the musty ozone of the ghost grew stronger. It blew at us, trying to force us deeper.

Elliott fought against the wind, and, whining, I did the same, but dirt and debris flew at us until we had to turn away. I could feel the lizard clutching my fur with his small claws as he tried not to be torn away. Elliott shielded the lamp with his body, but the wind died down as soon as we turned.

"It's as if it is herding us," Elliott said, voice strained.

The thought of being herded by anything, especially a ghost, made me growl, but as soon as I turned back, the wind picked up again.

My ruff stood on end as the musty ozone smell grew stronger. The ghost was coming back.

We walked further down the tunnel in the direction I'd wanted to go in the first place. The air grew stuffy, and Elliott stopped and swore quietly. Holding up the lamp, he looked at the wall of debris that blocked our way and sighed. "We're trapped between a ghost and a hard place, Brown. We're going to have to fight back, and we didn't find any salt deposits."

I echoed Elliott's sigh. We didn't have much to fight the ghost with, but we had to do something.

"The gun. It will help, just not permanently," the lizard said.

"I'll see if I can get him to understand." Walking up to Elliott, I nudged the gun again with my nose.

"Maybe. I can't imagine it helping though," Elliott said ruffling my ears. "What's that? Is that...is a lizard riding on you?"

Flattening my ears, I sighed.

Elliott laughed a little. "Well, as long as you're okay with it, I guess."

I wasn't sure I was okay with it, but for now, I had more important things on my mind.

The strange dried out smell was stronger. Following my nose, I sniffed around until I found the strongest concentration of scent. Digging at the ground, I quickly uncovered something that wasn't a rock or a piece of wood. It was soft and smelled faintly human, but I wasn't sure what it was.

"What did you find, Brown?" Elliott knelt next to me and together we cleared more of the rubble at the base of the old cave-in. "It's a body." Elliott sat back after we uncovered what seemed to be the top half of a miner crushed in the cave-in. Most of his body was buried too deeply in the rubble to uncover. A cowboy hat covered its head.

"Poor soul."

"Dieeeee..." The ghost's voice hissed around us and the wind it generated made the lamp flicker alarmingly.

Elliott glanced around then back at the body. "Maybe the miner is the ghost."

Woofing once, I agreed.

"Remember the ghost on the steamboat? We had to destroy the scarf to get rid of it. Maybe if we destroy the body."

Whining, I pawed at the dirt. Too much of it was covered.

"You're right, Brown. We don't have enough lamp oil to burn it anyway. I guess we need to capture this ghost so we can figure out how to destroy it. I'm going to draw a trap, but don't expect it to hold. I have to draw it in the dirt. Be ready."

Woofing again, I faced away from Elliott, alert for the ghost while he drew. I could smell it coming.

115

"Be careful, dog."

"Quiet, lizard."

A spray of dirt blew up from the floor and the ghost was there, laughing.

Its voice shook me to my bones, but I stood firm, barking to get its attention.

A face appeared in the spray of dirt and slowly turned toward me. Barking again, I stared and met the ghost's gaze. I could feel its mind and I grabbed it with mine, holding it with my Border Collie Eye. The ghost fought me, but my will was stronger and I turned and herded the ghost toward the trap like I'd done many times before.

Elliott shouted words as the ghost was pushed over the trap and a blue light flared up around it, breaking my connection, but keeping the ghost in the circle. The wind around us died and the ghost howled in rage, battering itself against the blue light.

Finally it stopped and laughed.

Whining, I wished I could block out the sound that made me quake in fear, but it was trapped, so I stood firm.

"Clever beast, clever human." It hissed. "But not so clever. The walls are weak. I can beat them." With that it threw itself against the blue light.

The light flickered, and I believed the ghost when it said it could escape. Elliott looked around frantically, searching for inspiration.

"Death to all who try to take my mine." It howled as it battered the light.

"The gun!" The lizard jumped off of my back and scuttled toward Elliott.

Faster than a lizard, I ran to Elliott's side and nudged the gun again.

Elliott drew the pistol at my suggestion and pointed it at the ghost. "No, no one else is going to die. We don't want your mine."

116

"Trespassers!"

The gun clicked when Elliott drew back the hammer. That seemed to get the ghost's attention. It froze, the wind and dirt stilling in the trap.

"You can't kill me with a gun." It hissed again. "Another tried, another died." More of that horrible laughter.

For a moment the ghost vanished, the dirt it had picked up falling to the floor, and then, with a loud shriek that echoed down the tunnel, it spun up into a small tornado of dust and slammed into the blue light of the trap again and again.

Elliott shouted the banishment words, but the light flickered and vanished before he could finish. The ghost howled in delight, flying straight toward Elliott.

Not knowing what else to do, I barked in alarm and leapt at the ghost. Before I'd been able to disrupt ghosts by jumping through them, but I'd had on my special boots that had been blessed. Still, I had to try.

Sand and dirt peppered me as I slammed into the ghost. It didn't disintegrate, but I deflected its aim just enough that it missed plowing into Elliott.

Something smacked my side and sent me flying. Yelping, I hit the wall and slid to the ground, vision going dark for a minute.

"Brown! Don't you hurt my dog."

The ghost simply laughed.

Forcing myself to my feet, I stared at the ghost, woofing to try and get its attention, but it wouldn't meet my eyes.

"Bring the wall down, crush the mangy mutt," the ghost said, almost singing to itself. It howled again before vanishing. The sudden silence was almost deafening, and I looked around, alarmed.

117

Rock groaned and, like before, I could feel that it was going to collapse soon.

"Like hell you will," Elliott shouted and pointed his pistol at the body. "Is this yours?"

The ghost reappeared in a spray of dirt directly in front of Elliott.

"No." The ghost sounded a little worried.

"That's what I thought." Elliott pulled the trigger. Light flashed from the gun and it made a sound like I had never even imagined. Sinking to the ground I tried to bury my head in my paws to get away from the horrible noise. Through the pain, I thought I felt the lizard climb onto my back.

Wind whipped at my fur and rocks and debris peppered my body, but then it stopped and the ghost scent vanished.

Elliott ran toward me. I could see his mouth moving, but I couldn't hear the words. He grabbed my ruff and pulled. Knowing I should follow, I sprang to my feet, though it hurt, and ran after him and we sprinted down the tunnel.

Almost running into Elliott, I skidded to a halt when the lamp died and plunged us into darkness.

"Brown, can you hear me?"

His voice sounded distant even though he stood next to me, but I could hear and I woofed quietly.

"Good girl. Can you follow the tracks?"

"The tracks lead out. He is smart, for a human," the lizard said.

Woofing again, I started walking as soon as his hand was on my ruff. Knowing we didn't have much time, I hurried.

Elliott paused after a short time. "I see light."

Whining urgently, I ran forward and Elliott followed. Feeling the deep rumble of an impending cave-in, I ran faster, barking urgently.

"Hurry!" The lizard yelled.

Elliott sprinted after me, and the rumble built to a roar. Dust and wind billowed past us, and I thought I heard the faintest hint of the ghost's laughter, but then we were out of the cave, just in time as the roof collapsed behind us.

We spilled out into the hot desert sand. Elliott fell to the ground, coughing, and I sneezed dust out of my nose.

"I'm outta here, riding with you is way to intense. Bye, dog."

The lizard scuttled off and I snorted more dust out of my nose as I laughed.

"Are you okay, girl?"

Woofing once I snuggled against Elliott's chest and licked his face.

"Hey, easy there." He laughed and hugged me. "Brown, I don't know what I'd do without you." He frowned and looked at me more closely. "You are completely covered in gold dust."

I didn't care as long as my human was safe. Of course, I knew that humans liked gold, so maybe it was a good thing.

Elliott leaned back and looked around. "Well, maybe we can save some of that. If we can find our horses, and figure out where we're at. Maybe that remarkable nose of yours can help out. No more mining for us though, I don't care to tangle with that ghost again. I'm pretty sure we didn't kill it."

Woofing, I put my nose to the wind, sniffing for our horses, happy to put that ghost behind us.

No matter what Elliott needed, I was the dog for the job.

# BROWN VS THE MARTIANS

*Arizona Desert, 1900*

"I could get used to this, Brown," Elliott, my human, said as he leaned back and stared up at sky.

I stared up too, wondering what all the little white lights in the sky were. They were pretty, like little fireflies. I shook my head at that thought. The last fireflies we'd dealt with had belonged to a demon that tried to trap people. Maybe they were more like the lights in a big city. A city in the sky. I grinned. That was such a silly thought. There was no way to get there, so how could there be a city in the sky?

Elliott scratched my ears. "I don't suppose you want a ranch in the great territory of Arizona do you?"

I shook my head. I wanted sheep and grass.

"We've been traveling out here for a while now. I like Arizona, but you're right. Sheep will do better with grass. Colorado it is."

I grinned and barked. Maybe he was getting better at knowing what I wanted.

"All right. We'll head for Colorado. With as much as we made on the last two jobs, we're set. You deserve your ranch."

I wagged my tail.

He lay back on the blanket that was our bed for the night and looked at the sky. We could have slept in our wagon, but it was nice, and we liked sleeping out when we could. I leaned against his side and dozed off.

"What's that?" He sat up and I jumped to my feet and spun around, looking for the ghost or demon that was attacking us.

There was nothing. I glanced at Elliott. He stared up. One of the little lights in the sky got bigger and bigger as we watched until it seemed to be streaking across the sky, leaving a trail of light behind it.

"That's a falling star!" Elliott sounded excited and jumped to his feet. "But it's huge. Maybe it's a meteor."

I didn't know what that was, but it was coming awfully close. I whined nervously.

"It'll be okay, Brown. They don't usually hit the ground."

This one sure looked like it was going too. The glow grew brighter until it was painful to look at. It screamed by overhead. I winced, the sound painful to my sensitive ears, and ducked.

"Wow!" Elliott turned, watching as it fell to the ground. Wind ruffled my fur and flapped my ears. The horses nickered nervously as a few dust devils swirled around their feet.

Suddenly the light got brighter and a huge boom had me diving for cover under the blankets.

I leapt out of the covers, annoyed with myself. I had to protect Elliott. He still stared toward where the light had hit the ground. It was far away and I didn't think we were in any danger, but I had to keep guard, even if I wanted to hide. The falling object, whatever it was, could obviously move quickly.

Elliott sat and looked off into the distance. "I wonder what that was, Brown."

I whined.

He scratched my ears. "Oh well, we'll probably never know. Let's get some rest. We have a lot of ground to cover in the morning."

He lay back down but I stared off into the distance for a long time, making sure whatever it was, wouldn't come after us.

"Didn't sleep last night?"

I opened one eye and looked at Elliott before closing it again. The answer to that should be obvious. The wagon bench wasn't the most comfortable but I didn't want to be in the back of the wagon with all the books and our bed. I wanted to be with Elliott. I shifted around and put my head on his leg.

"Good girl, Brown. Maybe they'll have some sheep in Flagstaff that you can herd. Or more cows."

I perked the ear that wasn't squished under my head and opened my eye again.

"Sorry, Brown. I'll let you sleep."

I huffed and tried to go back to sleep, but now I was thinking about sheep and cows. Sighing I sat up. Everything was the same dusty brown as my coat mixed with reds and purples and the occasional dash of green. We had a long way to go to get back to Colorado, but it would be a fun trip, as long as I was out with my human. Maybe we'd even find some more ghosts to hunt on our way back.

Although one of our last jobs had been to hunt a demon that looked like a dragon, I normally hunted ghosts with my Border Collie Eye. Elliott used rituals from his great-grand pappy's hunting journal to banish the ghosts.

Now we had enough money for our own sheep ranch, but I knew I'd miss hunting ghosts if we didn't keep doing it.

I lay back down and started dreaming of ghostly sheep and demon squirrels. I was having a great battle with a squirrel that had fangs the size of my legs when I was thrown forward. I sprang to my feet, barking.

"Brown, quiet."

I clamped my jaw shut, wondering why Elliott had stopped the wagon so quickly. At first I didn't see anything, but as I looked harder, I could see strange ripples in the ground and, beyond that, what looked like a hole.

"I'm going to find some shade for the horses. We need to look at that."

I sniffed the air. It smelled strange, but I couldn't identify the smell. It was almost like the farrier when he was making shoes for the horses, hot metal, but there were other things I didn't recognize. It reminded me of the one car I'd seen. Noisy, smelly, and not very practical, but the smell was similar. I didn't believe a car could have made the big hole though.

Elliott noticed me sniffing the air and he did the same. "Odd. I don't recognize that smell at all, do you?"

I shook my head.

Elliott turned the wagon toward a shady clump of rocks. Once we reached it, he watered the horses and gave them both nosebags of grain to keep them happy. I jumped off the bench and followed at his side when he headed for the big hole. The ground was hotter than normal; uncomfortable under my paws, but not so hot that I couldn't walk on it.

We stopped at the top of the big hole and stared down into it. Something in the middle glinted in the sunlight.

"What the...?" Elliott took off his round hat and scratched his head before putting it back on and heading down into the crater.

He had to slide down, dirt sliding with him, but I was able to run down into the hole without problems. Some of the ground was hard and shiny, not like normal dirt at all and I avoided those spots. I raced ahead, hackles up, on alert for any danger to my human. The shiny thing in the middle seemed to be buried partially in the dirt. I had buried a bone in the dirt once when we lived back east, and couldn't find it later. Though I suspected that a squirrel had stolen my bone after I'd left. Even though there weren't any squirrels here it was probably good that the shiny thing wasn't completely buried.

It made strange sounds, like the clicking I'd heard some of the desert beetles make.

"Brown, be careful."

I stopped and sniffed again. Over the hot metal and other strange smells, I thought I smelled an animal, almost like a dog, except that didn't smell quite right either. I stopped and waited for Elliott to catch up.

"What is that?"

The thing was shaped like a cow pie, although almost half of it was buried in the dirt. The part that stuck out of the ground went up into the air much further than Elliott could reach and made enough shade for us to get out of the sun. The ground wasn't any cooler in the shade though. Black streaked the shiny metal and it looked like there were gashes, like claw marks where the black streaks were.

"It's damaged," Elliott said.

Elliott walked around until we climbed a pile of dirt and ended up standing over the strange metal cow pie.

He crept forward and hesitantly touched it. Then he laid his hand flat. "It's cool. That's strange." He walked out onto the metal slowly and knelt where I could see some lines in the otherwise smooth surface. He touched one of the lines. "It almost looks like a...Ahh!"

Elliott jerked back and I barked in alarm when part of the cow pie moved. I jumped forward, trying to push myself between the danger and Elliott. The metal was smooth though and I ended up sliding.

"Brown!"

I yelped as I slid into the hole. I didn't fall far, but it was darker than outside and I landed on something soft.

"Brown, are you okay?"

I woofed once, trying not to bark too loudly.

"Hang on, I'm coming."

I woofed twice—a negative. I heard Elliott's footsteps hesitate. He leaned over the hole, blocking some of the light.

My eyes slowly adjusted. I wanted to make sure it was safe before Elliott came down into the metal cow pie. He waited while I looked around the small room I was in. I tilted my head, wondering what strange narrow chairs and a small table were doing in the metal cow pie. I knew I smelled something like a dog. A slightly more human smell came from another door I could see now that my eyes had adjusted. It was half open and I crept up to it, using my nose and ears to alert me of anything sneaking up behind. I had to scramble a little because the floor wasn't flat and the metal was smooth, but I managed not to slide too badly.

I squeezed through the opening. More chairs, and a strange black wall. The human-like smell came from one of the chairs. I scrambled around until I stood on something that looked vaguely like the controls for the steamship I'd ridden on once. The black wall was behind me. A person slumped over in the chair. Long hair covered her face, but even though she smelled strange, I could tell she was female. I whined, trying to see if she'd respond.

Nothing.

I carefully put a paw on the chair and leaned across the space between the controls and the chair, sniffing her face. She was bleeding, but it wasn't normal smelling blood. I whined again and licked her cheek. Still nothing. I needed Elliott.

I jumped down and went back into the main room, barking to get Elliott's attention.

"Brown."

I barked once.

"I'm coming." He lowered himself into the room, hanging by his arms and then dropping to the same chair I'd fallen on. "What."

I whined and pointed to the door with my nose. He followed me in and gasped.

"Brown. It's...She's...oh, God, she's bleeding blue. I must be wrong. It's dark. We have to get her out."

I whined.

"Let me check the other rooms and then we'll go." Elliott squeezed out of the room. I followed. One door opened but it didn't have anyone in it, though the dog smell was stronger from there. Elliott scrambled up to another door. I couldn't follow, it was too high. He had to use things to pull himself up. When he pushed his hand against the door, something beeped and a red light flashed, but the door didn't open.

"Huh. Okay, let's get the girl off." He stared up at the hole in the top of the cow pie. "I'm not sure how we're going to get her out though."

I sniffed the air, wondering where the dog was. The scent went to one part of the wall Elliott hadn't explored. I scrambled over to the spot and touched a shinier spot with my nose. It smelled strongly of the dog thing. Nothing happened for a moment, and then I heard a click and the wall slid. I jumped back, growling.

"Brown, what did you find?"

127

The wall screeched and I could hear things still moving, but the door stopped about halfway like the other one.

"It must be jammed," Elliott said. He shoved against the door and got it to move a little more before he gave up. "But, you found the bottom way out. Good job."

I grinned and wagged my tail.

"Okay, let's get the girl out. I think we can patch her up at the wagon and take her to Flagstaff. It's not far, and maybe we can get some help there." Elliott squeezed into the other room again. "Wow, she's light, and that really is blue blood. What the hell?"

He carried her out of the other room and I followed him out of the strange metal cow pie and back into the hot desert sun. Elliott had to struggle, but he managed to get her out of the big hole, though he ripped his pants and got dirty when he fell, protecting the strange human. Now he smelled like blood too, except his was normal. We hurried to the wagon.

"Brown, can you get down a blanket?"

He sounded hesitant, as if he thought I wouldn't understand. I barked once and jumped up into the wagon. I grabbed the blanket we used to sleep on the ground out of the back and dumped it on the ground. Then I jumped down and pulled it over to him. I couldn't quite spread it out all the way, but I managed enough for him to lay the girl on it.

"You're a special dog, Brown."

I grinned.

He brushed some of the hair out of the girl's face and shook his head. "There's no way," he muttered. Elliott went to the back of the wagon and got our small med kit and some water. Then he tried to fix her as best as he could.

128

"I think she needs stitches. We'll need a real doctor, but I'll wrap these as best as I can." Elliott worked on the strange smelling girl for a while. "I don't know if she's going to make it or not. There's no way she's human and I can't tell if she's okay."

I didn't understand how she couldn't be. Even if she smelled strange, she had to be human.

Elliott wrapped her in the blanket and got her in the back of the wagon. "Brown, ride back here and keep an eye on her."

I jumped up and sat on the end of the bed. Elliott got the horses ready and shortly we were bumping along faster than we normally traveled. The girl moaned every once in a while when we hit a bad bump, but otherwise she was quiet. I looked out the back and thought I saw something following us, but I wasn't sure.

It took us two days to get to Flagstaff, and in that time she barely moved. I caught sight of the thing that followed us once. I knew it was back there, but it never got close enough for me to figure out what it was. I wondered if it was the thing that smelled sort of like a dog that I'd scented by the metal cow pie.

The wagon bumped and lurched into town as Elliott hurried to find a doctor. He pulled the wagon to an abrupt halt in front of a building. He jumped off and ran inside, returning a few moments later and took the girl inside. I followed.

"She's hurt," Elliott said to the man inside. He had to be the doctor.

"Yes, you said that." The doctor pointed to a bed and Elliott set her on it gently.

"You have to treat her."

"Of course." The doctor sounded impatient. "Do you know what happened?"

"Um." Elliott hesitated. "I think she was in some sort of wreck. I found her in…" he hesitated again. "Wreckage."

The doctor glanced up at Elliott, one eyebrow raised. "I see. And you've never met this woman before?"

"No." Elliott almost laughed.

"Very well." The doctor uncovered the strange smelling human and stared. "What is that...Is that blood?" He took a step back.

"I think so."

"Where did you say you found her?" He took another step back.

"Wreckage. In the desert. Come on, I've had her for two days. She needs a doctor."

"Well." He took another step back and almost looked like he was going to bolt to the door.

I growled.

The doctor actually yelped when he spun around.

"Please. I can pay."

"You want me to treat some sort of demon?"

I growled louder.

"She's not a demon. Just… a person. Like us, only a little different. Maybe she's from Canada."

"Strange folk up there, or so I've heard. Cold too. Winter all year round." He sounded like he would allow himself to be convinced.

"Yes, they're so cold that their blood turns blue."

"Right." The doctor nodded. "Well, this Canadian had best be friendly." He rolled up his sleeves. "Get that water basin."

I watched while the doctor worked with Elliott's help.

"Have you fed her anything?"

"Just broth and water." Elliott sounded tired.

"Okay. We're almost done. We just need to get the rest of her clothes off of her and get her cleaned up."

They worked for a while longer before the doctor covered her with a clean sheet, tucking it around her shoulders.

"Let's clean up and get something to eat, and you can give her more broth. Then we'll see if your Canadian makes it."

She didn't move for the rest of the day, though she did drink the broth they fed her. I napped, knowing I'd need to watch her when Elliott couldn't.

That night, after everyone was asleep I watched the Canadian. She breathed steadily, and to me it sounded like she breathed more strongly. I hoped that meant she was going to get better. I stared so intently at her that at first I didn't notice the door open. A cool draft blew through my ruff and I spun around ready to defend the Canadian and Elliott from whatever was trying to get in.

A dog stood in the doorway, eyes shining in the dim light. I growled, warning him off.

"Please," he said. "I'm here to check on my person."

I didn't move out of his way, but I stopped growling. "The Canadian?"

The dog tilted his head. "What? No, we're not from Canada. We're from Pluto."

It was my turn to tilt my head. I'd never heard of Pluto.

"Please, may I check on my person?"

I wouldn't have been nearly as polite if someone had been standing between me and Elliott. I backed off.

"Thank you."

I sniffed as the dog ran past. He smelled the same as the scent I'd found at the strange metal cow pie and I relaxed.

He put his front paws up on the bed and sniffed the Canadian from Pluto all over.

"Will she be okay?"

"I think so. I'm grateful to you Earthlings for helping her."

I tilted my head the other way. "Earthlings?"

"Well, yes."

I sniffed again, and he stepped forward and sniffed my nose. Normally I wouldn't have welcomed that, but he was very interesting. He looked different, too, a strange color, though I couldn't tell what it actually was, and he had odd antennae like the desert beetles on his head, and more running down his back. I knew it wasn't polite to stare, unless sheep, or ghosts, or demons were involved, but I couldn't help it.

"Never seen a Plutonian before?" He sounded amused.

"No."

"Well, that's okay. I've only ever seen pictures of Earthlings before. First time here. I must admit I wish it had been under better circumstances."

"Your cow pie fell out of the sky."

"My what?"

"Your big metal thing. I guess it's like a wagon, but it's shaped like a cow pie."

"Whatever is a cow pie?"

I grinned. "Oh, they're wonderful. Smelly and everything. Since you've never done it before, when we find one, I'll let you roll first."

"Thank you?"

I wagged my tail.

"May I join you in your vigil?"

"Vigil?"

"You're watching over my person. May I join you? Or should I watch from over there."

"Ahh. Of course you may join me." I was educated, Elliott used to read to me and explain the harder words when I'd tilt my head, though I suspected he was mostly entertaining himself at the time, but this dog knew a lot more than I did. I was used to being the smartest, and it was a little strange to find a dog that seemed smarter than me. I wasn't sure how I felt about it.

I lay back down and the strange dog joined me.

"My name is Brown."

"Asa," he said.

"Nice to meet you."

"Likewise. You don't happen to have any food."

"I think there's some. Let me see." I got up and sniffed at the table. The dishes had been cleared so I went outside to see if the wagon was nearby. Elliott must have taken it to the livery. I followed the scent of horses until I found our wagon, jumped up in the back and located the dried meat. It was in a box, but I managed to open and close the lid and I carried a mouthful of food back to Asa. It wasn't much, but it would probably help.

He hadn't moved and I dropped the dried meat in front of him. "It's not much, but here."

"Thank you. It will be wonderful."

I could tell by the way he stared at it, that he wasn't sure if he thought he'd actually enjoy the food or not, but in the end he ate it all and licked his lips, obviously hungry for more.

I settled in next to him. Morning wasn't far and Elliott would be able to get us more food. I wondered what he'd think about my new companion.

133

"This is too much!" the doctor said when he saw Asa the next day.

"Canadian!" Elliott said desperately.

"Blue dogs? With antennae like bugs? Canadian?" The doctor looked like he was going to pass out.

"Brown, go get that, uh, Canadian dog, to roll in some mud. At least then he'll be brown."

I wondered where we were going to find mud in the desert. Maybe by the livery?

"Come on, Asa. Let's go make you dirty. It's better being dirty anyway."

"Thank you, Brown." He didn't sound convinced, but he followed closely behind me.

"Why does he keep calling us Canadian? It's obvious we are from Pluto. Canadians look like every other human."

"We've never been to Canada. We've never heard of Pluto. He had to explain why you looked strange."

"Oh. Well perhaps we shall find some of these cow pies you speak so highly of."

I wagged my tail. "Maybe. Where's Pluto?"

"It's the furthest planet from the sun in this solar system."

I stopped and sat down, shocked. "What?"

"We are from Pluto. In space."

I looked up.

"Yes, where the stars are. They are suns, just like ours. We Plutonians hope to explore them someday. We went to the Martians to see if they wanted to pool their resources with ours, to make this dream a reality much sooner. They have fairly advanced star drives, but they shot us down instead. And now we're on Earth."

"I..."

"Ahh, I remember, Earth is not nearly as advanced. No matter, I quite like you."

I thumped my tail on the ground because I couldn't think of anything else to do. "You're from space." I finally said, feeling dumb and not very advanced as I tried to comprehend how he could be from the stars."

"Yes."

"Oh. Well, we should still disguise you. Come on." I ran off toward the livery as fast as I could go, Asa right behind me. This was much stranger than hunting ghosts. I wondered if they had squirrels on Pluto. I wanted to ask but I didn't want to sound dumb.

There weren't any cows at the livery, and no cow pies or mud, but we did find a water trough. I had to jump in first to convince Asa to do it, and then we both had a good roll in the dirt. The dirt turned into mud, mostly hiding Asa's strange color. His antennae still showed but maybe we could tie a blanket to him.

The doctor was a little happier once he couldn't see the blue and Elliott must have had the same thought I did because he had a blanket and a rope in his hand when we returned.

"Brown, will he let me put the blanket on him?"

I glanced at Asa.

"Of course," he told me.

I barked once.

Elliott approached cautiously and carefully covered Asa with the blanket and tied it on.

"Well, that helps," Elliott said.

The Plutonian, who apparently wasn't also Canadian, groaned. Elliott and the doctor ran to her side. Asa and I followed.

"How do you feel?" Elliott asked.

Her eyes fluttered open. They were a strange violet color. She looked around but didn't say anything until she saw Asa.

"Asa!" Then she babbled something none of us understood, except Asa.

"Canadian?" The doctor said.

"They speak French up there, or so I'm told."

The doctor just shook his head. "Do you speak English?"

She looked back at the humans. "Yes." She had a strange way of saying her words.

"Asa, why are you so dirty?"

"It's a disguise." I heard him say, but he wasn't talking to me.

"Oh, good boy," the Plutonian woman said.

"Wait, you can talk to her!"

"Yes, of course."

I whined, feeling not very advanced at all. I wished I could communicate with humans. Feeling very useless, I walked away and curled up into a ball.

"Ma'am, are you okay?"

"Yes, I think I will be. Thank you. What happened?"

"Don't know. Elliott here found you in the desert. He wasn't real clear on the details."

"I was attacked. He must have saved me."

"I see. Well, as soon as you're able, you'd best be on your way. I've patients to attend to." The doctor left the room quickly.

She said something else to Asa and tried to sit up. Elliott helped her while I watched from the corner.

"Thank you for saving me."

"Of course. What's your name? I'm Elliott Gyles."

"Seija."

"Was that your...ship I pulled you out of?"

"Yes. I'm surprised you went in."

"Seemed like someone might need help." Elliott smiled. "I take it you're not from Canada?"

She frowned and glanced at Asa. "No, I'm from Pluto. It's a bit further away."

"How far?" Elliott sounded worried.

I whined.

"Well, surely you've heard of Mars?"

Elliott nodded.

"It's a bit further than that."

He took a few steps back and sank into a chair. "How is that possible?"

"How is it possible that you're here on Earth?"

"Well..."

"We're simply further along than you humans are. I'm an ambassador, to Mars actually. They, however, are not terribly friendly and shot me down. Now that I'm better, would you be willing to take me back to my ship? I might be able to send a message home to get someone to come pick me up."

"You speak very good English for someone who's not from here. Although you do have an accent."

I saw her smile. "Yes. All ambassadors study the major languages and customs of Earth. Just in case we end up here."

"Oh."

I went over and laid my head on his knee. He scratched my ears despite the mud.

"Well, of course we'll take you back to your ship as soon as you feel up to it. You should rest though. Are you hungry?"

"Yes, a bit. I believe Asa and your dog are hungry as well."

He glanced down at me. "Food?"

I barked.

"Okay, I'll be back in a bit." Elliott stood, pausing only to grab his hat from a peg by the door. I heard him muttering about aliens as he left.

137

"He seems to be taking this rather well," Seija said looking at me.

I huffed.

"I don't think Brown can communicate telepathically, but I will translate."

"We hunt ghosts, and demons. Aliens aren't that strange. I guess."

Asa passed my message on, and I wondered what he meant by communicating telepathically. Obviously I wasn't advanced enough.

"Ghosts and demons?" Seija said. "That sounds dangerous."

I nodded.

She stood, holding the sheet around her. I hadn't noticed until she stood, but her red hair fell to her knees, and she was as tall as Elliott, but very thin, not like most human women.

The door banged open. "Oh, dear, lay back down. You're not well."

I spun around. A priest stood in the doorway carrying one of his books.

Seija sat on the bed, clutching the sheet, her violet eyes wide.

He came into the room. "I'm Father Caleb. I've come to pray for you. The good doctor said you're from Canada?"

"Say yes!" Asa said urgently.

"Yes."

"Well, lay back and I'll say a few prayers for your quick recovery."

"Thank you." She sounded scared. I went and sat next to Asa and we sat near the bed.

Father Caleb glanced at us and wrinkled his nose. "I'm surprised the doctor allowed filthy dogs in here, but it's not my place to say, I suppose."

"Like we'd leave her alone," Asa growled.

The priest opened his book and started reading. He glanced over at Seija and stopped, staring at her. He waved his hand in front of himself, as priests often did and stood, backing away.

"Your eyes."

"They're quite normal for Canadians." She sounded afraid.

"They're red, possessed, you've the devil in you, girl."

"They are not red. They're purple, and there's no such thing as the devil you ignorant fool." Apparently now she was mad.

"Blasphemy!" He pointed at her.

Asa and I put ourselves between the priest and Seija, growling.

"With devil dogs!"

Elliott chose that moment to return. "What? Where?" He looked around, his arms full of food and a few packages.

My stomach growled and I licked my lips. I could smell steak.

"Demons!" The priest shouted and ran for the door, almost running Elliott over. "I'll be back to exorcise the devil. We'll save your soul, if not your body." He slammed the door and ran down the street. I heard him yelling for the doctor.

"Um. What'd I miss?"

"That ignorant human saw my eyes and decided I was possessed. Of course Asa and your dog protected me."

Elliott swore. "Here, put these on. We need to leave, now."

Seija stood, dropping the sheet. Elliott's eyes went wide and he spun around, turning his back. She didn't seem to notice.

139

J.A. Campbell

"Thank you for your kindness." She unwrapped the dress Elliott had bought for her and put it on.

"Sure. I just hope that if I, um, ever crash land on someone else's planet, they'll help me too."

"Avoid Mars." Seija laughed.

"Noted."

"I'm dressed."

"We should hurry. Dogs, you guys can eat in the wagon. Let's go." Elliott clutched his other parcels to his chest and looked out the door. "It's clear for now, but we should take the back alley. Seija, are you well enough to walk?"

"Yes, as long as I don't have to walk the whole way." She sounded tired again after her outburst at the priest, but she smelled very strange and I couldn't tell for sure how she felt.

I scouted ahead with Asa, but we didn't encounter anyone on the way to the wagon.

"Here, you and the dogs, get in the back. Feed them, help yourself to food. I'll get the wagon hitched." He helped Seija climb into the back and we jumped in. Then he shoved the parcels at her and pulled the cover over the back so no one could see in. I heard him shout at the livery man and they hitched the horses, but my stomach and the wonderful food Seija unwrapped occupied my attention.

Before too long we were bouncing down the road out of Flagstaff. I heard Father Caleb and the doctor shouting but we weren't followed.

After a while Elliott pulled aside the flap to the front bench. "Did you save any of that food for me?"

It took us three days to get back to the cow pie ship. Elliott didn't want to push the horses as hard, and I thought he was enjoying Seija's company, even though she was from another planet. He seemed very happy to talk with her and told her all about our ghost hunting adventures. She seemed very impressed and gave me lots of scratches, but I couldn't help but feel inferior to Asa. He could actually communicate with his person and all I could do was bark once for yes and twice for no, or nod my head. He knew all sorts of things and was always willing to tell me about stuff, but I didn't have anything I could tell him about in return. We didn't even find a good cow pie to roll in.

I spent as much of the trip as I could running alongside the wagon so I didn't have to talk. Asa, naturally, stayed with Seija. She slowly got better, but she still hurt. If it had been Elliott I would have stayed right by his side too, no matter how much I wanted to run.

Elliott pulled up the wagon by the shade he'd left the horses in the last time we were at the giant hole.

"Here we are. Let me unhitch the horses so they can rest and we'll go investigate your ship."

"Thank you."

It didn't take long before we were ready. The horses stood swatting flies, happily resting in the shade. There was a small pool of water we hadn't seen last time and Elliott threw out some feed.

Elliott and Seija slowly scrambled down the side of the crater while Asa and I bounded ahead, running toward the ship. I put my nose to the wind and sniffed. The hot metal smell was still there, and I guessed that must be the way that the ship smelled all the time.

Asa stopped and sniffed, tilting his head.

Elliott and Seija came behind us. Elliott had Seija's arm in his and she smiled. They stopped when they reached us and Elliott frowned.

"Something wrong?"

"The ship shouldn't smell so hot," Asa said to me.

I whined.

A low hum slowly drowned out the sound of the wind. I glanced at Asa. He whined.

"It's a ship!" Asa said to me and turned back toward our people and the wagon.

"Oh, no!" Seija shouted. "Come on, we have to go. It's the Martians." She stumbled and Elliott helped her up.

"Be careful. You'll hurt yourself again."

"You don't understand!" She said something else in another language and pulled on Elliott's hand. "Run, Asa!"

He sprinted for the wagon, leaving the people and me far behind.

I barked at him, angrily. "We have to protect them."

"Brown, run!" Seija yelled.

I would do no such thing. I stayed with Elliott and Seija as they scrambled back toward the wagon.

The hum grew louder until I could barely hear Elliott shout. Wind blasted around us, sending dirt flying in hundreds of little dust devils. A shadow raced across the ground, blotting out the sun. I looked back and saw a flying cow pie rapidly approaching.

I barked in alarm, flinching when the shadow reached me. It was no use, Elliott and Seija couldn't outrun it so I turned to fight and give them time to get away.

The wind went still and the sound vanished as the ship stopped over the crater. I barked and growled, warning it off. I wanted to run but I had to protect my people.

A door opened in the middle of the ship, and a light flashed so bright I couldn't look at it. Something came down out of the middle. It almost looked like a basket.

"Brown!" Elliott shouted. "Come now!"

I had to obey. I turned and sprinted toward them. Elliott carried Seija as he ran.

I turned to check on the Martians. The basket sat on the ground and little Martians swarmed out of it. They looked vaguely greenish, and were shaped similar to humans or Plutonians, but were much shorter. I barked. Elliott tried to run faster.

Sharp buzzing sounds shattered the quiet, and bright lights flashed past me. I yelped when one got close, burning my fur, and dodged as more buzzing lights flashed around me. They chased me all the way to the side of the crater. I sped up it as quick as the loose dirt would allow, almost getting hit a few times, but I managed to make it to the top and the lights stopped.

I spun around, barking angrily. The Martians were close to Elliott! I charged back down into the crater, but it was too late, the little Martians had my human and Seija. I ran harder but the ship moved the basket faster than I could run, and before I could reach them the Martians had my people in the basket and it went up toward the ship. I leapt, trying to catch it. One of the Martians shot that buzzing light at me. I yelped, though it didn't hit me and I fell to the ground. I didn't get up, ashamed that I couldn't protect my people.

I thought I heard Elliott call my name, but I didn't move, just laid there until the ship was gone. There was no way I could go up into the sky to rescue them.

I'd lost my human.

"Brown. Are you okay?" Asa touched me with his nose a while later.

143

I growled. I didn't want to talk to the coward.

"Are you hurt?"

"No. Go away." I snapped at him when he touched my shoulder with his nose.

He yelped and jumped back. "You need to get out of the sun," he said from a safe distance.

I growled.

"Brown, come on. Let's get back to the shade. We need to make a plan."

I jumped to my feet and lunged at him. "You ran away. Now they are gone. There's no plan!"

Asa plastered himself to the ground, rolling onto his back and whining submissively. "Brown, you don't understand. I had to run. The Martians hate us. They kill us on sight. At least now we have a chance to rescue our people."

I stood over him, teeth bared. "How. They're in space if you didn't notice."

"Our ship is broken. But there's another one. It's supposed to be intact."

"I'd think that if there was a ship, a human would have found it by now."

"It's not far. The people in the area call it Crater Diablo." He stayed on his back but looked at me hopefully.

"Great. So there's a ship. How are we going to convince a human to fly it for us?" I wrinkled my lips, seriously considering tearing Asa's throat out.

He must have seen something in my eyes because he turned his head away, offering no challenge at all. "I can fly it, Brown."

"You can fly a ship, but you can't keep Martians from taking your person?"

"They kill us."

"Better dead, than a coward."

That got a reaction. Asa growled for a moment then stopped. "Brown, we can't fight. You're very brave and fierce, but we are a peaceful people and don't know how anymore. Their lasers..."

"If you can't fight, how are we going to get them back?"

"I have mind powers. I can fly the ship. We can get on board their ship and sneak our people out. It will work. It's why we're always killed, because we can rescue our people."

"If the Martians hate you so much, why were you trying to talk to them?"

"We have to try, every once in a while. It's the only way we'll ever know true peace, and reach the far stars."

I growled. His plan was dumb, but if there was a chance... I spun and sprinted back to the horses. I was hot and thirsty and tired and I wanted nothing to do with a coward, even if he could fly a ship. I'd have to work with him later, but right now being around him was more than I could stand. And of course he could fly a ship. I was so not advanced.

I got a drink then jumped into the back of the wagon and dug around until I found some of the dried food I ate occasionally. I heard Asa come back to the camp while I ate, so I stayed in the wagon and took a nap.

Finally it started to get dark out. We couldn't travel during the day without the wagon. The horses would be okay here for a couple of days. I jumped down and went and got another drink. Asa jumped into the wagon and I almost told him to leave the food alone, but he needed to eat too.

"How long will it take us to get to this crater?"

"If we run fast, we can get there tonight."

"Good. Which way?"

"Brown, I'm sorry. I really am. We'll get them back."

I glared at him.

He sighed. "This way."

He ran and I followed. We ran for hours. Occasionally stopping if we smelled water. Asa was tired, but I was used to running all day so I pushed him to run faster. Finally as the sky started to lighten in the east, Asa stopped. "We're close. Please, Brown, I must rest."

We'd been climbing a hill for a while and I could use a quick break too. I smelled Plutonian blood. Asa limped up to me but didn't say anything about his bleeding feet. I ignored them too. My feet were only a little sore. I sat and stared at Asa while he panted. His antennae were limp where they normally stood straight up and though he was still standing, I guessed he'd rather lie down and sleep.

After a short rest, Asa limped forward. "We're here. Look, Crater Diablo."

I followed him to what I thought was the edge of a mesa, but it was really a giant hole kind of like the one his ship made, only much bigger.

The sides were steep, but we could get down. I didn't see a ship though.

"Where's the ship?"

"Buried at the bottom. I can get it out, if it still works."

"It had better work." I growled.

Asa sighed and started down into the crater. I followed and soon we slid down, rock and dirt falling with us.

The sun was low in the sky; rapidly warming the day by the time we made it to the bottom. It would take us a while to reach the middle and I started toward it.

"Brown, wait."

I spun.

"Let me get the ship out first."

I still didn't really understand what he was talking about, but I sat and gave him time to do whatever it was he wanted to do.

Asa stared at the center of the crater for a long time before he lay down with his head on his paws.

"It's starting. We need to wait for a few minutes. Then, if the ship starts properly it will surface on its own."

"What if it doesn't start properly?"

Asa sighed. "Then we will have to go back to my ship and see if we can send a message for help. I'm afraid the Martians have destroyed the other ship, though. They usually do.

"These Martians seem mean, like squirrels. Maybe they're related."

Asa stared at me, then shook his head and laughed. "Maybe they are."

We waited forever but Asa didn't seem worried so I tried to relax. The sun was visible overhead when he sat up and stared at the center of the crater. I did the same and soon saw the dirt moving. It was hard to see at this distance but it seemed like it bubbled upward. I felt a low rumble in my paws and then the ground seemed to crack open and a silver ship rose out of the earth. This one was shaped more like a pinecone than a cow pie. It rotated until the pointy end was straight at us, and then it came toward us. I stood up, alarmed and glanced at Asa. He still didn't seem worried so I tried to relax, but it was hard with a giant silver pinecone floating toward us.

Asa sighed and the ship slowly lowered to the ground a short distance away.

"I think we have a chance. Come on, before a human sees this."

We ran to the ship. A door opened and a ramp lowered when we got close. I sprinted inside behind Asa before I could think too much about it, and followed him into a room with a lot of controls like the one we'd found Seija in. He left blue bloody paw prints on the shiny floor but didn't complain. Asa jumped up into a chair and I did the same. We could see the crater through the front window.

"Hang on Brown. We're going into space."

I whined. "Hang on to what?"

Asa grinned and the ship slowly rose. I watched the ground until I could only see light blue sky. Then the ship rumbled again and I was shoved backward. I yelped as the ship leapt forward. The sky rapidly changed from light blue, to dark blue, and then black.

"Brown, welcome to the great blackness. You may very well be the first Border Collie in space," Asa said.

I whined as I started to float away from the chair.

The Plutonian dog laughed at me.

I growled.

"Oh, stop. It's fun to float around, maybe I'll teach you once we have our people back, but for now I suppose we should walk on the ground."

I didn't know what he was talking about, but the ship lurched then after a moment I fell back to my seat.

"What was that?"

"There's no gravity in space. Gravity is what makes it so you can walk on the ground instead of float away from the planet. I put the ship into a spin so we can walk normally. It's an old ship. We have artificial gravity on our newer ones and don't need to spin."

I tilted my head, not understanding at all. I decided it didn't matter as long as I got Elliott back.

"Can we catch the Martians?"

Asa nodded. "I found them and we're on a course to intercept."

I didn't ask what that meant. "Won't they see us?"

"I'm counting on it."

I tilted my head the other way. That didn't sound like a good idea, but then I had no idea how to fly ships, or talk to people, or anything. What did I know about intercepting

Martians? Although I supposed it was good when the sheep saw me when I tried to catch them. Maybe it was the same thing.

"Come on, let me show you around. I bet there's still food onboard."

I hoped so. I was hungry.

We found food and explored the ship. The side windows were hard to look out of with the ship spinning but the front window stayed steady. I stared out it for hours while the Martian ship slowly grew larger, from a small point of light that Asa assured me was the ship, until I could see the cow pie shape.

"They slowed. They saw us. Come on, Brown. They'll take us onboard. We need to hide so we can sneak out later and rescue our people.

"Where are we going to hide?" There were plenty of places onboard, but if I were a Martian I'd check them.

"We make special compartments to hide in, just in case we have to rescue our people. The best one is in the floor. Come on."

I followed Asa, thinking that I might have to forgive him if this actually worked. When we got out into the hallway one part of the floor I'd walked across many times rose into the air. Asa jumped down into the hole underneath and I followed.

"How will we know when to come out?"

"It'll be a while, but after the Martians search the ship we'll be able to sneak off."

"Won't they expect that?"

"It has been a long time since one of our people has been caught. Hopefully they won't expect us, but it's a possibility."

"Then how will we rescue our people?"

"We have to be very careful."

This was such a bad plan.

The ship shuddered and I started to float. Asa somehow clung to the floor but I bumped into what had been the roof. Then I heard several loud clanks and yelped when I fell back toward the floor. I stopped falling before I hit.

"Sorry, Brown. I should have held you to the ground." He didn't sound sorry, he sounded amused.

I fell the rest of the way, but I didn't hit hard. I wondered what Asa had to do with that. He said he could move things with his mind, but surely not dogs.

"We have to be quiet now."

I nodded and lay down in the small space. We waited so long that I fell asleep, dreaming of chasing flying sheep and fighting squirrels that shot buzzing lights at me.

"Brown."

I jumped to my feet, growling. Stupid squirrels.

"Easy. It's time to go. Please follow me so we don't get caught. I can sense where they are."

I nodded and followed Asa off the Plutonian ship and onto the Martian one. We darted across the open area. I saw many little cow pie ships in the big open area and guessed we weren't on the little ship that took Elliott and Seija. I hoped Asa was right and that they were close.

The metal on the Plutonian ship was silver. This ship seemed to be made of red metal. I could smell the Martians, but I didn't see any. My skin crawled and I couldn't keep my hackles down. Any minute those buzzing lights could shoot at us and then Elliott and Seija would be trapped forever.

We darted around a corner. I kept my nose in the air, sniffing for Martians. Asa seemed to be doing the same. Every once in a while he'd stop and we'd wait while Martians walked past our hiding spots. They did look like short Plutonians, or tall human children, with green skin. They all wore identical clothes, except some had different colors or shiny bits and they all seemed to carry those things that shot buzzing light. Their eyes were red instead of violet like Seija's, and they had no hair. When they spoke their voices sounded angry, though I didn't understand their scents well enough to tell if they were or not.

Asa led us through several more doors. They all opened for us and I hoped we didn't find one that was locked. We hid from several more Martians and then I caught a hint of Elliott's scent.

I perked my ears forward. "Do you smell them?"

Asa nodded. "This way."

We went around one more corner and there they were, in two cells like a prison, only on a ship.

Elliott saw us first. His eyes went wide. "Brown, I thought you were dead!"

Seija sat up slowly.

"Asa. You found us!" She sounded surprised and happy. "The other ship?"

Asa nodded.

"We have to get out of here. They won't leave us alone for long," she said.

"I'm working on the doors. They're more complicated than the normal ones." Asa stared at the doors.

I turned around when I heard a sound.

The door opened. Before the Martian could react, I launched myself at him, hitting him with all four feet in the chest. He fell to the ground, his head hitting hard, and didn't move. I grabbed the buzzing light gun off of his belt

151

and dragged it back into the room. Elliott could use it when they escaped.

The cell doors opened and Elliott rushed out and hugged me tightly. "Oh, Brown. I thought you were dead."

I licked salty water off of his face and grinned, happy to see him too. I pointed to the light gun with my nose and he picked it up.

"Good girl, Brown." Elliott scratched my ears.

"Asa, lead the way," Seija said.

"Brown, stay back and protect Seija. I'll lead since I have the gun."

I wanted to protect Elliott, but he had the light gun and Seija didn't have anything. I followed while Asa and Elliott led. We went quickly, since we wouldn't be able to hide our people in the small places we'd hid in before. We were almost back when the lights began to flash and a horrible wail made me yelp.

"They know we've escaped! Hurry," Seija said.

We ran, but Martians blocked our path, shouting in their language.

"I don't want to hurt you," Elliott shouted, pointing the light gun at them.

The Martians shot at us.

"Okay, I lied. I do." Elliott returned fire as we retreated down the hallway. I heard a few Martians scream.

Several came up behind us, but I barked a warning and attacked them. They weren't expecting it and one of them shot his partner while trying to hit me. I tackled the third to the ground. His head hit hard and he went still. The other stared at me, looking surprised. I snarled and ran into his legs. He fell on top of me and a buzzing light hit him. He jerked, dead.

Elliott shot at another Martian that came up behind me and turned back to the others.

I wagged my tail.

"Brown, let's go!" Elliott shouted.

Elliott had managed to clear a path and we ran for the ship. He fired the light gun and I knocked down a few more Martians who tried to sneak up behind us.

We ran out into the big open space with all the ships, going as fast as Elliott and Seija could run. Seija was bleeding again, but she didn't complain. Asa's feet bled too, leaving blue paw prints, but we were almost there.

More Martians ran out, firing their light guns and one hit Elliott in the arm. He stumbled and I lost my mind. I charged the Martian, barking as loudly as I could. The Martian's eyes went wide and he ran. I grabbed his ankle and he sprawled out on the ground, light gun sliding away. He rolled over and I pounced on the Martian's chest, clamping my teeth around his neck and tearing. Martian blood was even greener than their skin and it tasted terrible.

That Martian gurgled and died. I wrinkled my lips at the nasty blood all over me.

"Brown!" Elliott shouted.

I ran to the ship, passing several dead or injured Martians from Elliott's light gun. I got on board and the ramp closed. I heard the buzzing light a few more times and then the ship clanked and grumbled and I thought we were in the air.

Asa came to the back, leaving more blue paw prints. "We need to check the ship while Seija flies. We don't want any Martians on board."

We ran through the rest of the ship, and just when we thought we were clear a Martian ran out of one of the rooms. I crouched, staring at him, daring him to come any closer.

He met my eyes and held still. I wasn't sure if I actually controlled him with my Eye like I did with ghosts and sheep, but he responded by backing up when I took a step forward.

"Go, I'll hold him. Get Elliott."

The Martian tried to grab his light gun. I growled and stared harder. He froze, holding his hands out to the side.

Asa stayed by my side. "He's on his way. I told Seija."

I still didn't understand how he could do that, but as long as Elliott came, it was okay. I heard Elliott running toward us.

He pointed his light gun at the Martian. "Keep your hands out. Asa, get his gun."

Asa frowned. "Gun?"

"The thing that shoots lights," I said.

"Oh, his laser." It floated from the Martian's belt and landed on the floor in front of me.

Elliott swore. "Okay, Martian. Hands up. Try anything and I'll shoot you."

The Martian stared blankly at Elliott for a minute before he put his arms up higher and walked past us, edging carefully around me. Elliott found something to tie his hands together with and pushed him back toward the room with all the controls.

"You're very brave, Brown." Asa licked some of the blood off of my jaw before stepping back.

I sighed. "I can't do any of the things you can do." I walked off before Asa could reply and found a corner to curl up in.

Asa left me alone for a while, but he came and got me when we got close to home. "Brown, you'll want to see this."

I sighed but followed, jumping up into a chair and looking out the front window. In the blackness I could see a green and blue ball with white swirls and a gray one that was a little smaller. "What's that?"

"Earth. Where you're from. And the smaller one is the moon you see every night."

I stared.

"This is incredible," Elliott said to Seija.

"Yes. I never really get used to how beautiful your planet is. Ours looks much like your moon. We live underground."

"I'd like to see it."

She smiled. "Maybe someday. I will ask the leaders if I can bring you and your very brave dog, Brown."

I thumped my tail, her praise making me a little happier.

"She seems upset." Elliott scratched me on the ears and turned back to the view.

"Asa says she is upset because she can't fly ships and talk to you."

"I still can't believe you can talk to Asa. Can he really talk to Brown?"

"Yes."

"Come here, Brown." He patted his lap and I jumped from my seat to his lap. He hugged me and we watched the Earth get bigger in the window. "Brown, I understand you just fine, and we don't have any ships for you to fly anyway. Besides, Asa can't herd sheep or fight ghosts. I like you just the way you are."

I licked his face and thumped my tail, feeling much better.

"And I promise we're going straight to Colorado to get a ranch."

I dropped my jaw in a grin.

"And Seija and Asa can visit any time."

I woofed once.

"But not the Martian." We all glared at the Martian who sat, tied up, in one of the seats. He glared back.

Elliott smiled and hugged me.

"Asa, can you tell Elliott that he's the best person ever and that I really like hunting ghosts and I hope we don't stop even after we get our ranch, and that Colorado is perfect?"

Asa told Seija, who told Elliott. He hugged me tighter and I had to lick more water from his face.

"I love you, Brown."

I wagged my tail and licked his face even more.

"Brown says she loves you too," Seija said for me.

Elliott held me tight and looked out the front window. "Let's watch this, because I bet we'll never get to see it again."

I got the feeling he didn't know what else to say. I didn't know what else to say either so I tucked my head under his chin and watched the Earth grow bigger in the window.

It was dark when we finally landed. Seija took us to our wagon. My ears popped and I shook my head as we left the ship, but it was good to smell the desert smells again and feel the wind in my hair.

Elliott stood at the base of the ramp with Seija. "What will you do with the Martian?"

"I'll take him to Pluto. The leaders will question him, and maybe we can learn how to get along."

"Will it be safe?"

Seija nodded. "Yes."

"I'll miss you."

She smiled at him. "It was wonderful to meet you, Elliott. I hope we meet again."

"Me too." He hugged her.

Asa grinned at me. "Brown. Thank you for teaching me to be brave. Those Martians don't have a chance now."

I touched noses with him. "I'm glad I got to meet you, and go to space. I hope you get to come back and visit."

He nodded. "Count on it."

Elliott and I moved away from the ship and Seija and Asa went back onboard. Elliott waved and we watched as the ship slowly lifted from the ground, and then rapidly streaked away.

"Well, Brown. That was one heck of an adventure. Let's go hitch up those horses and cover some ground before the sun comes out." He scratched my ears. "My very brave, perfect girl." He knelt and hugged me, then stood quickly. "The horses!"

He ran back to our little makeshift camp, but I knew the horses were okay. They'd found the grain, I could smell it, and I could hear the sounds they made when they slept.

"Oh, they made a mess." Elliott shook his head and started cleaning it up while I followed him around. He finally got the horses hitched and I sat up on the bench with him as he guided the horses north. We stared up at the sky and Elliott put his arm around me.

"Think they'll come back?"

I whined. It occurred to me that I'd never found a cow pie for Asa to roll in. They'd better come back or he'd be missing out on one of the best things ever. I'd even teach him to herd. He'd never taught me to float in space either. Maybe I could learn to fly his ship and talk to Elliott.

"Well, Brown. Let's go get some sheep."

I licked Elliott's face and leaned against him. Maybe we'd find a ghost or two to hunt on the way.

J.A. Campbell

# BROWN TAKES TO THE SKIES

*Denver, Colorado, 1901*

I hated leashes.

Elliott, my human, tried to argue that since we'd been invited to fly on the airship, I shouldn't have to be on a leash.

Captain Peyton, the owner had countered that allowing me on board was exception enough.

Elliott had almost walked away. In the end it was my desire to fly on the airship that made him agree.

Besides, they had a ghost problem, and I was the dog for the job.

My human held my leash while I stood with my paws on the rail, nose to the wind, drinking in the glorious scents of the sky.

A few ladies tittered nervously as they strolled across the deck, distracting me from my nose. One glanced up at the air bag that kept us aloft. The other said something in soft tones like Elliott might have used on nervous lambs, and they moved on.

"Sure is beautiful up here, isn't it, girl?" Elliott said.

I dropped my jaw in a doggy grin and wagged my tail before putting my nose back into the wind.

Though only a short time since we'd lifted off, already I felt at home in the sky. Perhaps it was strange for a dog to like to fly, but I'd done far stranger things recently, and I liked the scents the air brought me.

"We should begin our preparations," Elliott said.

Huffing, I dropped back to all fours and padded next to my human as we headed for the door that led below.

The ladies stopped us.

I sniffed, one smelled very nervous, the other merely annoyed. Both wore fancy dresses I associated with the clothing from back in the east where we'd come from and they smelled faintly of flowers.

"They really let you bring a dog onboard?" The annoyed one asked.

"She does tricks." Elliott knew we weren't supposed to talk about the ghost, so he couldn't tell them why I was here.

Obediently, I sat up on my back legs when Elliott gave me the signal.

The nervous one laughed. "What's her name?" She held out her hand for me to sniff.

"Brown."

She glanced up at Elliott. "That's not a very original name for a brown and white dog."

He shrugged. "She's a Border Collie from the old country. They all have simple names."

The woman still held out her hand so I put my paw in it and she giggled. "How wonderful."

"She'd better not have fleas," the annoyed one said.

I flattened my ears.

"Easy, Brown. She takes exception to that, ma'am. Now if you will excuse us, ladies, we were off to find some lunch." He touched the brim of his round hat and I followed him away.

Lunch sounded like a fine idea to me. I hoped they had steak.

Elliott and I walked across the deck and down into the ship. It wasn't very large, I'd been on a steamship on the Mississippi river that was larger.

Captain Peyton, the owner of the airship, had approached us almost as soon as we'd gotten off the train in Denver. Apparently we'd made enough of a name for ourselves that he'd been looking for us and discovered we were headed for Denver. He hadn't wanted me to come along, not believing that I was part of the ghost-hunting team, but finally he'd consented, if I wore a leash.

Food smells, including meat, distracted me from my memory of the stinky Captain and how demanding he'd been when he asked us to banish his ghost. He'd smelled of sweat and fear and guilt when he'd told us of his problem. At the time I'd wondered why, but now I only cared about eating and handling the ghost problem.

Elliott left me outside the door to the room where they prepared the food. Sitting, I waited patiently until he returned with two wonderful smelling plates. Drool splattered the floor as I followed Elliott back to our room.

"Well, Brown. This should be straight forward." He stared at his great-grand pappy's hunting journal while I made short work of my lunch.

"We should simply be able to summon, trap, and banish the ghost without much trouble." He put his plate down on a small table and rummaged in his hunting bag.

I rested my chin on the arm of one of the two chairs and stared at his half-eaten food. Surely he was going to finish that?

Kneeling next to the bed in the small room, Elliott shoved a small rug out of the way and cleared some space to draw. I knew I should be more concerned about what Elliott was doing, but the uneaten food had my nose's full attention.

"Brown, are you still hungry?" Elliott finally noticed where my nose was pointed.

Strictly speaking, I wasn't hungry, but there was always room for steak.

He laughed. "Go ahead and eat that while I finish up this drawing."

Gleefully, I jumped into the chair and devoured his lunch. Once I'd licked the plate clean I joined Elliott and looked over his drawing. I knew the circle with the strange designs was supposed to be complete, no breaks in the lines at all. Elliott had explained it all to me once. I looked closely, and then woofed quietly to let him know I thought it looked okay.

"Good girl, Brown." He scratched my ears and I thumped my tail on the ground before scooting back so I could watch for the ghost. It was my job to catch it with my Border Collie Eye and push it into the trap, the same way I herded sheep into a pen.

Elliott read from his book, trying to keep his voice down so passengers wouldn't hear, but also keep his voice forceful enough to command the ghost that haunted this airship to appear.

The air chilled and the gas lamps flickered. White smoke drifted in under the door of our small cabin and crawled across the floor. Jumping up, I got out of its path and growled, trying not to sneeze as the ghost's musty-ozone smell filled the room. Pausing in front of the trap Elliott had drawn, the smoke began to swirl as more continued to pour under the door. Finally, the smoke stopped flowing under the door and the white swirl spun faster like a dust devil. Many of the other ghosts I'd fought did the same.

Two eyes opened and stared at me. Growling when I felt the ghost's wind pull at my fur, I met its eyes and pushed. Most ghosts fought me when I caught them with my Eye, but this one simply floated backward until the trap sprung around it with an audible pop.

Sitting, I tilted my head while I stared at the ghost. I was very good at hunting ghosts, but it was never that easy.

Elliott frowned, as if he were also confused at how easy that was. "Good girl, Brown."

We both stared at the ghost, but it simply swirled contentedly in the trap, not howling in rage, or otherwise trying to escape. Elliott glanced at me and I looked back and thumped my tail on the ground once because I wasn't sure what else to do.

According to the owner of the airship this ghost was supposed to be extremely violent and had almost thrown him off the ship several times when they were high in the sky. It didn't bother passengers often, but it did chase the crew around.

This hardly seemed like a violent ghost.

"Well, I guess I'll get on with it." Elliott looked back at the book in his hands and said the first few words that, when complete, would banish the ghost.

"Ah, excuse me."

Elliott snapped his mouth shut and I yelped in surprise, looking around for the source of the voice. It almost sounded like one of the men who had taught Elliott about books and things when we lived back east, with words carefully formed and pronounced. Not like a lot of the people we came across in the west.

We both glanced wildly around before looking back at the ghost. It was no longer spinning, and seemed to be more like the cloud of smoke from earlier. The eyes were gone.

"Who's there?" Elliott finally asked.

"Ahh! You can hear me. Excellent. Most humans can only see me."

Sniffing the air, I whined uncertainly. The only thing I could smell besides myself, Elliott, faint traces of lunch and the background scents of the airship was the musty-ozone of the ghost.

The smoke drifted around the trap before becoming taller and almost human shaped. Wavering slightly, slits opened where its head would be if it were human, and formed eyes and a mouth.

"Hello."

I flattened my ears and stared at the ghost. I'd never seen one do this before. Sure, I'd had ghosts talk to me on occasion, but usually they hurled insults like squirrels. Though, once I'd met a friendly ghost. He'd looked completely human though.

Elliott lifted his book.

"Please, don't. Hear me out." Raising what looked like a hand, the ghost interrupted Elliott before he could begin the banishment words again.

"Okay." Elliott sounded uncertain.

The ghost made a sound like it was clearing its throat.

That seemed really strange to me.

"My name is…was Charlie Victors. I'm the owner of this fine ship."

"I see." Elliott took a couple of steps toward me, carefully stepping around the ghost-trap.

"That murdering bastard, Peyton, stole it from me after he killed me." The ghost shut its eyes for a moment and the smoke swirled as if it were agitated.

Elliott shifted uncomfortably and smelled nervous. Pushing my nose up under his hand, I tried to reassure him by leaning against his leg. He scratched my ears and that seemed to calm him a little.

"Yes, well, I've heard of you two and I hope you can help me."

"Heard of us?"

I tilted my head, wondering if I'd understood the ghost properly.

"Well, yes, even spirits talk amongst themselves."

"How?" Elliott sank down onto one of the chairs.

"That's not relevant at this time. Just that I've heard of you, and all that. No hard feelings of course, all of those you've sent away were giving ghosts bad names. As, I suppose, I was. Unfortunately, I was unable to take care of Peyton myself and now I need your help."

Elliott shook his head. "I'm sorry, this is a lot to take in. Exactly how do you think I can help you?"

"Why, prove that Jerrod Peyton murdered me of course. And then perhaps I can go to my rest instead of haunting this ship for eternity."

I whined.

Elliott was silent for a while before he glanced at me. "Mr. Victors, I'm sorry. I don't know how to prove that Captain Peyton murdered you. All we do is fight ghosts."

And demons, and Martians, I thought to myself. For a while there, I'd wished for a simple ghost to fight after all of the strange creatures we'd encountered. If we could handle Martians especially, I thought maybe we could handle a murderer. Martians were worse than squirrels.

"Of course I'd be willing to help. I know where some of the evidence is. If it will see Peyton hang, I'll even pretend you've already banished me. I've only made myself a nuisance because I wanted to get rid of him."

Frowning, Elliott leaned back and rubbed his forehead with his hand. "What proof can you offer me that you're telling the truth?"

The ghost shifted around until its eyes met mine. I refrained from capturing its mind because it wasn't trying to escape. It studied me for a minute, and then did a curious thing. It spoke to me.

"Dog, can you understand me?"

I thumped my tail on the ground once, shocked. "Of course."

For some reason, though I couldn't communicate directly with humans, ghosts always seemed to understand me. "My name is Brown."

"Her name is Brown," Elliott said at the same time.

The ghost laughed, but it was a friendly laugh instead of the evil hate-filled ones most ghosts used.

"So she says." The ghost seemed to smile. "And you are?"

"My apologies, I'm Elliott Gyles."

"Nice to make your acquaintance."

Thumping my tail on the ground again, I woofed quietly, though I wasn't sure what to think about this very strange ghost.

"Brown, when you met Peyton the first time, did he seem strange to you?" The ghost asked.

"He smelled afraid, but most people are afraid of ghosts. He also smelled guilty." I glanced at Elliott, who was staring at both of us intently.

"Mr. Gyles, your rather fabulous dog says that he smelled guilty. Would he have smelled so if he weren't feeling guilt about creating a ghost?"

"Is that correct, Brown?"

I woofed once in agreement.

The ghost's eyes widened. "You already have a system of communication worked out?"

"Yes, of course," I replied. "Just because humans can't listen properly and understand animals, doesn't mean we can't communicate with each other."

"You are remarkable."

"That's all well and good," Elliott said. "But that doesn't prove your story."

"No," the ghost agreed. "But perhaps it helps. By all means, keep me contained in this trap but go investigate my desk drawers in the office. You'll find documents that support my claim. He was an investor, to be sure, but he decided he wanted all the money for himself. Go on, you'll see. He should be enjoying his lunch at this time."

Elliott glanced at me before shrugging. "Very well. Come on, Brown."

"Ah, Mr. Gyles, if the door should be locked, there is a spare key hidden along the top of the door frame on a hook so it won't fall. I had a singularly bad habit of losing my keys."

Elliott nodded to the ghost and let us out of the small room.

"So, you can talk to ghosts?" Elliott glanced at me as we walked down the hallway toward the office Charlie the ghost wanted us to investigate.

I woofed quietly, once.

"Do they talk often?"

I woofed twice to say no.

Elliott was quiet after that, seeming to think. It didn't take us long to navigate the small airship. We knew which room to go to because we'd had a tour when we first came aboard.

Pausing outside, Elliott put his ear up to the door and listened.

"It's quiet. Do you hear anything, Brown?"

Listening and sniffing told me the room was empty and I woofed twice.

"Good, watch and make sure no one comes this way."

I sat next to the door.

Elliott unclipped my leash and looped it on his belt. Then he knocked lightly on the door. "Just in case," he said, smiling at me.

I doggy-grinned back, though he smelled nervous.

Elliott tried the handle but it didn't turn so he felt along the doorframe. Turning my attention back to the hallway, I listened with half of my attention to what Elliott was doing. He let himself into the office and opened drawers, muttering to himself. Finally I heard an 'ah-ha!'

I also heard footsteps coming down the hallway.

Alarmed, I woofed quietly.

Elliott shut drawers and rustled papers.

The footsteps grew closer.

Urgently, I woofed again.

Elliott left the office, shut the door and returned the key.

"Come on," he whispered.

We walked away from the office quickly but before long Elliott slowed and looked around as if he were looking for a ghost. I recognized what he was doing and sniffed the floor, playing along.

"Mr. Gyles?" Captain Peyton said.

We both turned and I wrinkled my lips when I caught a hint of his sour scent.

To my canine nose, most humans smelled best after they hadn't bathed for a few days, but I wished the Captain would jump in a lake or do something to wash away the sour scent that clung to him.

"Yes, Captain?"

"I trust you are having luck searching for the nuisance?"

He called the ghost 'the nuisance' when guests could potentially overhear.

"Yes, we have had some luck. I suspect we will have success tonight."

"Tonight? Why not now?"

For a moment the Captain smelled suspicious and his eyes flicked to the office door he stood near.

"It's the best time to capture a ghost," Elliott said.

"Of course." His scent eased. "Carry on then."

"Thank you, Captain." We turned away.

"Mr. Gyles."

Elliott stopped and looked back, his nervousness rising.

"Dog on a leash, please."

Sighing and smelling angry for a moment, Elliott clipped the leash to my collar. "Sorry, not used to using one." We quickly left the narrow hallway.

Elliott was silent until we were back at our room. He hesitated, hand hovering over the handle, before he took a deep breath and opened the door.

Pushing past him, I sneezed as the musty-ozone ghost smell tickled my nose. The trap still contained a swirling cloud of smoke that solidified into a sort of human figure when we entered. Two eyes opened and the ghost regarded us until Elliott closed the door.

"Well?" It asked.

"I've found enough evidence to suit me, but I'm not sure it's enough to see Peyton hang." Elliott took some papers from the inside pocket of his vest and waved them at the ghost before putting them into his hunting bag.

"Well, it's a start. What do you plan to do next?"

"If I let you out, will you give your word that you will pretend that I've banished you?"

"Yes, I promise. However I plan to monitor your progress and I will tell you if I see anything important."

Smudging the drawing with his foot, Elliott disabled the trap and it opened with an audible pop.

The ghost melted into a cloud and poured out before swirling around my paws.

Picking up my paws, I tried not to let the ghost touch me, but I could only lift so many paws off the ground. I whined.

"I quite like you, Brown," the ghost laughed, briefly flowing into a semi-human form.

Wagging my tail uncertainly, I tried to like the ghost too, but it was still a ghost.

"In the morning, I will tell Peyton I succeeded. We will be on board until we return to Colorado. I will try to question the crew and see if I can find any more evidence."

"Be careful. I'm sure I don't need to tell you that Peyton is ruthless."

Elliott nodded.

"Very well. I will leave you for now. Thank you." The ghost made a gesture similar to one Elliott made when he tipped his hat to ladies and melted back into a cloud of smoke. It crept along the floor and vanished into the wall.

"Well, Brown. That's a new one." Elliott took off his round hat and scratched his forehead.

Huffing, I sat and stared at the wall, head tilted, trying to figure out how we were suddenly working for a ghost instead of a human.

The next morning we found Captain Peyton on the deck of his airship. He stood toward the front, Elliott told me that was called the bow, and looked out ahead of us.

Sniffing the air, I could imagine what he saw, though I couldn't see it yet. What Elliott called cotton puff clouds would fill the sky. The sun shone brightly, and I scented water from far below. All the extra spring scents of the world coming alive after sleeping through the winter colored the air too. I loved the smell of spring.

Peyton glanced at us, checking to make sure I wore the leash. I glared at him, much like I stared at a recalcitrant sheep, except this time I really was angry. Quickly glancing away, he cleared his throat and addressed Elliott. "You did say she was friendly, correct?"

Elliott glanced at me and shrugged. "You're making her wear a leash. She's not terribly happy about it."

"Well, it's not like I put it on her. She can't know it was my doing."

"She knows," Elliott said. "Regardless, we've handled your ghost problem."

"Oh, most excellent!" His scent shifted from nervous to relieved.

Elliott smiled, though I could smell his anger and uneasiness. He didn't show it though. Once, we'd convinced people we hunted ghosts that weren't actually there and he'd had to act all the time. Peyton would never know how Elliott really felt, especially since humans couldn't smell emotions.

"We will be in St. Louis shortly. The winds favored us in the night. We will head directly back to Denver once we've loaded cargo and passengers."

"Excellent. Thank you, Captain."

"Thank you, Mr. Gyles. I'm quite glad to be rid of the nuisance."

Continuing to glare at Peyton, I jumped when a quiet voice in my ear whispered… "I wonder if he called me that when I was alive, too."

Huffing in annoyance I sat, looking around for the ghost. I couldn't see it anywhere, but the faintest hint of musty-ozone colored the beautiful spring scents. I sneezed.

Elliott glanced at me. "Come on, Brown. Let's get something to eat."

Turning, I walked next to him, sensing that the ghost trailed along with us.

171

Bright colors filled the sky and the sun had set by the time the ship landed. It was a noisy affair with men shouting commands, lines snapping in the wind and a sudden jolt when the ship finally settled and was secured. We picked an out-of-the way spot on the deck watching while passengers got off. The two women from the first afternoon spotted me. The nervous one approached with the other lady trailing behind.

"My uncle, the Captain, told us how you helped," she said to Elliott. "We are so grateful. Brown, I have a treat for you." She held out a piece of cooked meat.

Normally I would have taken it without thought, but something smelled strange though I wasn't sure if it was her or the treat. Laying down on the deck, I covered my nose with my paws and whined.

"Oh," she tittered. "Maybe she's airsick."

"Maybe," Elliott said sounding suspicious.

"Here, you can give it to her later."

He accepted the scrap and watched as the ladies left the airship.

"You're not hungry?"

I whined.

After glancing over the side of the airship, Elliott tossed the scrap of meat away. "Never seen you refuse food before."

I huffed.

After the passengers all left, the crew unloaded the cargo.

"Brown, let's go inside. I don't feel well."

I followed Elliott to our room and watched as he collapsed into the bed. Jumping up next to him, I lay my chin on his chest. He smelled odd and I could feel his heart racing.

I'd been sleeping for a while when the ghost woke me up.

"What's wrong, Brown?"

"I don't know," I said. "Elliott's not well."

"I wasn't around for a short time," the ghost said. "What happened?"

I told him how we've been standing on the deck of the airship and the nervous lady had tried to give me a scrap of meat and that I hadn't wanted it. Something had smelled strange she'd given it to Elliott instead and shortly after he'd become sick.

"You didn't touch it?" The ghost asked.

"No I didn't. Elliott only held it and then threw it over the side of the airship."

The ghost swirled around in a cloud of smoke for a moment before solidifying into its human-like shape again. "Perhaps it was poisoned."

I flattened my ears. "Poisoned?"

"Yes, he could have gotten a little bit of it through touching the piece of meat. It's a good thing you didn't eat it, Brown."

I whined. "Is he going to be okay?"

"I don't know. We should try and find the antidote if there is one."

I tilted my head. "An antidote?"

The ghost nodded. "Yes, some poisons come with a cure. Something that counteracts the poison. It's called an antidote. I don't know if this poison will have some but it's a good chance that if Peyton is behind this he will have wanted something he could counteract it with just in case. Was the woman wearing gloves?" The ghost asked.

"Yes, she was."

The ghost nodded, or what seemed to be a nod with his smoky form.

"Why do you ask?"

"I bet she's not now," the ghost replied. "Probably to protect herself from the poison, though why he'd want to harm you I don't know. Perhaps he simply didn't want to pay. Maybe he's suspicious that you know more than you should."

I huffed in annoyance. "Well and let's go find this antidote."

"Do you know how to open doors?" The ghost asked me.

I nodded like the humans did and hopped off of the bed. Waiting by the door for the ghost, I studied the doorknob. It returned to its smoky form and crept across the floor behind me. After a moment it disappeared but I could still smell a faint hint of musty-ozone.

"The antidote, if there is one, should be in the office," the ghost said. "If it's not there it may be in his cabin."

Relieved to discover that the doorknob was one of the lever type handles, I stood on my hind legs and put my front paw on the lever and pushed down while pushing forward. It didn't work. The lever clicked but the door remained shut.

Remembering that the door swung inward, I knew I needed to pull instead. I hooked my paw on the handle pushed it down and hopped backward. This time the door opened enough for me to get my nose in it and to sneak out into the hallway. I stopped, looking and sniffing, but no one was around.

"I will keep my senses open and if I see or hear anyone coming I will let you know. Things are different as a ghost, though, and sometimes I don't notice as much as I should. Stay alert, Brown."

I woofed quietly in agreement and headed back toward the captain's office. Of course, I had no idea how I was going to get in since I couldn't reach the key.

The ghost alerted me to several presences in the hallways and we were able to take side routes. If it weren't so late, more people would have been out and would've spotted me. Perhaps they would have tried to capture me.

I wasn't sure what I would do if someone captured me or tried to. I'd have to fight back and I didn't want to hurt people, but to save Elliott I'd do what I had to. It didn't take long for us to navigate the hallways of the small airship. Shortly I sat on my haunches staring at the door to the captain's office. After a moment's hesitation I sniffed the knob and listened at the door. No one was there, and the knob smelled normal. I stood on my haunches again, my paw on the top of the knob, and pushed down. This type of knob was much harder to turn and it was locked.

The ghost swirled into its humanlike shape, two eyes opening and staring at the door. I got the impression that it was significantly annoyed.

"I had forgotten about that. If I get the key down do you think you can open the door?"

I stared at the ghost, my head tilted, ears perked forward, trying to figure out what to say. I had to get the door open, but did I think I could do it? Not with the key.

Even though I didn't answer the ghost seem to understand what my hesitation meant. "Well, you are a remarkable dog but I suspect using a key would be beyond your physical capabilities though I'm certain you understand how to use one."

"Yes, of course I understand how to use a key. I don't think I can actually do it."

The ghost considered the door for a moment longer and a mouth appeared, smiling. "Well of course," it said. "If I can get the key down for you, certainly I can manipulate a simple lock. I wasn't too terribly concerned about someone breaking into my office and therefore did not buy an expensive lock for the door. I merely wanted to deter curious travelers from disturbing me while I worked."

The ghost vanished before I could ask what it meant and because I was listening very carefully, after a moment I heard the distinct click of the lock opening on the inside of the door. Surprised I tilted my head and wagged my tail, before jumping up on the door again and trying the knob. This time it turned easily and I was able to push the door open.

"Well done, Brown," the ghost exclaimed when I entered the study. "Shut the door behind you and let's look."

I used my nose and the ghost used whatever senses ghosts have. I caught hints of the strange smell I'd scented on the nervous woman but every time I caught hints of it there was nothing in the drawer, or on the table, or on the shelf that looked even remotely like it contained poison. I was careful not to touch anything just in case, at the ghost's cautioning. It, being already dead, took care of that part of the search for me.

After a while we had to admit defeat. Even the hidden compartments the ghost knew about were empty or only contained papers which were not at all interesting to me since they would not save my human's life.

"Well, Brown," the ghost said. "I do believe we're going to have to try his cabin. Ah, that rankles me to say his cabin. It's my cabin, this is my ship!" The ghost's cloud swirled rapidly, the light smoky color darkened for a moment before it seemed to get itself under control and returned to its humanlike form. "Sorry, Brown. I had a moment there. Very well, onward we go. I will lock the door behind you if you would shut it."

I stopped by the door, listening. I heard footsteps but they were far enough away that I should be able to get the door shut before they got here. I managed and dashed around the corner just as I heard the captain's footfalls and smelled his distinct sour scent come around the corner. He

176

paused in front of the office door and I hoped the ghost had gotten it locked before Peyton tried to open it. I heard the clink of keys, and then a soft wind ruffled across my fur.

"Brown, Peyton should be occupied for a while."

I followed the musty scent down the corridor toward the captain's cabin. We made it without any problems. This door was one of the lever ones and wasn't locked so it was easy for me to go in. I wrinkled my nose in disgust at the scents from his room. It smelled even more sour than the captain himself. I sneezed. I couldn't help it.

The ghost looked at me. "What do you smell?"

I wrinkled my lips and sneezed again. "His scent is very sour. Enough that he's the first human I've ever met that I actually wanted to take a bath."

The ghost laughed. "I seem to recall that he did stink but your nose is much more sensitive than mine."

Once I was able to ignore the smell we searched the room. My nose was impeded by not being able to use it completely but finally I caught the scent of what I had smelled on the nervous lady and smelled hints of in the office. I woofed quietly to get the ghost's attention and it came over to me.

Gesturing with my nose, I pointed toward the cabinet.

He momentarily disappeared inside. "That's it Brown." He returned. "There are two bottles. They aren't specifically labeled poison and antidote of course but they're probably what we're looking for. You shouldn't touch them but now we know where they're at. Let's see if we can wake Elliott long enough to get him here, and then maybe he can give himself the antidote if that's what it is. If not it may not matter."

I flattened my ears at the ghost's words and whined. We had to help Elliott. The trip back to the room I shared with Elliott was short. It was late out and it seemed like everyone was sticking to their cabins or were up on the deck watching the night sky. I pawed the door open, ran across the room, and shoved my nose under Elliott's chin, whining and trying to get his attention.

He groaned and tried to push me away but I was insistent and shoved harder at his chin with my nose.

"Brown, what are you doing? I'm trying to sleep."

I whined and tugged on his sleeve.

He pushed me away and rolled over.

I jumped up on the bed and put my paws on his shoulder, pushing him onto his back, and then I put my paws on his chest and licked his face.

"Brown, leave me alone. I'm tired and I don't feel good." His voice sounded weak.

I growled, knowing that would get his attention. I never growled at him. He was my human.

Elliott forced his eyes open and looked at me, clearly unhappy, but I tugged on his sleeve again. "Oh, okay," he said. "I'll try. I know it's important. You're a good girl, Brown. I'm sorry."

Elliott sat up in bed and clutched his head. I tugged on him urgently and he managed to get to his feet. He looked like he might fall at any moment.

The ghost swirled around my feet. This time I ignored it and it swirled toward the door. I understood that it wanted me to follow although I knew where we were going.

I opened the door and Elliott stumbled after me. It was pretty obvious he wasn't paying attention to where we were going. Although he managed not to step on me when I stopped in front of him to let a lone passenger get down the hall before we entered it. The one stairway was a little bit of problem and he almost fell halfway down but he caught himself on the railing and stumbled to the bottom. It didn't take long for us to get to the captain's cabin and I opened the door.

Elliott seemed to be aware that we are doing something strange because he stopped and looked around. "What are we doing, Brown?"

I nudged him in the back of the knees, and then led him over to the cabinet where we'd found the poison. At my urging he opened the door and stared blankly at the two bottles that sat on the edge of the shelf. I whined in frustration but the ghost came to the rescue, solidifying next Elliott into his human form.

"Elliott you must look at bottles. We believe you've been poisoned. One is probably the antidote but you need to look and see. I don't read so well as a ghost. Brown smelled the poison so we know these are what we need."

Elliott perked up at the word poison but not by much. He carefully took the two bottles off the shelf though his hands shook and he nearly dropped one. He held them both up where I could see. I pointed my nose at the one that did smell like the poison and growled. He put that one back on the shelf before looking closely at the other one.

"I'm not sure I can get my eyes focused enough to read the small label," Elliott said.

The ghost whirled around us and disappeared for a moment before returning. "Hurry, he's coming this way."

Elliott took the stopper off the bottle, sniffed, and then shrugged. "Well, I suppose it can't hurt me anymore than I'm already hurt if I have been poisoned."

Whining, I watched while he drank the contents of the bottle.

Elliott sputtered, wrinkled his nose and gagged. "That tastes awful. It must be good for you as bad as it tastes."

The ghost chuckled. "I don't suspect the effects will be immediate but we should get out of here. The captain is coming."

Elliott staggered to his feet and followed us out of the room. I was certain he was going to fall over but he

179

managed to keep his feet and we led him further way from the cabin. It would be obvious that someone had been there as we hadn't taken the time to shut the door but there was little we could do about that now.

By the time we made it back to our room, Elliott seemed to be feeling better and to my nose he smelled a little bit healthier. He sank down onto the bed and stared at me for a moment before getting back up. He washed his hands and face in the basin before coming over and wrapping me in a hug. "I don't know what I'd do without you, Brown. I can't believe they tried to kill you. It must have been the piece of meat you refused."

I woofed once in agreement and he buried his hands in my ruff and held me close.

"Thank you, Charlie, for helping," he said to the ghost.

"Of course, Mr. Gyles. After all you're helping me as well."

"Please call me Elliott and I will continue to help you as best I can but he's already tried to kill us once. We're going to have to lay low until we get back to Denver. I'm not sure if we'll be able to do anything right away but I will certainly help you see him hang for trying to kill my dog and having obviously killed you. I have a friend in the area, a sheriff, and I'm certain he'd be willing to look into it."

"Excellent, Elliott," the ghost said. "Perhaps you should get some more rest. In the morning I would act as if nothing happened otherwise the captain may become suspicious."

"What is this?"

Snarling, I spun but didn't launch myself at the smelly man. Two other men stood with him in the doorway. The ghost vanished immediately but the damage was done. Obviously Captain Peyton had seen him.

"So you banished the ghost, did you?" Peyton glared at Elliott.

Elliott climbed his feet and though he was steadier than before he still moved more slowly than normal. "You tried to kill my dog."

"Nonsense. Whatever are you talking about? I've done nothing of the sort yet you are apparently conspiring with the ghost who you claimed you already banished. For a considerable fee I might add, that I was planning on paying you when we returned to Denver. Yet I hear you talking about seeing me hang for something I did not do."

Elliott glared at him but before he could say more the captain gestured. "Seize him and that dog."

"Brown, run!"

As the men came forward I darted underneath them. I knew Elliott was right, we couldn't overpower them right now and as long as they didn't kill him they couldn't take him far while we were in the air. We'd be back in Denver soon. I had to stay hidden long enough to escape in Denver and find help. Although who would help a dog I didn't know.

I remembered someone from the last time we were in Colorado, a little blue cattle dog named Scoot and his person, Sheriff Tolbert, but they weren't in Denver and I had no idea how to find them.

I could tell the ghost followed me as I darted down the hallway because I smelled the musty-ozone and felt a slight breeze through my ruff as it fled with me.

Men shouted and chased after me and I had no idea what they did with Elliott. I darted around a corner and ran up a flight of stairs, and then down into the hold while the ghost whispered suggestions to me. Finally, finding a dark corner, I hid under a tarp. The ghost assured me that at least for the moment we had lost our pursuers.

"Ghost," I said.

"My name is Charlie."

"Charlie," I said, though it felt strange. "Can you check on my human and see what they're doing to him?"

"Of course, Brown." The ghost vanished.

Miserable, I curled up into a tight ball and waited. I didn't like not being able to help my human. The ghost returned a while later and actually seemed excited it swirled around quickly and its colors darkened in agitation.

"Brown, we can rescue him once we're on the ground. The captain doesn't know I can unlock the door. We can get him out once we land, and then he will be able to tell the authorities what has happened. I don't believe Peyton will let him go otherwise so we need to act quickly. Do you remember where he put those papers?"

"Yes. His hunting bag."

"We need to get them before the captain searches his room. He hasn't yet, but I'm sure he will soon. I will make sure the way is clear."

I knew the ghost was right even though I didn't want to leave my safe hiding place, so I crept out from underneath the tarp and followed him back through the ship. Sticking to the shadows as much as I could to stay hidden from view, I ran, though the hissing gas lamps that lit the hallways made that difficult. Once we were back at the room, Charlie checked to make sure no one was inside before I went in. I found Elliott's hunting bag where he left it and clutched it in my mouth.

"Hurry, Brown. They're coming."

I darted out of the room not bothering to close the door behind me and followed the ghost as we ran back toward the hold. Picking another spot to put the hunting bag once we were at the hold, I scraped back some canvas as if I were burying a bone. Fortunately there were no squirrels to dig it up and steal it. I was starting to think I liked the captain less than I like squirrels, which was saying something.

"Should we rescue Elliott now?" I didn't want him to be captured any longer than necessary.

"He'll have to hide on the airship until we land if we rescue him now," the ghost said.

Huffing in annoyance, I glared at Charlie the ghost. "Isn't there any other way off of the airship?"

"Well, it is possible to make it land early, but who knows where we will come down. Brown, let me go investigate and see how far away we are. I overheard the crew saying that the winds were favorable. Perhaps we'll be down soon."

"Okay." Curling back into a ball, I tucked my nose under my tail and sighed.

Charlie vanished and I was again alone. I hoped once we had our sheep ranch in Colorado that Elliott wouldn't be in any danger anymore.

I didn't have to wait long before Charlie returned.

"Excellent news, Brown. We should arrive soon. Well, there is some bad news. We'll be landing during the day. That will make it harder for us to hide our escape."

"Just as long as it is soon. Please keep an eye on Elliott for me while we wait."

"Of course, Brown. Get some rest."

Shutting my eyes, I tried to sleep so I'd be ready to go when it was time to rescue Elliott and escape.

It seemed like I slept forever, but finally Charlie woke me.

"Brown, we're landing. Be ready."

Crawling out from under the tarp I hid under, I shook and listened carefully. Distantly I heard the crew shouting and a few excited noises from female passengers. The sounds of the airship changed and my ears felt funny like they had the last time we landed.

Finally, the ship jerked and it felt like we came to a halt. I retrieved Elliott's hunting bag from its hiding place.

"Okay, Brown, let's go before the crew comes down."

We had to go up onto the deck to get from the hold into the main part of the ship, but in the chaos no one noticed me slinking along behind boxes and baggage. Creeping was awkward with the hunting bag clutched in my mouth, but no one was currently looking for a brown and white dog. They were all staring over the sides and marveling at the city of Denver or waiting for their turn to get off the airship. Sneaking down into the passenger area of the ship was harder but I managed with Charlie's help.

"He's in here." Charlie led me to one of the passenger cabins at the very back of the ship.

"Keep your senses open," I said to the ghost. "They're probably expecting me to try and find Elliott."

The ghost swirled around me and then vanished into the wall. After a moment I heard the lock click and I scratched at the door. Before long I heard the handle jiggle and saw it turn.

"Brown!" Elliott left the room and hugged me tightly. "Good girl," he took the hunting bag from me and slung it over his shoulder. "Let's get out of here."

I woofed in agreement.

This time we were prepared when the Captain's men tried to capture us. I grabbed a couple of ankles with my teeth, tripping them, and if I bit a little harder than I would have on sheep, well, who could blame me. Elliott hit a few others and then we burst out onto the deck.

Not having much of a plan other than to run, I barked ferociously, scaring women and men alike as they scattered out of my path. Elliott sprinted behind me, and I could smell the faint hint of musty-ozone as the ghost fled with us.

People screamed, or yelled in anger and a few tried to grab me, but I was quicker and soon we had managed to lose ourselves in the bustling streets of Denver.

Elliott leaned against a wall and panted. "I think we need to find the police, and then I need something to eat. I'm sure you're starving too, Brown."

My stomach growled when Elliott mentioned food.

He laughed, but it was a bitter laugh. "Let's go."

I pressed against Elliott's leg while we walked, and though it made it harder for him, he didn't object. Finally, we found the police station and though I'm sure they didn't normally allow dogs, I wasn't about to stay outside and no one objected when we entered together.

"Can I help you?" The man behind the counter asked.

"Yes, I have a murder to report."

He smelled surprised. "One moment." He went further into the building and came back after a short time with another man. They both wore uniforms with shiny buttons.

"I'm Officer Toms. Please, come with me." He barely glanced at me so I stayed pressed up against Elliott's leg while we went further into the building. We were shown into an office and Officer Toms gave me a dish of water.

Not having had any in a while, I was very grateful and wagged my tail at him while I drank.

Elliott told the story of how he'd overheard some of the crew talking about the previous captain's murder and how he'd stumbled on some evidence and then how we'd almost been poisoned. He left Charlie the ghost out of it. Finally, he presented the papers he'd come across in the office.

Officer Toms studied them for a while before nodding. "This will take some investigation of course, but I believe we have enough to arrest Captain Peyton and keep his airship on the ground until we can determine more. Please, wait here."

"Officer, it's been several days since I've had a decent meal. May I go across the way to the café?"

"Yes, Mr. Gyles, but please, come back once you've eaten."

The thought of food drove everything else out of my mind and I happily followed Elliott back out into the crowded streets. He left me by the door, and apparently procured permission for me to enter because he returned to get me after a moment.

Food occupied my attention completely though I remained pressed up against Elliott's leg while we ate.

Charlie reappeared once we finished.

"They captured him. At first he protested, but then a couple of the crew who I'd hired spoke up and he confessed." The ghost cloud spun and seemed to laugh.

Someone gasped, and a woman screamed.

"Oops." Charlie vanished.

Several of the people in the restaurant stared at us. Elliott sipped his coffee as if nothing had happened, though I could tell he was amused by the slight tilt of his lips and his scent.

"Perhaps we should return to the station," Elliott said his scent souring to nervousness.

I remembered that Elliott didn't really like the police. It had something to do with when we used to hunt fake ghosts for money.

After draining his coffee we went back across the street.

Officer Toms was waiting for us. "Thank you, Mr. Gyles. We've captured Peyton and he confessed. We won't need anything else from you."

"I'm glad to have been of assistance."

"Good day, Mr. Gyles."

"Good day to you, Officer Toms."

Elliott sighed in relief once we were outside. "Come on, Brown. Let's get our wagon and horses and head for Miller."

Musty-ozone filled the air for a moment, and Charlie swirled into view.

"Elliott," it said. "Might I trouble you for one more favor?"

"Of course."

"I was wondering if you had a spell other than the banishment that might allow me to cross over. My task is done, but still I remain."

"I…" Elliott frowned. "Actually, I believe I do. I was going to ask if you wanted to join me and Brown. We make a good team. I imagine you'd like to go to your rest, however."

"Yes, though I'm honored by the offer."

"I still need some supplies from my wagon, and I would like to put some miles between us and Denver. Will tonight be soon enough?"

"Of course."

"Elliott, Brown, I can't thank you enough. And there is little I can do to repay you."

"No need," Elliott said.

I woofed in agreement. I wasn't sure how I felt about Elliott sending Charlie away. I was getting used to having him around. I did know I would be glad to be out of the city though. Elliott scratched my ears and we headed for the livery.

"…and go to your final rest."

Charlie the ghost swirled one last time and vanished.

"Brown, I think we need a vacation." He sat next to the small fire we'd started and put his great-grand pappy's journal into his hunting bag.

Woofing in agreement, I rested my chin on Elliott's knee. I liked hunting ghosts but I didn't want my human hurt anymore.

"I'm going to miss Charlie though." He ruffled my ears. "But who needs a ghost when you've got the best dog in the world as your best friend."

Jumping into his lap, I covered his face in kisses, trying to tell him that he was the best human ever.

Elliott laughed and hugged me close. "We will go to Miller, get our ranch and maybe you can teach that little dog of the Sheriff's how to herd sheep."

And maybe they'd have another ghost in the saloon. If they had a ghost problem, I was the dog for the job.

# ELLIOT HEADS UP SHEEP CREEK WITHOUT A BORDER COLLIE

*Miller, Colorado, 1901*

"Well, Brown, we did it." Elliott scratched my ears and I sighed, content as we stared out over the lush grassy pastures of our new home.

"Now all we need are the sheep. I'll make inquiries in town tomorrow."

Wagging my tail, I woofed excitedly. Sheep of my very own! It was every Border Collie's dream and for me it was about to come true. Elliott had promised me my own sheep once we earned enough money hunting ghosts. He had gone so far as to buy me an entire ranch in Miller, Colorado, not far from our first real ghost and our friends Sheriff Tolbert and his cattle dog, Scoot.

Elliott gave me one more scratch before turning back to our house.

"I think I'm going to have to get a riding horse. Hitching up the wagon every time we go into town will be annoying. We are just far enough out that walking will take too long."

We wandered down the slight rise and headed west toward our house. I admired the way the mountains framed it just right. It really was beautiful and would look even better with sheep.

189

Daydreaming about fluffy lambs and recalcitrant ewes, I didn't notice that Elliott had stopped walking until I heard him sigh.

"I wonder how Seija is. I sure would like to show this to her."

Trotting back to Elliott's side, I echoed his sigh. I missed Asa too. At first we had been too busy to notice, but one day out in the desert on our way here we'd both stared up at the stars, carefully avoiding looking at the angry red planet with its angry little inhabitants. Instead we searched for Pluto though we knew we couldn't see it from Earth. It was too far away. Seija and Asa were too far away, and we both missed them.

"I hope they made it home okay." Elliott said that every time we thought of them. We'd probably never know.

Pushing my nose under his hand, I wagged my tail and grinned when he glanced at me.

"You're right, Brown. I'm sure they are fine. Let's get inside. Big day tomorrow."

Jumping around happily, I barked for sheer joy at the thought of my very own sheep. Soon. Very soon.

Our trip to town was successful and Elliott ordered a flock to be delivered from Denver in just a few days. I was so excited I could barely sleep and I was actually a little tired by the time the appointed day arrived.

"We'll walk today, Brown. We have the time and my riding horse should be in as well." Elliott threw a pack over his shoulder and we headed out. On our way off of the property he opened one of the gates. "Put the sheep in here when you bring them back. There's plenty of good water and grass. It will let them get settled after a long trip. Then we can sort them out and see what we've got."

Woofing, I danced around happily.

Elliott laughed. "How do you have so much energy?"

I grinned.

The trip to town wasn't too long though we stopped to rest once or twice on the way.

Miller wasn't a big town, in fact Elliott said it was barely big enough to qualify. He wasn't quite sure why it rated a sheriff, but Tolbert and Scoot did have duties in other local areas and were often gone. There was a deputy we hadn't yet met named De, too. Tolbert told us she traveled a lot more than he did. Elliott had smelled surprised to learn that De was a woman, but I wasn't sure why.

The train from Denver didn't run often and it was only by luck that we'd had good timing. Elliott also wasn't sure why a train spur ran out this way, but I was happy it did or it would have taken a lot longer to get our sheep.

We arrived at the station just as the train was unloading the cars. Perking my ears, I listened to the sheep *baaing* nervously and smelled their earthy scent coming from the next car to be unloaded. Barely able to contain my impatience, I quivered as I stared at the car.

"You Mr. Gyles?" A well dressed man walked up to us but after a quick glance I ignored him, completely focused on the boxcar.

"Yes."

"Good. Got a whole bunch of ewes for you. Ram will come up with the next train. It'll be a month or so. Owner is sending a few extra ewes by way of apology for the delay."

"Excellent."

"Is it okay to unload them now? Do you need to hold your dog?"

"She'll be fine. The sheep are hers anyway."

"Yes, sir." The man hollered at the rail workers. They shouted orders and others moved a ramp to the car and finally, agonizingly slowly, the door opened and there were my sheep.

*Baaing* and frightened, the first one bolted down the ramp.

Men shouted as the others followed and soon they had a mini stampede.

The humans ran around frantically waving their arms and trying to move the flock, which just scared the sheep more.

Elliott laughed and the man standing by him sighed.

"They said they knew how to handle stock or I would have brought some hands," he said.

"As amusing as this is, we had better help out. Brown, show them how it is done. Come by."

At his command, I ran out and circled the sheep, pushing them away from the men and the train and driving them toward Elliott.

"Take them over to the water," Elliott shouted above the train yard racket. He pointed.

Following his directions, I soon had the entire flock under control and contentedly drinking after a long train trip.

"Good job, Brown," Elliott said when he joined me.

"Sir, are you happy with your purchase?" The man asked.

"How about it, Brown, are we happy?"

Barking excitedly, I startled the nearest sheep.

Elliott laughed. "They'll do."

"Excellent. I will inform Mr. Ansel. She's a nice dog. If you ever have pups, I can guarantee Mr. Ansel will be interested in purchasing one."

"Thanks. I will keep that in mind." Elliott and the man shook hands and he departed.

"Okay, Brown. Think you can get them home?"

Sitting, I stared up at him and tilted my head. Was he seriously questioning me? If I could handle ghosts, demons, Martians and everything else, of course I could handle my flock.

"I'm teasing. Of course you can. I'm going to pick up my horse. Why don't you start for home. I'll catch up." He scratched my ears and I wagged my tail.

Woofing softly, I got up and slowly gathered my flock so I wouldn't spook them and pushed them through the middle of town toward home.

I let the sheep stop and rest about halfway home. A nice stream fed into a lush meadow and I thought it would be a good place for them to graze while I waited for Elliott.

The afternoon stretched and shadows lengthened while the flock sated themselves. My stomach rumbled and I finally decided I would have to press on without Elliott. His absence worried me. He should easily have caught up with the horse. Maybe there had been a problem with the horse that had delayed Elliott. I was sure that was it. He'd catch up soon.

Heart somewhat heavy, I gathered the ewes and pressed on toward home. The trip went reasonably quickly, the sheep gave me no trouble, and soon the pasture Elliott told me to put them in was before us. The gate still stood open so I carefully angled the flock toward it. At first the sheep resisted, but then they saw the opening and it was puppy's play to get them in.

J.A. Campbell

Nosing the gate shut behind them, I even managed to secure the latch. Not only did this pasture have a stream running through it, but it had a few sheds as well so the sheep would have some shelter if the weather turned bad. I could leave them there and they would be safe from everything but predators.

Tonight I would eat and rest. Tomorrow, if Elliott hadn't returned home, I would go look for him.

Trotting to the ranch house, I circled around the outside until I came to the back door where Elliott had installed a flap so I could go in and out as much as I liked.

Once I was inside I sniffed around just in case Elliott had come home before me. I already knew he hadn't, all the scents were old and no new horse grazed in the pasture, but I had to check anyway.

Whining when I finished searching the empty house, I gave up and my stomach insisted that I feed it. I pawed open the cupboard where Elliott kept some dried meat for me. I usually shared his dinner, but we kept trail rations around, just in case.

Eating my fill, I then took a quick drink and lay down by the back door to rest. I would check the yard and my flock in a few hours.

Darkness had fallen by the time I woke up out of a strange dream. A voice in my head had kept asking me where I was. I had responded 'right here.' It was a familiar voice, but I couldn't figure out whose it was. The day must have worn me out more than I had thought.

Stretching a bit of stiffness from my legs, I got up and went outside. Perking my ears hopefully, I listened for the sound of a horse and rider. Nothing. I did hear my sheep.

194

Despite my worry for Elliott, I was excited about the sheep. Running out to their pasture, I circled wide around the group, nose to the air. I didn't smell any predators and the sheep were calm, so I laid down to watch them.

Rolling over on my back, I wiggled, having a good scratch in the sweet smelling grass. Then I lay there, staring up at the stars. I wondered where Elliott was. It wasn't like him to be gone for so long without taking me along.

Sighing, I watched one particularly bright star. It flashed a few times and then seemed to move. Sitting up, I tilted my head and watched, momentarily forgetting my worry as I watched the bright light flash across the sky.

Glancing over my shoulder, I saw that the sheep were still calm, so I went back to watching the light. It became steady in the sky, but grew as if it were coming toward me. Slowly, my sensitive ears picked up a low whine as the light approached.

It *was* coming toward me!

The sheep stirred, either sensing my distress or hearing the increasingly loud whine. I had to protect my flock.

I wondered if the approaching light was one of the ships that the Plutonians and Martians flew around in. I hoped that if it was, it wasn't Martians. I ran toward the sheep, slowing when they noticed me and pushed with my Eye. They lifted away from me and I drove them toward their shelters. Hopefully whatever it was wouldn't hurt my sheep. I would defend them, of course, but the Martians had strange buzzing lights that burned and I couldn't fight them.

The light grew until I could make out individual lights that flashed in a circle around the big one. The whine turned into an earsplitting howl and the wind blew my fur around.

The sheep cowered in their sheds and I crouched alongside one of them, trying to remain small so they wouldn't notice me.

Agonizingly slowly, the ship lowered legs to support it and sank to the ground.

*Baaing* frantically, the sheep broke out of their sheds and bolted for the far end of the pasture. I had no reason to stop them so I remained hidden by the side of the shed.

The spinning lights slowed and finally winked off. The big light in the middle turned off and the noise faded away until all I could hear was a strange ticking sound.

Finally, I heard something that sounded like the hiss of steam and a piece of the ship lowered, casting light into the field. Once, before I'd known about space ships, I had thought they looked like giant shiny cow pies. Now I knew what they were, but they still reminded me of cow pies.

Warily, I studied the ramp, hoping it was a friendly Plutonian and not the Martians and their buzzing lights.

"Brown!" A canine form appeared in the entryway followed by a taller, thin human-shaped form.

"Brown!" The canine bounded down the ramp straight toward me.

"Asa?"

"Yes, we came back!" The Plutonian dog ran up to me, tail wagging so much his entire body wiggled, causing the antennae atop his head and all down his back to wiggle as well.

I sniffed noses with him and then he pressed against my shoulder and licked my chin. Normally I didn't let other dogs get that close, but I liked Asa so I leaned against him.

Seija came down the ramp more slowly and I went over to her and let her pet me.

"Brown, it is so nice to see you. Where is Elliott?"

"He's missing," I told Asa. Plutonian dogs could talk into their people's minds, so he relayed my message. Briefly, I told him how I had taken the sheep home, expecting Elliott to join me and that he hadn't. "I'm going to go look for him tomorrow."

"Oh, Brown, that's terrible. We'll help of course. I have a way to disguise myself and Asa this time so no one will see our blue skin or his antennae."

I wagged my tail, happy for the help.

"And we both want to see your sheep," she added.

Perking up a little, I woofed softly. "Wait here." I sprinted away from the ship to the far end of the pasture. It didn't take long to find the flock, circle around them and drive them back to Asa and Seija.

The sheep were a little nervous, but allowed me to push them into the light that shone from the ramp. I didn't know how well Plutonians could see in the dark but I knew humans had a hard time, so I stopped them once the light shone on their wooly backs.

"Oh, marvelous." Seija clapped her hands and laughed. "You are so clever, Brown."

Asa stared at the sheep, nose twitching. "They smell ... strange," he said.

Tilting my head, I sniffed. "They smell like sheep to me," I replied.

"Ahh, yes. I spend much of my time on a ship. Sometimes I forget what animals smell like."

"Oh. Isn't it wonderful?" I wagged my tail.

"Uh, yes. I suppose it is." He sniffed and then sneezed.

I laughed at him. "We can go inside if you want. Elliott won't mind. He kept saying he wanted to show Seija our home."

Asa relayed my words.

"He did?" Seija smiled. "I'm sorry he isn't here. We will begin searching as soon as it is light."

Truthfully, now that I had rested, I wanted to go right away, but it would probably be okay to wait for light.

"This way."

I spent time showing Asa and Seija around our house and then we went to the kitchen.

"Are you hungry, Brown?" Seija asked.

Shaking my head, I sank down and rested my chin on my paws.

"We will find him," Seija said.

"Brown, what's that?" Asa tilted his head.

Perking my ears, I listened. "Hoofbeats! That's a horse." I burst out of the dog door, Asa on my heels.

Barking, I sprinted around the house and charged up the path. I didn't expect to recognize the horse because Elliott had bought a new one, so it took me a moment to see that Elliott wasn't the rider. I slowed.

"Brown!" The little cattle dog running next to the horse put on a burst of speed and ran out to meet me.

"Brown, did you see the lights? They came out this way... Who's that?" He slowed, wagging his tail hesitantly.

"Scoot, this is Asa."

They looked at each other and Asa wagged his tail hesitantly.

Scoot titled his head and then his ears perked. "You're Plutonian. Brown, how do you know a Plutonian?"

I returned his confused look. "How do you know the Plutonians?"

Asa looked and smelled surprised too.

"Sheriff Tolbert and I met them once a long time ago. We were afraid the lights were Martians. They're mean'uns."

"Yes, they are," Asa agreed. "It is nice to meet you, Scoot."

"Likewise." They sniffed noses.

198

"Howdy, Brown." Sheriff Tolbert slowed his horse and rode up to us. "Who's your friend?" He seemed to squint in the low light. "That what I think it is?" He muttered to himself. Tolbert swung his leg over his saddle and dismounted. Leaving his horse standing, he came over to us and knelt. "I suppose it is. Howdy, fella." He held his hand out to Asa.

After a quick glance at me, Asa sniffed Tolbert's hand and let the Sheriff pet him.

"Well, at least you ain't the Martians. Come on, let's go talk to Elliott." Tolbert gave me a quick pat before clucking to his horse. The well-trained animal followed behind us as we walked back to the house.

I saw Seija standing in the doorway, watching, her shoulders hunched and arms crossed over her chest. Her eyes darted toward the pasture where her ship was but she stayed in the house.

"Howdy, ma'am." Tolbert touched the brim of his hat as he got closer. "I'm Sheriff Luke Tolbert."

"Seija," she said, voice sounding a little afraid.

"Don't you worry. I'm in charge of Uncanny Affairs in these parts. We were just worried you might be someone unfriendly."

Seija seemed to relax. Her shoulders straightened and she came forward a few steps.

"I know Brown, of course. Who's your companion?" He glanced at Asa.

"That's Asa. You've met our people before?"

"Yes. I've had the pleasure a time or two. Also had the distinct non-pleasure of meeting up with the green folks."

Seija laughed. "Yes, they are very unpleasant. It's not my house, but I'm sure Elliott wouldn't mind if I invited you in." She glanced at me, as if asking permission.

I woofed softly and led the way inside.

"Where is Elliott?" Tolbert shut the door behind us.

199

"We're not sure." Seija lit a lamp and set it on the kitchen table. "Brown said that Elliott sent her home with the sheep they bought and he promised to catch up once he picked up his horse. He never showed up. She brought the sheep home and was going to start looking for him in the morning."

"Said all that, did she?" Tolbert scratched his head.

"Yes." Seija said.

"What are the two of you doing out here anyhow?"

"We came back to visit Elliott. He saved our lives last year."

"Did he now? Guess I'm not surprised he didn't mention it when he was telling me about his adventures."

"It was quite the adventure. The Martians kidnapped me and Elliott. Asa and Brown had to find an old ship that had landed out in the desert years and years ago and use it to rescue us before we were taken all the way to Mars."

Tolbert stared at her for a minute before shaking his head and glancing down at me. "Well, that's quite the tale."

"It's true," Seija said defensively.

"I believe you, ma'am. It's just ... well ... I'm not sure I would have believed Elliott even knowing what I do. I wonder if you're that girl he's pining after."

"What?" Seija sat up, starting at Tolbert.

The sheriff smiled. "He's never said anything, mind, which leads me to think he misses you a fair bit. But now and again he gets that look in his eye that says he's missing someone pretty fierce. I've seen it before."

That seemed to please Seija. She smiled and leaned back in her chair. "We have to find him. We were going to help Brown, but maybe you can help too."

Tolbert nodded. "I have an idea of what may have happened. Good kid, Elliott, but he's gotten himself into trouble in the past. Wondering if it maybe caught up to him. Can you ride a horse?"

Seija nodded. "I think so."

Tolbert took a long look at her. "Course, your appearance doesn't bother me, but it'll raise a few eyebrows in town. His, too." He pointed at Asa.

"Ah, I have a device that will disguise us. It's relatively new. I convinced the council to let me come back and try it out." Seija smiled. "It was a good excuse."

Tolbert chuckled. "Any way to disguise your ship?"

"Yes."

"Let's get to it then. We've got miles to cover. You'll have to ride with me back to town but I've a horse you can borrow. My old mount. He's retired now, but still very fit."

"Thank you for helping us."

"Elliott has done us a good turn in the past, and I like him real well. Liked all of your folk that I've met too, only a couple mind, but still, you seem like decent sorts. I'll do what I can. De can mind the fort while we're gone."

Seija frowned. "De? I've heard of her, and now that I think about it, you as well. Rama and Ersa mentioned the two of you in their report. This must be Scoot." Seija glanced down at the cattle dog. "They spoke very highly of all three of you and were, obviously, very grateful that you helped them escape from the Martians."

Tolbert's scent shifted pleasantly and he smiled. "Yes, ma'am. Helping anyone escape from the Martians makes my day."

"Okay, let's get on the road. I don't suppose we have to wait until light."

"No. Get what you need and we'll head out. Daylight's not far off anyhow." Tolbert stood and pulled Seija's chair out for her.

Having a brief moment of inspiration, I woofed softly to catch their attention and then trotted through the living room and into the study. Seija and Tolbert followed and I led them to Elliott's hunting bag. It hung from the wall on a hook next to his desk. Touching it with my nose, I wagged my tail.

"What's that, Brown?" Seija asked.

Glancing at Asa I said, "Could you ask her to bring it along? It's Elliott's ghost hunting bag. We might need it. It has some of my ghost hunting things in it, too."

Asa passed the message.

"Of course, Brown." Carefully, Seija took it from the wall and slung the battered bag over her shoulder.

After that, we all headed outside and Tolbert locked the door behind us.

Seija went into her ship and returned with two small boxes. One she secured around Asa's neck with a collar, and the other she attached to her belt. After touching a button, the air around both of them shimmered and then Asa looked like a normal dog, no antennae, or anything unusual. Seija's appearance didn't seem to alter as drastically to me, but Sheriff Tolbert exclaimed in surprise.

"That's remarkable. You both look, well, normal for this planet."

Seija grinned. "Yes. It won't fool someone if they pet Asa, so he has to remember that, but visually, we look like Earthlings now."

"Lookin' forward to seeing what you do with your ship."

Seija gestured toward her ship. "Right this way."

It didn't take long to disguise Seija's ship as a hill. She had some sort of blanket that came out of the top. She and Tolbert simply had to secure it to the ground, and after a moment, the fabric shimmered and then it looked like a grassy field. Scoot and I sniffed at it. It didn't exactly smell like a grassy field, but it sure looked and felt like one.

"Asa says that it wouldn't fool anything with a decent nose, but it'll fool a human and the animals won't care."

Tolbert nodded. "Pretty nifty." He mounted his horse and held out a hand for Seija. She put her foot in the stirrup and swung up behind him, sitting on his bedroll.

"Have you ridden before?" He asked her.

"Yes. We don't have horses, but those of us who are explorers learn how to utilize the major forms of transportation on Earth. Of course I've only ever ridden a mechanical horse, so, this will be different."

"I see. Well, hang on to me, and we'll get going."

Seija gasped as the horse started moving, but shortly we were all headed to town at a decent clip.

"Looks like he's got himself into a world of hurt," Tolbert said as he walked back into the small sheriff's office in town. He'd left us there to wait while he collected his other horse and asked some questions.

"What's wrong?" Seija stood and clasped her hands in front of her.

"Well, some police officer down in Denver apparently moved here from back east recently. Recognized Elliott from a warrant he had on him for fraud, and finally tracked him down."

"Fraud?"

Tolbert removed his hat and looked at the ground. "Well, back before he came out here, he used to pretend to hunt ghosts. Tricked a few folks out of their money. Guess they want it back. Can't see as how he'd mind repaying them. He's a decent sort, and he's got the money to do it now. But still, never know what angry folk will do. Heard some rumors of some people getting antsy and religious too. Nothing normal folk would hear of, but in my line of work it pays to keep on top of things like that. Never know who's actually stirring up trouble."

"Where did they take him?" Seija twisted her hands around.

"Pennsylvania." Tolbert sighed. "They got him on the train back to Denver and I'm sure he's already on his way east. We'll have to ride to Denver. It'll take a couple of days. We can catch a train from there and only be a few days behind. Should be enough to keep him out of too much trouble."

"We could take my ship. That would save us a fair amount of time."

Tolbert laughed. "As tempted as I am, I believe it would attract far too much attention. It, and the sheep, will be okay while we're gone. I'll have De check in on everything now and again."

He looked at me when he said the last bit, and I got the idea that he was trying to reassure me.

Woofing softly, I looked at the door, anxious to head out.

"I believe she's ready to go," Seija said.

"Reckon so. You have everything you need?"

Seija nodded and patted her belt pouches.

"Light traveler."

"High tech. Please, let us hurry." She headed for the door and opened it for me.

Outside, two horses stood by the tie rail. Neither were tied, and both wore similar saddles. I recognized Tolbert's normal horse right away.

"A matching pair. Are all of your horses black?" Seija went over and pet the new horse's nose.

"Yes. The Department of Uncanny Affairs has a thing for black." He patted his vest. "Very obviously, they haven't spent much time in the high plains sun dressed in dark clothing, but, they pay for it, so I can't complain much I reckon. Mount up, we'll head out. He's very well trained."

Tolbert helped Seija onto the horse and then they turned and headed through town toward Denver. Once Seija got a feel for her mount, Tolbert picked up the pace and we hurried toward our destination, racing the train, and time. We had to rescue Elliott before anything happened to him.

We rode and ran throughout the day, taking breaks for the horses and Asa. Scoot and I could run all day, but the Plutonian was used to ship life. He never complained but when we finally stopped for the night, he collapsed to the ground and didn't move. Worried about him, I lay down against his back. It had cooled off, as it always did, once the sun set, and I didn't want him to get cold.

Though I couldn't see his antennae anymore because of his disguise, I could feel them when I pressed against him. It was strange, but he still smelled the same, so I didn't mind much.

"Can I join you?" Scoot stood back a short way.

"Sure," I said.

He curled up on Asa's other side and soon we dozed while the people cared for the horses, built a small fire and prepared our dinner.

My stomach rumbled and I licked drool from my lips as the food smells became stronger. It even woke Asa, and he raised his head, blinking sleepily. I licked his chin and he wagged his tail before glancing at Scoot. The cattle dog was focused entirely on the food and before too long Tolbert brought us each over a heaping plate.

Asa ate more daintily, but Scoot and I devoured our dinner. Once we had all finished Seija collected our plates and Tolbert showed her how to clean them. Not that they needed much cleaning after we'd finished, but they had to rinse them off.

"This would be fun if I wasn't so worried about Elliott," Seija said, leaning back against her saddle and staring at the sky.

"Yes. He'll be okay. They have to treat him decently while he's in custody and I doubt he'll give them much trouble."

"I hope you're right."

Tolbert nodded. "We should make a plan though. We'll have to adapt once we see the lay of the land, but I reckon you should let me do most of the talkin'. If anyone asks, tell 'em you're my sister."

"Okay."

"And ignore folks who give you a hard time about wearing pants. Traveling in skirts just ain't practical anyway."

"Okay." Seija sounded concerned. "Should I change my disguise to look like I'm wearing a dress?"

Tolbert shrugged. "Maybe when we get back east a ways. For now it doesn't matter."

"What else can we do?"

Tolbert shrugged. "We'll try and get him released if they sentence him to jail time. Hopefully they'll just fine him, and it'll be done and we can get him safely home."

"Do you think that's likely?"

Tolbert nodded. "He ain't committed any hanging crimes, just some fraud. Probably can't even prove most of it, especially since he and Brown really do hunt ghosts. Might even be able to prove he's legit, get him off completely. I had De send out some messages. We'll have proof waiting for us when we get there."

"Thank you. I don't know what I would have done without your help."

Tolbert chuckled. "Whisked him and Brown away in that fancy ship of yours, I reckon. She'd miss the sheep, but I think she'd take to your life okay." He glanced at me.

I wagged my tail.

Seija studied me. "Maybe. I think we like it here pretty well, honestly. I was hoping to stay for a while."

Tolbert nodded and stared into the fire. The campfire crackled merrily and he hummed a quiet tune. I recognized the song, I'd heard Elliott sing it before.

"What song is that?" Seija asked.

"Old campfire song called Home on the Range. Goes like this. 'Oh, give me a home...'"

"Sheep," I barked, unable to resist.

They all looked at me and when I didn't continue barking, Tolbert started over. "'Oh, give me a home...'"

"Sheep!" I barked more insistently, wagging my tail.

Asa woofed softly, laughing.

Tolbert glanced at Seija. "Okay, what's she sayin'? I know my singing voice isn't that bad."

"Sheep," Seija said after consulting with Asa.

"Sheep? Oh give me a sheep?" Tolbert laughed.

I woofed happily.

"Oh give me a sheep, where the buffalo roam. It doesn't quite work, Brown."

Asa perked up. "Where the Martians don't roam!"

Seija laughed and shared his variation with Tolbert.

The sheriff shook his head. "'Oh, give me a sheep, where the Martian's don't roam,'" he sang and snorted. "It doesn't quite ring the same, but I'll take sheep where the Martians don't roam any day."

"Yes, agreed," Seija said.

"Well, best be getting some rest. We have another long day ahead of us, and many more after that. Trains are quicker but not a whole lot more comfortable."

"Good night Sheriff Tolbert. Good night, Asa, Brown and Scoot."

"Ma'am, you're welcome to call me Luke."

"Then you should call me Seija. Good night, Luke."

"'Night Seija."

I lay there awake long after the others had fallen asleep, staring up at the sky. At one point I saw a bright light flash, and hoped it was a falling star. Elliott had told me to wish on falling stars once, because it was lucky. I wished that we'd get Elliott back, safely, and return home soon.

Elliott stared at the crowd in the small courthouse and sighed. He should be more worried about himself, but all he could think about was Brown. He'd managed to get his captors to let him send a telegram to Sheriff Tolbert asking him to look after her, but it had taken a couple of days before they'd consented. He had no doubt she'd taken the sheep home and she knew how to get to the food, so she wouldn't starve, but something could have happened to her and, until he managed to get out of this mess, he'd never know. It was driving him crazy.

It seemed like they'd been on the road forever, mostly traveling by train and he'd already offered, several times, to repay the people of Sheep Creek. The officers simply said that was for the court to decide. He'd given up after the third day and spent most of his time pacing the confines of his cell on the train, which was really just a converted room and not terribly uncomfortable except that he was used to open spaces and he didn't like feeling trapped.

They finally reached Sheep Creek, Pennsylvania several days into the trip and he'd been transferred to a small local jail. There, he'd largely been left alone while they prepared for his trial. He hadn't minded the lack of visitors, but not having any news about Brown was tearing at him.

Just before his trial was to begin, a heavyset man with ruddy cheeks and a fantastic handlebar mustache, red, like his hair, had shown up and introduced himself as Tommy McClarian, his attorney. Elliott hadn't even thought of trying to get an attorney, so he had no idea where Mr. McClarian had come from, but he hadn't complained. His mystery attorney had come with several letters from people Elliott had legitimately helped in the past, Captain Arnault from the steamship, Ruby, Mr. Taggart and Mr. Markie from Golton, Arizona, Mr. Dalton from the railroads, and Sheriff Tolbert. The messages gave Elliott hope that Tolbert had received his telegram and that Brown was probably okay.

Finally, they were getting on with things. This was day of his trial. It seemed like it would be a short trial. Mr. McClarian had defended him well, saying Elliott had merely made a mistake, he'd shown the evidence that Elliott did in fact hunt ghosts, and somehow managed to convince the crowd that Elliott was an all around decent guy. Elliott had apologized and offered to pay the town back. His accusers even seemed to be considering his offer.

The jury had just recessed and Elliott and Mr. McClarian were about to retire to a waiting room when five men filed into the back.

Alone, Elliott would never have remarked on any of them, but together, there was a distinct uniformity that brought to mind a western outlaw gang. They didn't quite

J.A. Campbell

dress the same as each other, but they were close enough that it was obvious they were a group. Unlike outlaws of the west, with their cowboy boots and low slung holsters and dusty trail clothes, these men seemed well dressed, with long coats covering clean, dark colored trousers and tidy vests. Several even appeared to be carrying pocket watches. None were visibly armed, though the long coats, not quite dusters, not quite suit jackets, could have hidden a short sword.

A couple of the men were tall, one seemed slightly stooped over and the others were a touch shorter, all wore dark colored fedoras. Several had trimmed mustaches, and a couple had bare faces. All the men were white, looked fit—even the man with stooped shoulders—and all had identical hate filled stares. It was those angry, narrowed eyes, more than all the other similarities that made Elliott think they were together. He'd almost rather face down a western outlaw gang, as try these men.

Shivering he glanced at his attorney. Mr. McClarian studied the men as well, before turning and gesturing for Elliott to precede him into the waiting area.

"Uncanny gentlemen," McClarian said. "I'd steer clear if I were you."

Elliott nodded. "Yes, I'm glad they're not on my jury."

McClarian laughed. "Indeed. Do you know them?"

"No, I'm quite certain I've never seen them before. I wish Brown where here. She'd know. Her nose never forgets a scent."

"She sounds like a remarkable hound. I'd certainly like to meet her. Plenty of old ghosts in Sheep Creek and the surrounding areas for her to dispel."

Elliott laughed, though his stomach roiled. "Yes. I'm anxious to return to my ranch."

"I imagine so. Well, have a brief rest. I'm certain the jury won't take long to decide."

Elliott paced around the confines of the small room. "I hope they let me repay them. I do feel bad."

"Relax, Elliott. All will be well."

Sighing, Elliott sank into a well worn padded chair, before springing to his feet again. "I can't relax."

"Understood. Be grateful your life isn't on the line. Those that face death are the ones who wore those tracks in the floor." McClarian pointed at a worn path by the barred window.

"True. I do have it better than all that. Still. I'm worried about Brown. I wish Tolbert had sent word."

"I believe that the help he sent is evidence enough that he has Brown well in hand."

"What if something happened to her and he didn't want to tell me in a telegram? Perhaps he is saving the bad news to tell me in person." Elliott twisted his hands around, his stomach fluttering.

"Don't work yourself up over something you can't control, Elliott. If something happened to Brown, it has happened. If nothing happened, which is the more likely, then Tolbert is caring for her."

Elliott sighed again. "You're right, but I can't just not think about her. She's always right with me. It feels as if I'm missing a limb."

"I understand. I'm sure she's just fine."

"I hope you're right."

Before Elliott could turn to pace back the other direction, he heard a discrete knock on the door.

Elliott's stomach did all sorts of new summersaults.

"Mr. Gyles, Mr. McClarian, they are ready for you."

"Thank you. You see, Elliott, I told you they would be quick."

Elliott tried to absorb some of Mr. McClarian's confidence as he followed them back the short distance to the court room.

"All stand."

Elliott followed the bailiff's instructions and soon the judge stood before them.

"Mr. Elliott, this court deems that you are a decent human who made an honest mistake. The evidence, from upstanding citizens indicates that you do in fact have a knowledge of the paranormal and have rid many people of troublesome events."

Elliott noted that he didn't actually say the word ghosts. It amused him slightly.

"The town of Sheep Creek will accept reparations in the form of returning the fee they paid for your services plus a small fine."

The figure the judge named would have given him a heart attack a year ago, but now he could easily cover the repayment.

"Thank you, sir. And, ah, should the town ever again have legitimate ghost trouble, my services are free."

The judge smiled slightly. "You have five days to repay the town. If you fail to do so, you will face imprisonment."

"Yes, sir."

"Very well, this court is adjourned." He banged his gravel on the desk and people began filing out.

"See, Elliott, I told you everything would be fine. Come, there's a bank in the next town over where you can wire funds."

Elliott heaved a great sigh. It felt like a ton of bricks had been removed from his chest. He just had to get the money and then he could return home to Brown.

Remembering the strange group of men, he turned to look at the courtroom, but they were nowhere to be seen.

Shaking his head, he put them out of mind. "Okay, let's go to the bank. I want to get on the road for home."

"Tomorrow?"

"Yes, sir. The funds will be available for pickup tomorrow. The bank has confirmed your wire, but it does take a bit of time for the transaction to complete."

Elliott sighed. "Very well. I'll be back when you open."

"Here is your receipt. You'll need it to claim the funds." The clerk handed him a piece of paper.

Tucking it into his inner pocket, he left with McClarian.

"Thank you for your services. How much do I owe you? I hadn't even thought to ask. I may have to wire for more money."

McClarian laughed. "I've been paid, Elliott m'boy. Don't worry about it. It was a pleasure to meet you. If you need anything else while you are in town, here's my card."

"Who paid you?"

McClarian patted Elliott on the back. "Let's just say you have some excellent friends in the west. Take care of yourself, Elliott."

Elliott accepted the piece of stiff paper and after a quick glance, tucked it into his pocket next to the receipt.

"I'm going to head to the court house and show them the receipt and let them know I'll have the money to them tomorrow. Again, I can't thank you enough."

"It was my pleasure."

They shook hands and Elliott began the long walk back to Sheep Creek. Tomorrow, he mused, he would hire a driver of some sort so he could be on a train home as soon as possible.

The light faded, though the temperature remained warm and muggy. Elliott sighed, missing the cool, crisp air in Colorado. Though he had grown up in the east, he truly felt at home in Colorado and couldn't wait to return.

Glancing up at the sky, he briefly wished to see Seija again. He hadn't known her for very long, but he couldn't get her out of his mind. Except, of course, when he was worrying about Brown.

Still the countryside was beautiful. Soft, lush grassy hills. A creek, aptly named Sheep Creek, sparkled in the fading light. He could just make out the peaceful sound of it running over rocks. He wasn't far from the bridge that crossed over it, and he planned to stop and admire the masonry. Cobblestone bridges weren't something you saw often out west. Trees clustered around the water source, and fields, some dotted with sheep, spread almost as far as the eye could see. Sighing, he wished Brown were here to see it with him.

Kicking a stone, he forced himself to focus on the present. His plan to show the courthouse his receipt would have to wait until morning. Surely they would be closed by now. He hadn't realized how long of a walk it would be or he would have asked to borrow the coach, or waited. Nothing for it but to press on, he supposed. He was almost back.

Something made his skin tingle and he paused, looking around and yet again wishing Brown was with him. She would know if danger were near.

Maybe while he was in the area he should find a male Border Collie for Brown. Shaking his head, he decided that she needed to be in on the decision, so he would have to bring her back sometime soon. Undoubtedly she would have some sort of test or other qualification for a male.

The thought made Elliott grin and he continued on. He was almost to the bridge.

A branch snapped and Elliott froze. Turning, he looked around but didn't see anything.

He twisted back around just in time to see a club flying at his face.

Elliott's pounding head woke him out of a restless dream of being chased by little green men with laser guns. He didn't feel much better when he finally cracked open his eyes. He almost had to pry them apart, they were so crusted and his hands wouldn't cooperate when he tried to rub them.

Groaning, he tried again, despite the flashes of light he saw every time he moved. Still unable to get his hands to cooperate, he slowly took inventory of himself. He was sitting, in a chair, he thought, and his hands wouldn't work because they were tied to the arms. Blinking, he managed to get his eyes to focus and he tried to crane his neck around to see behind him. The explosion of pain was too much and he almost blacked out again.

Once he recovered, he carefully tried to take in his surroundings. Except for a taper that flickered on a wooden table, it was dark. Its meager light showed a small room in what appeared to be a cabin by the construction of the walls. Curtains covered the single window and he didn't see anything other than the table. He knew better than to try and look behind him.

Elliott went back to his personal inventory. He couldn't hear anything over the pounding in his skull, but it seemed like his jaw still worked when he opened his mouth and all of his teeth were still present, though the movement brought tears to his eyes from pain.

Thoughts of Seija and Brown and Asa distracted him for a while, though he had a hard time holding on to a coherent thought for more than a few moments. After a while he drifted back to sleep, welcoming the relief from his aching body.

"Here we are," Tolbert said as the train screeched to a halt. He had somehow managed to get permission for Scoot, Asa and me to ride in the passenger car. The train ride had lasted forever, but we were finally here to save Elliott.

Tolbert and Seija gathered their things while I paced by the door to our private room.

Finally, they were ready and we left our room and filed out into the crowded passenger car. We all ignored the few disdainful looks the passengers gave us. Tolbert's sheriff's star kept anyone from commenting, just as it had the entire trip. The train attendants opened the doors and finally, we were outside.

I put my nose to the wind, taking in the relatively fresh air outside. It still smelled of too many people, smoke and hot metal from the train and livestock, but the air smelled less stale and soon I'd be able to run and stretch my legs. That thought was almost as exciting as finding Elliott right now.

Working my nose harder, I searched for traces of my human.

"We'll get the horses and then go look for Elliott. First stop will be the jail. Hopefully they'll know where he's at, if he's not still in a cell."

"Thank you, Luke. I can't wait to see him again."

"Soon, Seija." Tolbert smiled.

Once the horses were unloaded and tacked, we all headed to the jail with Tolbert and Seija riding along at an easy clip. The three of us canines ran ahead as soon as we were clear of the traffic. We had to ride to Sheep Creek to get to the jail, as there was no actual rail stop in that town.

We raced along fields, through a couple of streams and generally burnt off energy while the horses followed behind.

Intent on my destination, I didn't pay much attention to my surroundings though halfway, just past the creek, I thought I smelled Elliott and paused. Sniffing, I tried to find the scent again, but it eluded me and I hurried to catch up to the others.

It was mid-afternoon by the time we arrived in the small town of Sheep Creek. I remembered being here a long time ago before I'd met real ghosts. It hadn't changed much, still a one street town surrounded by farms and pasture fields.

I remembered Elliott telling me that the only reason they even had a jail was because the train stop was built many years after Sheep Creek.

Tolbert led us straight to the jail. He and Seija dismounted and left their horses standing while we hurried up the worn wooden stairs. Tolbert pushed open the door and I burst inside, tail wagging. I could smell Elliott's scent but it was at least a day old.

Working my nose, I searched anyway.

"Hey, control your dog."

"Relax." I saw a flash of silver out of the corner of my eye as Tolbert flashed his badge. "She's with me."

The jail was empty except for the one officer and my group. Scoot and Asa joined me.

"He was here," Scoot said.

"Yes, but the scent isn't fresh. Perhaps they already released him?" Asa sniffed the bars of the cell.

"Thanks for the information." Tolbert shook the officer's hand. "Come on, everyone. Let's go."

"What did he find out?" I asked Asa.

217

J.A. Campbell

"Seija says that they already had Elliott's trial. They gave him a fine and sent him on his way. That was yesterday. He said he would pay them as soon as the money was available and he hasn't show up yet today. He has four more days to repay the town."

"Oh." I wagged my tail happily. "Excellent."

Once we were outside, Tolbert helped Seija onto her horse. "Okay, gang. Officer Schmidt doesn't know where Elliott is staying, but the bank is in the rail town so we'll head back and see if we can't track him down. There's only one inn, shouldn't be hard." He mounted and we followed him back the way we'd come.

As we traveled, I scented Elliott again by the creek. The scent seemed strong, but it wasn't fresh and Tolbert thought Elliott was in the rail town. Maybe he had rested here, allowing his scent to linger. Putting it out of my mind for the moment, I raced to catch up.

Once we reached the rail town we went by the bank. The teller, once Tolbert showed his star, told us that Elliott had planned to return first thing to collect his money, but so far hadn't arrived.

His scent was fresher at the bank, but still a day old.

Our stop at the inn resulted in a dead end. He'd never taken a room.

"Luke, what if something happened to him?" Seija clenched her hands in front of her and her scent went tangy. I was beginning to be able to understand Plutonian smells and I thought she was worried.

"I'm sure he's fine, Seija. He's resourceful. Let's go talk to Mr. McClarian and see what he knows.

"Who's that?"

"The lawyer we hired for Elliott. I recommended him and some friends of Elliott's in Arizona paid him."

"When did you do that?" Seija smelled amazed, I thought.

"During a few of the stops we made. Everyone has telegraphs these days."

"He's lucky to have such friends."

Tolbert ducked his head and didn't answer, though he smelled pleased at her words.

Finally we stood outside a small office building nestled up against what smelled like a general store. A round man wearing a suit was just locking up for the evening. He turned and straightened his hat when he saw us. For a moment he studied our group, forehead creased, smelling a bit worried, but he smiled when he saw me and his scent shifted to pleased surprise.

"You must be Brown. Elliott has said so much about you." He knelt and held out his hand.

After a quick glance at Tolbert, who didn't seem worried, I trotted forward and sniffed his hand. I caught a faint trace of Elliott that set my tail to wagging.

Mr. McClarian scratched my ears before standing. "You must be Sheriff Tolbert."

"Yes, sir." Tolbert dismounted. After a moment, Seija did the same.

"These are my companions, Seija, Asa and Scoot. Obviously you recognize Brown."

"Ma'am." McClarian touched the brim of his hat before chuckling. "Not too many people introduce their dogs."

"If you traveled with this pack, you would. Remarkable, all of 'em."

McClarian laughed again. "What can I do for you all this afternoon?"

"We're lookin' for Elliot."

"I haven't seen him since yesterday. Perhaps he's already on a train?"

"He never collected his money. From all I can gather, you're the last to see him."

McClarian's scent shifted back to worry and he frowned. "He was headed back to Sheep Creek to show the court house the receipt and let them know he would pay the fine in the morning. This morning in fact. You said he never went to the bank?"

"No."

"Hmm, last I saw he was on the road to town."

I titled my head when that triggered a memory. "Asa, please tell Seija that I smelled Elliott on that trail. Almost a stronger scent like he had touched the ground with more than his shoes. I didn't pay much attention at the time because we were supposed to find him in other places. I've smelled him all along, so it didn't seem important then. It does now, though."

Asa passed the message.

"Luke, I believe Brown found a strong patch of scent on the road between here and Sheep Creek. She thinks it is important."

"Right. Thank you, Mr. McClarian. We'd best go check the scent."

McClarian's frown deepened and he smelled a little confused. "You're welcome. If I think of anything, I will let you know."

"Thank you." Tolbert mounted.

"Oh, one thing. There was a strange group of five men who came to the end of Elliott's trial. I don't know who they are, though I may have seen one or more of them about town. I hadn't thought much of it, but they didn't seem terribly friendly. If you'll wait a moment, I will try and find out more."

"Thank you." Tolbert tilted his head, but McClarian hurried over to the general store without further explanation.

We waited and after a few minutes McClarian returned. The breeze carried his worried odor ahead of him, but I could tell by the tight set of his shoulders that he was upset.

"I shouldn't have let him go off on his own," he said once he was closer.

"What's wrong?" Seija's voice sounded shrill.

"Well, those men are part of some religious group. Well, Seth thinks they are a religious group anyway. He said he's never been brave enough to ask. They behave themselves in town, but he's heard them make comments that makes him think they are very conservative in their beliefs. A ghost hunter would be very evil to them."

"Oh no." Seija mounted her horse as if she were going gallop to Elliott's rescue right then.

"How do we find these folks?"

"They live out past Sheep Creek … an hours ride or so. Stay on the main road until you get to Sheep Creek—the creek, not the town. The road will fork just past the bridge and a smaller trail heads off to the west. I believe you simply follow that until you reach their village. Seth said he made a delivery there once. They have a communal farm and a small herd of cows and a small group of houses. There aren't more than thirty people total, including children. Perhaps you should take someone with you."

"I don't think I have time to round up a posse. We'll be okay."

McClarian nodded. "Be careful."

"Thank you." Tolbert turned his horse and Seija followed.

We ran ahead of the horses toward the edge of the rail town but Tolbert slowed once we were on the path to Sheep Creek.

"We should take a break once we're by the water. The horses could use some rest and we could all use a meal. We've been all over the place today. We'll stop for a bit and continue on so that we reach this village just before dusk."

"What if he's in real danger?"

Tolbert nodded. "I understand your concerns. Believe you me, I feel the same way. However, I reckon we'll be able to sneak up on them better in the dark, and I know we'll be better prepared to deal with everything when we've had some rest and food. Dark isn't far off. An hour won't make a difference."

I wasn't sure I agreed and I could tell by Tolbert's slightly sour odor that he didn't completely agree with himself, but he was right, we were all hungry. I could hear bellies rumbling.

Reluctantly, Seija agreed with Tolbert and we trotted down the path. I worked my nose as we went, searching for traces of Elliott. I picked it up in the same spot as before, just before the bridge. This time, while Scoot, Asa and I sniffed around, Tolbert and Seija dismounted and cared for the horses.

"I smell him here." Small puffs of dust curled up from the ground as I sniffed the path.

"Here as well," Asa said.

I got the impression that Asa wasn't terribly used to using his nose for this sort of thing, but he sniffed delicately at a rock and his tail wagged.

"Yeah, this way." Scoot was probably the most used to tracking by scent, and he quickly had the trail. "I think they dragged him and finally picked him up here." Scoot trotted down a side trail for a ways. "And here I mostly lose the scent on the ground, but I still get it from tree branches and stuff. He was bleeding, but not bad."

"I'm impressed, Scoot." Asa studied the scents as Scoot pointed them out.

"I help Luke track down bad guys and do other sheriff and marshal things." His tail wagged furiously.

"Thanks, Scoot."

"I will tell Seija."

Before long, I heard Seija relay what our noses had discovered to Tolbert.

"Having telepathic dogs sure is handy. Come on over here and get some grub."

He didn't need to tell me twice. I licked drool from my lips at the thought of food. Even trail rations tasted good when you were hungry.

We ate and rested in silence, but as the sun sank lower into the sky, Tolbert paced around our little grassy area.

"Okay, so there's one of me and a bunch of them. We'll need a plan and I'll need you to make some diversions or something. Your folks are pacifists, yes?"

"Well, we are peaceful. Fighting is not in our nature. I suspect I could throw rocks at someone and not feel terribly upset about it. Especially since they have Elliott."

Tolbert chuckled. "Okay. Fill your pockets with rocks. That may come in handy. I'm going to try the direct, 'I'm the law' approach first. If that don't work, we may have to improvise. You'll need to stay hidden if we have that option. Depends on the terrain. Varies a bit around here."

Seija nodded. "I'll do my best."

"Know you will. Okay, time to head out. Mount up."

"I am not a witch."

"You are accused of witch craft and consorting with the devil. We find you guilty. Penalty is death by burning."

"But I'm not a witch." Elliott couldn't believe he was in this situation. He looked around the larger room they'd taken him to and fumed. Situations like these happened years ago, not now, not in modern America. "This is ridiculous." He couldn't even feel afraid, the situation was so unreal. He sat, again tied to a chair, now in front of a group of men—apparently his jury. They were same men who had been in the courthouse with their fedoras and long dark coats, though most didn't currently wear their coats. They claimed to be witch hunters, an order older than time, or some nonsense.

"All claim innocence, but you've already admitted guilt by confessing to your devil worship to the people of Sheep Creek. Your sentence will be carried out this evening. I suggest you spend your time repenting your sins. We will not forgive you, but perhaps God will." The man who spoke was not much older than Elliott, and his voice carried all the righteous fervor of a zealot.

Elliott knew he wouldn't be able to get through to these people. His only hope was to escape, and he wasn't quite sure how he would manage that, as his head ached so badly he could still barely stand.

The men stood, almost as one and filed out, except for two, who quickly untied him and dragged him back into the small room he'd first woken in. Elliott hoped that they would let him move around at least, but apparently they weren't taking any chances. The men roughly shoved him back into the chair and before Elliott could work past his spinning vision to try and struggle, they had him tied and left the room.

"Damn it." Elliott sagged in the chair, his situation finally catching up to him. They were going to burn him alive. He didn't even want to think about how unpleasant that would be, but the worst thought was that he would never see Brown again. Tolbert would take care of her but he didn't think that the Sheriff knew how special Brown really was. All he wanted was to see his best friend again. Tears leaked from the corners of his eyes and he prayed with all his might that Brown knew how much he loved her.

Elliott didn't recall falling asleep, but he sure did recall getting woken by a bucket of cold water to his face.

Coughing he jerked backward, though the chair restricted his movement.

"What?"

"Time to face your judgment, witch."

Elliott didn't bother trying to protest the label. At least they had used relatively clean water. He wouldn't have to die covered in filth.

They jerked him to his feet and he was mildly pleased to note that the world didn't lurch around him this time, and his headache had faded to a dull pounding in his temples. Now if only he could escape.

Alert for the possibility, his heart sank when they led him outside. They were in a small town square and people milled about everywhere. Though many were women and children, there was no way he would be able to elude everyone, even if he could get away from the men who held him.

Everyone stared as they paraded him through the crowd and to a pyre in the middle of the square. Some made the sign of the cross, others some sort of warding gesture. A few spit on the ground and turned their backs. All of the adult faces were filled with hate. The children simply seemed curious.

At least they weren't throwing things.

Yet.

Elliott did struggle when they tied him to the wooden post and almost broke free, but one of his captors clubbed him on the head, sending him to his knees. Nausea made him retch, but there was nothing in his stomach to come up. The world lurched again as they hauled Elliott to his feet and before it stopped spinning they had him securely fastened to the pole.

Fear clenched Elliott's chest and made his heart race. Sweat that had nothing to do with the humid air soaked his hair to his scalp. The sun had set while they were securing him to the pole and the light from the torches shone brightly as two men carried them closer.

Elliott jerked at his bonds, trying not to let his fear paralyze him. He had to think, had to escape, had to see Brown again.

"Alrighty, here's the plan. Brown, Asa and Scoot, I want you three to sneak into town and have a look around. Asa can tell Seija what you see. Make sure you stay quiet. We don't want to give ourselves away. Once you get the lay of the land, we'll refine that plan a little. Seija, stay with me."

She saluted Tolbert with a slight grin on her face, though I could smell her worry.

"Be careful." Tolbert scratched our ears before sending us on our way.

The three of us carefully left the small woody patch we were hidden in and ran across the open field between us and the village. As we ran, Asa mentally relayed what we saw to Seija. No one stood guard around the houses.

We wove through the buildings and paused in the shadow of one, panting, looking out into the town square.

Elliott!

"Brown, stay please. Tolbert will rescue him. There's nothing we can do at the moment." Asa nosed me. "It will be okay."

Quivering, I stared at my person. They had tied him to a pole, and it looked like they'd made a small pile of wood, like for a campfire around his feet. "Are they going to cook him?" I wrinkled my lips in anger.

"Oh, that wouldn't be good. I didn't think humans ate other humans." Asa sounded disgusted.

"Neither did I."

Scoot huffed. "They don't. Not usually, but Tolbert and I have seen this before. Sometimes they'll burn another person to death."

"That's horrible," Asa gasped.

"Yes."

"I'm telling them everything I see. Seija says to stay put for now. They have a plan."

It was getting harder and harder to obey that command. Elliott struggled against his bonds and even from across the town square, I could smell the sour stink of his fear. Two men approached with torches, and I knew what they were going to do.

I was just about to bolt, to try and do something, when Tolbert stepped out from between a couple of houses.

"You'll stop that nonsense if you know what's good for you."

Everyone froze and looked at Tolbert.

He stood with his hands on his pistols, legs set in a wide stance for balance. His sheriff's star glinted in the dim light.

Scoot stood and wagged his tail. "He's so wonderful."

I remained focused on Elliott. His expression turned from fear to elation and, after he studied Tolbert for a minute, he looked around frantically. I thought he was looking for me. I wanted to show myself so badly, but I hadn't picked up any other dog scents, so I thought the locals would notice me right away.

After a moment, Elliott froze, nodded his head as if he were responding to something, and went back to staring at Tolbert. His scent drifted to me over the sweet odor of burning wood and I inhaled it, holding it in my nose. I'd remember his sheer joy forever.

"Seija is trying to free Elliott. If Tolbert can keep the zealots distracted long enough, they'll slip away. If he needs help distracting them, we're to start running around in the crowd and barking and knocking things over as best as we can," Asa said.

"Okay."

The zealots recovered from their surprise and one of the men approached Tolbert.

"That's far enough, son." Tolbert tensed, not quite drawing one of his pistols.

"You are trespassing, and interfering in the work of God."

"Ain't no work of God, burning a man alive."

"I don't see as it's any business of yours." The man took another step and Tolbert drew one of his pistols, though he still pointed it at the ground.

"Federal Marshal Luke Tolbert. Unlawful executions is murder. Let the boy go, and perhaps we'll forget about this. Keep tryin' me and I'll have you all up on charges."

"Federal marshal?" Asa looked at Scoot. "I thought he was a sheriff."

"Well, he's actually not quite a Federal marshal, but he's allowed to use that title when the situation warrants." Scoot wagged his tail again. "Being a sheriff is just a cover for his real job dealing with Uncanny Affairs."

"Oh, I see. I suppose he did say as much earlier. I had forgotten," Asa said.

"What are you talking about?" I only half wanted to know. Mostly I watched Elliott. I thought he was free. I hoped they ran soon so we could all escape.

"You know, dealing with aliens, watching for Martians, things like that," Scoot answered.

"Oh. Oh! Look, they're escaping. Let's distract." Not waiting for an answer, I ran out amongst the people, barking my head off as if there were a wolf in the herd, but this time, I was the wolf.

People shouted, children screamed, two more canine voices joined mine and we raced through the village.

Over the chaos, I heard someone shout. "The witch is escaping!"

Now we had to deal with witches too?

A loud boom and a scream halted everyone in their tracks except me, I kept running toward Elliott. I had to get to my person. I dodged through legs and finally broke out of the crowd to see Elliott leaning over someone on the ground. A man pointed a shotgun at his back and I smelled Plutonian blood. Seija!

Elliott glanced up and his eyes went wide. He gestured for me to hide and, at the last minute, I ducked into a shadow. The light was fading quickly, but I could still see well enough to know that Seija was alive, but obviously injured.

Tolbert argued with the men across the village, but he was too far away to understand.

"Tie them both up. We'll deal with the Marshal once we're done with the witches," one of the zealots yelled.

Two witches? I wondered what a witch smelled like. I'd never met one before. Crouching, I watched as men forced Elliott and Seija to their feet. They tied Elliott and Seija to the pole, back to back."

"I'm not a witch!" Seija shouted.

"Oh?" The man ripped a very familiar bag from her shoulder. It was Elliott's hunting bag. "Then I suppose we'll find a bible and a cross in here."

"Brown, we have to do something." Asa, panting, joined me. "Scoot is trying to help Tolbert."

The zealot flipped open the flap and pulled out Elliott's hunting journal. He opened it to the middle and read a few words. "Hardly the bible. What exactly does this mean?" He read a passage.

Elliott tensed. "That's nothing. A journal from the old country. It was my great-grand pappy's. Look, she's hurt. We need to get her help and then you can burn me all you want."

"We're going to burn you both, so it doesn't matter if she's already injured."

Seija moaned.

The zealot tossed the book into the pile of wood at Elliott's feet and pulled something else out.

"Hey, that's my feather! An Indian gave it to me and told me it would protect me. It has magic in it." Growling, I thought about trying to retrieve it, though I was more worried about Elliott. He needed the protection more than I did at the moment.

"The western savages gave you a feather?"

Glaring at Asa for a moment, I wrinkled my lips at him. "They aren't savages."

"My apologies. Perhaps I've read too many of your eastern newspapers. I will retrieve it for you once he tosses it to the ground."

Dumping the rest of the bag out on the pile of wood, the zealot turned back to Elliott. "You say this is all yours, and not the woman's, yet she was carrying it to you to aid in your heathen rites. You shall both be judged before God."

Before anyone could do anything else, another man thrust a torch into the wood. It whooshed alight. The fragrance of Elliott's incense from the bag joined the burning wood.

Seija gasped.

The feather the old Indian ghost had given me floated across the ground and fell at my feet. I had forgotten Asa could make things move without touching them.

"We have to rescue them!" Asa whined, but didn't do anything.

"Can you untie them with your trick?"

Asa tilted his head. "Yes, maybe. I will try. It may be their only hope." He stared at Elliott and Seija.

"They're free. I'm holding the ropes so they can't tell. Seija says it is getting very hot. We have to hurry. Brown, can you knock the man with the gun down? It's not pointing at us, so it should be safe, if you are quick."

"Yes, I will." Regretfully, I left the feather at Asa's feet. I couldn't tie it around my neck by its string so I would have to come back for it. Something made me think it would be very important or I wouldn't have worried about it at all.

Dashing forward, I jumped, barking at the last minute to distract everyone, and slammed into the man with the shotgun, sending him and it flying. I thought I saw the shotgun zip away and guessed that Asa had retrieved it.

Just then something in the fire popped, sending a wave of pressure out from the pyre. It shoved me to the ground, and the humans around me fell. The smell of musty ozone mixed with the fire and incense.

Unsure what had happened, I barked in alarm and jumped to my feet, looking around.

The wind picked up, whipping around me, and almost drowned out a sharp whistle. I thought that was Tolbert.

A mournful howl, not quite like a pack of wolves singing, split the night air and seemed to travel with the wind as it stoked the fire into a tall column of flame.

People screamed and ran from the fire as it danced in the wind.

"Brown, Asa, let's go!" I heard Elliott shout.

Elliott! Turning, I sprinted toward his voice. Asa joined me, my feather in his mouth.

Elliott carried Seija and was running toward the woods as fast as he could. We joined him and, though I wanted to tackle him to the ground and cover his face with kisses, I knew I'd have to wait. We had to escape.

The thud of hooves alerted me and I barked to get Elliott's attention. When I turned toward the horses, he followed and soon Tolbert rode up with his other horse close behind.

He threw himself off of the horse and helped Elliott mount with Seija before getting back on. "Is she stable enough to make it back to town?"

"Yes, I will survive. It hurts, but it is not fatal." Seija's voice sounded weak but I didn't smell a lot of her strange blood.

"Let's ride." Tolbert wheeled his horse and we galloped back toward safety.

We galloped until we made it back to the rail town. Tolbert led us to the inn. He dismounted and took Seija from Elliott.

"We'll get a room and I'll see about getting doctor."

"No, no doctor." Seija gasped when Tolbert shifted her around. "I can't hide the blue."

"You need medical attention."

"Can't trust them."

"Luke, the last doctor didn't take her blood color so well. I managed to convince him that she was Canadian, but then a priest showed up. It went pretty bad."

"I have some supplies. You two can clean the wound. I'll be okay, really." She sounded determined.

"Okay." Tolbert didn't sound happy, but he followed when Elliott opened the door.

We all went inside. The common room was empty at this time of night, but Elliott rang the bell on the counter insistently until someone, cursing, stumbled down the stairs.

"It's the middle of the night." The round man that stomped toward us wore his dressing gown and a glare. "Oh, it's you. Find your missing friend I take it. What's this?" He peered at Seija, still cradled in Tolbert's arms.

"Our friend has been hurt. We need a room and stalls for the horses."

The innkeeper stared at Tolbert for a minute and I saw his eyes flick to his sheriff's star before he nodded. "Fine. I'll settle up with you in the morning. You'll have to stable your horses yourself." He pushed a key across the counter. "Down the hall." He gestured and surprisingly didn't object when Asa, Scoot and I followed our people.

"Need me to call the doctor?"

"No, we'll be fine. We just need a place to clean up and rest," Elliott said quickly.

The innkeeper grunted, but didn't say anything.

Elliott opened a door and we all crowded into a small room with two beds.

"Let's get you cleaned up, Seija." Elliott was already washing his hands while Tolbert gently set her on the bed.

"I'll get our things from the horses. Back in a bit." Tolbert left and Elliott went to work helping Seija.

I pressed up against his leg and he glanced down at me.

"Good girl, Brown. You're such a good girl."

He didn't pet me, but I could see the love in his eyes. Content for now, I settled against the wall with Asa and

Scoot to stay out of the way while he helped Seija. Asa dropped my feather next to me. It was a little damp from being in his mouth, but otherwise unharmed. I leaned against him and rested my chin on my paws.

"Will Seija be okay?" I asked Asa.

"Yes, she says she will be fine. She was lucky. Elliott tackled her to the ground before she could get seriously injured."

"Good." Exhausted from the day, my eyelids drooped. It would take a while for Elliott to help Seija anyway, so I'd nap while I waited to properly say hello. I was so happy to see Elliott again. It felt like my world was once more complete.

Bacon woke me the next morning. Delicious, sweet bacon. I cracked open my eyes to see a plate sitting right before me. Bacon, eggs and steak. Every Border Collie's dream.

Woofing happily, I snatched a piece before looking around. Asa and Scoot were licking their plates clean and Tolbert, and Elliott sat at a small table. Seija was propped up in bed finishing off her breakfast.

Elliott! Leaving my plate, I ran across the room and threw myself into his arms, slobbering all over his face in my delight.

Laughing, he wrapped his arms around me and held me close.

I licked salty water from his eyes and couldn't stop my tail from wagging.

"I thought I'd never see you again, Brown." Elliott cried into my ruff.

"Asa, will you get Seija to tell Elliott how happy I am to see him?" I wiggled more, trying to press myself into Elliott so we'd never be separated again.

"Brown, I think he knows." Asa woofed softly but passed the message.

Elliott just squeezed me more tightly when Seija told him.

"Gang, we need to get Elliott's debt settled and get out of here. Brown, you might finish your food before Scoot gets to it."

Twisting my head, I glared at Scoot. He backed up a step, but continued to stare at my plate, licking drool from his lips.

"Go on, Brown. Finish up. We all want to get out of here." Elliott hugged me again before releasing me.

I jumped down and gobbled up my delicious breakfast, never taking my eyes from Elliott. After I finished he knelt next to me.

"What's this? Oh, is that your feather? You saved it from the fire. Here, let's tie that on you for now." He fastened my feather to my collar and gave my ruff a pat. "I'm so happy to see you, Brown."

Grinning up at him, I woofed softly.

"Seija, can you travel?" Tolbert stood.

"Yes. I will be okay. Especially since we will be on the train for a while."

"Let's hit the road, everyone," Tolbert said.

"What about the, eh, witch hunters?" Elliott asked.

"I'll put in a word with some folks I know. They'll handle it."

"Good," Seija said vehemently.

It didn't take long for us to gather our things. Elliott helped Seija outside and onto her horse once they were tacked. Elliott swung up behind her and held her protectively. Seija leaned back against him and smelled content.

It was a beautiful day with a nice breeze and my nose worked while we trotted to the bank. I wasn't looking forward to the train ride, but I was looking forward to being home, with the sharp scent of pine and my sheep. Now that I had Elliott back, I couldn't wait to see my sheep again. I hoped that Tolbert's deputy, De, was taking good care of them. He had promised she would.

Our transaction at the bank was quick and we rode as swiftly as Seija's wound allowed back to Sheep Creek. Once we arrived, we headed straight to the courthouse and Elliott and Tolbert hurried inside.

Seija attracted a little attention from passers by but no one came near and before long Elliott and Tolbert emerged, both smelling relieved.

"Let's head home," Elliott said.

"Yes." Seija gave him a big grin.

Elliott swung up behind Seija and Tolbert mounted his horse. We all turned for the now familiar path between the rail town and Sheep Creek.

Finally, we were going home.

"Witch! Witch!" a young voice cried.

Elliott sighed and I saw Tolbert draw one of his pistols.

"Witch! Please help!"

We all turned.

"Who's a witch?" I glanced at Asa wondering if he would know.

Asa tilted his head like he did when talking with Seija before answering.

"Apparently Elliott."

"Oh, strange. I didn't know he was a witch."

Asa laughed. "Neither did he."

"Oh." I was still a little confused, but I didn't care if Elliott was a witch or not, so I didn't worry.

"Please help!" A young girl, skirt torn and face dirty, ran up to us. "We can't fight them. They're destroying our village."

"First, I'm not a witch," Elliott said. "Second, I'm not terribly inclined to care if your village is destroyed. Third, who?"

The girl's lip trembled at Elliott's angry tone. Her hopeful scent turned sour and she scrubbed at her eyes with her grimy fists.

"Ghosts. Lots of ghosts."

Elliott shook his head. "Fool was reading the summoning incantation."

"How many ghosts?" Tolbert asked the little girl.

"Dunno. Lots."

He glanced at Elliott and winked. "Wouldn't be the first ghosts someone accidentally summoned that we had to banish."

"One ghost. That was only one." Elliott smiled back.

"Well?"

"All of my supplies are gone. The only thing we have left is Brown's feather and while the Indian who gave it to her said it would protect her, I'm not sure that will be of any use in this situation. My journal is gone and they tried to kill me. The ghosts can have them."

Tolbert seemed surprised at Elliott's answer but he nodded. "Reckon you're right. Sorry little lady, you might try the priest." Tolbert clucked to his horse.

The girl sniffed, standing in the middle of the street as she watched Elliott and Tolbert ride away. The breeze gusted around her, carrying ghost scent to my nose. It must have come from all of the ghosts in the town.

Growling softly, I walked over and sat next to the girl. They had a ghost problem, and I was the dog for the job.

Elliott glanced over his shoulder. "Come on, Brown."

Barking twice for no, I stayed.

237

Elliott stared at me for a moment before looking at the girl and sighing again. "Your folks will try to capture us again."

The little girl shook her head. "No, they won't."

Barking once, I tried to let Elliott know she smelled honest.

"Asa says he believes she is telling the truth," Seija said.

Elliott and Tolbert shared another long glance before Elliott shook his head and sighed again. "Fine, but your people burned my supplies, so I need a few things. Chalk, incense."

"Welp, the church is that way." Tolbert rode over to the little girl and, leaning over, held out his hand.

Hesitantly, she took it and Tolbert pulled her up into the saddle in front of him. "What's your name, darlin'?"

"Zoe," she whispered.

"All right, Zoe. We'll help."

"Thank you." She sniffed and rubbed at her eyes.

The church proved helpful and soon we headed back to the zealot's village. I didn't want to return but if they had ghosts it was my job to get rid of them.

It was well into afternoon but a dark cloud hung low in the sky and we smelled smoke long before we reached the village.

As we rode through the cluster of trees and came out into the clearing, it became evident why they wouldn't be trying to capture Elliott and Seija again. The village was mostly in ruins and the stench of ghost clung to everything, overpowering the burnt wood.

No one was in sight.

"Is everyone gone?"

"They're in the church," Zoe said.

Tolbert's horse snorted nervously as we rode into the smoky ruins of the village. Many of the buildings still smoldered though some had burned completely out.

The column of fire I saw grow from the bonfire last night must have done this. I didn't know ghosts could use fire.

Whining uneasily, I avoided hot embers and dodged around other debris.

"What happened?" Seija whispered.

"The ghosts burnt everything. They were very angry." Zoe sighed. "They had a lot of bad energy to feed on and it made them very strong."

"Everyone is hiding in the church?"

"Trapped."

The ghost stench grew stronger as we went further into the small village. I saw a few buildings that were almost intact. They were coated in ghost slime. Nasty goo that only came off in salt water. I'd been covered with it a time or two.

It didn't take long for us to find the church. Sitting just outside of the small village, it was the only intact building. It wasn't fancy and I suspected that it was painted white, but it was hard to tell from all the slime that covered it. Clouds of ghosts swarmed around the building, spinning dust devils, ones that looked like fog, one that looked vaguely like a man.

"Holy Mary." Tolbert pulled up his horse and made the sign of the cross in the air.

Elliott stopped his horse. "Wow. I'm not sure we can fight all that. I have the trap circle and the banishing incantation memorized, but that's it.

"Perhaps we should retreat into the town, so that we aren't noticed," Asa said.

239

"Good idea," I replied.

Seija said the same to Elliott and Tolbert, and carefully we backed away until the church was out of sight behind a smoldering ruin.

"Okay, so what's the plan, gang? We can't leave 'em there." Tolbert took off his hat and scratched his head. "Sun's fading. Should do whatever it is we're going to do in a hurry."

"I don't know the entire summoning ritual, seeing as I've only done it once and that was over a year ago. Doing only part of it could be worse than doing nothing at all. The dogs are going to have to round up the ghosts and herd them this way. I'll make a large trap if we can find an open space big enough for me to draw on, and the dogs can push them this way. The incense will help attract them to our location and then we banish them, I guess."

"Sounds too simple." Tolbert grunted.

"Yes, well, there are a very large number of ghosts."

"I will help," Seija said.

"I'll put you in charge of the salt. You and Tolbert. At the very end you have to throw the salt at the ghosts, it helps banish them."

"I can do that." She didn't sound certain.

Elliott touched her shoulder reassuringly.

"Let's find a spot and get this done before we are discovered." Elliott helped Seija off his horse and then he dismounted. Tolbert did the same with Zoe and soon we were all scouting for a flat space big enough to draw on.

"There's a flat space in the town square. It might work." Zoe headed that way and we followed.

"It used to be inside a large building. The people who owned it before we bought the town used it for dancing," Zoe said when we arrived.

Using his foot, Elliott pushed some debris off of the flat wooden area and studied it. "Half of it is charred really badly, but we might be able to use this section. The boards are joined close enough that there isn't a gap, so the circle will be unbroken. It is probably the best we are going to get. Hurry, help me clear it off."

We went to work, dragging off pieces of wood. Scoot, Asa and I took the wood that wasn't warm. It had been a while since I'd had a good stick to chew on, and the wood momentarily distracted me.

"Brown, later," Elliott said.

Woofing softly, I dropped the stick and went back to helping.

Shortly, we had a clear space and Elliott knelt, pulling chalk out of his pocket. "Seija, would you get the salt and incense from the saddle bags?"

She and Tolbert went to do that while Asa, Scoot and I watched Elliott draw. He took his time, frowning and occasionally muttering like he often did. "I wish I had my book. I'm pretty sure this is right, but I always double check with my book." He grumbled.

It looked right to me, and I always double checked his work. I woofed encouragingly and wagged my tail when he glanced at me.

"I'll take that as a good sign. Okay, I think I'm as ready as I will be with this. Be careful not to smudge the lines. Put that incense there, and some there. It should burn for a while, so let me work on lighting them."

We'd been able to borrow some censers from the church and Elliott lit them, filling the air with spicy smoke.

Elliott sighed. "Brown, think you can get them back here?"

Woofing confidently, I wagged my tail.

"Okay, be careful." He came over and hugged me.

I licked his cheek before glancing at Asa and Scoot. "Let's get them! We'll need to circle wide around and push them from behind. Use your Eye and if they meet your gaze, stare at them and control them that way."

"I will do my best," Asa said.

Scoot simply wagged his tail.

"Let's go!" I dashed back toward the church, Asa and Scoot on my heels.

We ran out wide and circled behind the church so that we could push the ghosts toward Elliott. I hoped the circle was big enough for all the ghosts I saw swarming the building. I'd never seen so many and I wasn't sure if we'd be able to move them all, but we would try. It might take more than one trip.

The ghosts howled their frustration as they beat against the side of the church. The noise was deafening.

Barking, I tried to get their attention but none seemed to notice me over their cries.

I'd just have to do it the hard way. Gathering myself, I leapt at the ghosts, knowing that would disrupt them enough to make them pay attention to me. Closing my eyes, and folding my ears flat to my head, I slammed into the ghosts and stumbled when I hit the ground right next to the church. Ghost slime coated me, but I ignored it. Snapping my eyes open and barking, I ran back toward Asa and Scoot.

The ghosts howled in rage, drowning out our barking.

"Brown! They are all coming right for you!" I heard Asa's voice in my head.

Glancing over my shoulder, I stumbled, alarmed. There were so many ghosts, there was no way I'd be able to control them.

"Run back toward Elliott, they will chase us!" Asa said.

Scoot and Asa ran for Elliott. I sprinted right on their heels. This wasn't how I had envisioned getting all the ghosts to the trap, but I supposed if it worked it would have to do. There was no way I could stop now or they'd be all over me. I didn't know what an entire herd of ghosts could do to me, but I didn't want to find out.

Putting on a burst of speed, we tore around the ruined buildings and down the road until Elliott and the ghost trap were in front of us. I could see from Elliott's stance that he was shocked. Tolbert shouted something I couldn't understand over the howling ghosts. Seija scooted over next to Elliott and I didn't see Zoe.

Not sure what else to do, I ran straight at the ghost trap. Normally I pushed ghosts into it. This time I would just have to lead them. Leaping at the last minute, I cleared the trap and landed on the other side, still running.

Hearing a pop as the trap activated, I slowed and turned to see a brilliant light surrounding the trap. Ghosts milled inside, their screams of rage muted by their prison.

Everyone stared in shock for a minute. The ghosts began to batter at the sides, and I'd seen them break out before, so I barked at Elliott, encouraging him to banish them quickly.

"Right, thanks, Brown."

Elliott scrunched his eyes closed and chanted the familiar words to the banishing spell. The ghosts' cries intensified and soon Elliott had to shout to be heard over them. Their howl and his words built in intensity until the sounds melded together and I couldn't take it anymore. Lifting my nose, I howled.

Tolbert shouted something to Seija, and I saw her shake her head. She couldn't hear. He gestured and she nodded. They both threw their salt at the trap as Elliott shouted the last words of the banishing spell.

We all staggered, and I stopped howling as the light containing the ghosts flashed and vanished, taking the ghosts away with a loud crack.

The silence after all the noise was almost as deafening and we all stared at the empty place that had been writhing with ghosts.

"That was intense," Asa said after a few moments.

Wagging my tail, I sat and looked around. I'd never howled before, and I kind of wanted to do it again, but I didn't have a reason to, so I remained silent.

"Elliott that was amazing." Seija wrapped her arms around him.

I couldn't smell anything over the ghost slime that coated me, but I thought he looked pleased as he hugged her back.

"Are you feeling okay?" he asked her.

"Yes. I'm all right. A bit tired."

"I think we all are," Tolbert said, grinning. "Well done, Elliott."

Elliott shook his head. "Couldn't have done it without the rest of you."

"Yes, well done, Elliott," a low voice hissed. "Quite amazing." It didn't sound pleased at all.

"There's another one!" Zoe ran toward us, shouting.

"Yes, indeed. You missed me."

Frantically looking around, I tried to find the source of the other voice, but my nose was still clogged with slime and I didn't see anything.

The others looked around too and Tolbert had a gun in his hand, though I knew it wouldn't do much against a ghost.

"There!" Zoe pointed.

Small puffs of dust lifted from the dirt path as if someone walked there and the air shimmered a little.

Growling, I stalked forward.

"Ingenious, getting the ghosts to chase your dog. I've never seen one face us like that." The voice sounded almost conversational for a moment, and then it laughed, cold and cruel, lifting the hairs on my ruff.

I deepened my growl.

"But your trap is spent." Dust swirled up around the shimmer in the air and a man stepped out of the cloud, though I could sort of see through him. He wore clothing much like the people who lived in this town, dark, long coat, vest, fedora hat, but his face was gaunt and skeletal and his eyes had sunk into his skull, skin stretched tight, revealing his teeth even when he wasn't talking. "And I'll not chase a dog. This is my town, now. Begone." He spread his hands wide and the wind picked up around us.

Elliott grabbed Seija and, sheltering her with his body, ran toward the nearest partially standing house. Tolbert and Zoe followed.

"Dogs, come on!" Elliott shouted.

We dashed after them, hiding behind the partially standing wall. It provided meager shelter from the wind, but kept us from being pelted by the debris that flew through the air.

"He's going to call up a twister," Tolbert shouted.

"He wants to kill everyone," Zoe cried.

"Looks like it. I'm not sure what to do. My notes are in Colorado. My book is destroyed."

"Well, nothing for it but to banish him, son. You know that incantation. We'll just have to keep you safe while we do it."

"There's no way we'll be able to build another trap."

"Dogs will have to hold him. Think you three can do it?" Tolbert looked at us.

I glanced at Asa and Scoot. "You have to control him with your Eye."

"Brown, we aren't Border Collies," Asa pointed out.

245

"I saw an Indian dog in Arizona use Eye and he wasn't a Border Collie either. Scoot has some Eye. Asa, you can do it too." I tried to encourage them.

"But, that ghost, he's terrifying."

"We won't escape if we don't try."

"I'll do it," Scoot said. "It'll be like the one time I worked cows, only not quite." He wagged his tail uncertainly.

"Well, I'll give it my best try, of course. I'm just not sure how good I'll be at it." Asa glanced at the ground.

"They said they'll try," Seija relayed for us.

The wind screamed around us. Debris pelted the wall, and I had a feeling our shelter wouldn't be standing for long.

"Be careful." Elliott hugged me again. "Tell Seija as soon as you are ready and we'll do our best. Seija, Luke, do you still have the salt?"

"Yes, we both still have a little left," Tolbert said.

"When I get to the same spot in the incantation throw the salt at that ghost. It will help."

"Got it." Tolbert nodded and the wind ripped his hat from his head. He didn't even try to grab it. Elliott's was already gone. Seija's long hair whipped around her. Something heavy pelted the wall we hid behind.

"Let's go," I said. Asa and Scoot bravely followed me out into the windstorm.

Dust turned the air brown, and I could barely see, but Asa and Scoot led the way with their noses and soon we saw our target.

The ghost still stood with his arms spread wide, head tilted back, laughing. I noticed that the wind didn't rip the hat from his head.

Stalking forward, I snarled.

Looking at me, the ghost laughed and met my eyes. "What, dog..."

Triumphantly, I snared his mind, struggling to hold him like I did any other ghost. This one was powerful and, while I had a lot of practice, I didn't think I'd be able to do it for very long.

The wind died down around us, as the ghost struggled with me and I heard Elliott start shouting.

"Asa, I can't hold him for long!" I barked as I stared at the ghost. My head ached as the ghost pushed against me. Soon, sharp pain split my skull.

"Brown, my turn!"

Trusting Asa, I broke eye contact and Asa took over. I wasn't sure what went on, but they stared at each other, and he held the ghost.

Soon, Scoot took Asa's place. Both were able to control the ghost, but not for as long as me.

Elliott shouted the incantation and we struggled to hold the ghost. Asa and Scoot were already exhausted, and my head ached, but it was my turn again and I took over.

The ghost's mind felt more slippery and I had a hard time holding it. I tried, but Asa took over, just as I almost lost control.

The ghost's rage washed over us and I whimpered. We weren't going to be able to hold it long enough. Already, Scoot had replaced Asa and I could see him panting with effort.

*Brown, circle the ghost three times and call to our gods for help. I can't do much, but I will speak for you.* Something around my neck warmed. The feather! The Indian ghost! He would help.

"Asa, help Scoot!"

Not waiting for him to answer, I raced around the ghost in a circle, hoping I made it three times around. Then I stopped and wondered how to ask the Indian gods for help. The urge to howl filled me, and not knowing what else to do, I threw back my head and let the howl escape, as loudly as I could.

The feather around my neck grew warmer and I saw light shine from my neck and from the circle I'd run around the ghost.

Asa and Scoot fell back, exhausted, but after a moment, both joined my urgent cry, filling the air with our voices.

Released from our control, the ghost raged, beating at the light I'd created and trying to escape.

Elliott's voice melded with ours until we filled the evening with our cries.

Tolbert and Seija threw salt at the ghost.

It screamed in rage and pain.

Scoot, Asa and I howled.

Elliott shouted the last words of the incantation.

The circle I'd created exploded with a boom that knocked us all to the ground and splattered us with slime. Silence settled around us and after a quick glance to make sure the ghost was gone, I shut my eyes and lay on the ground, panting.

"Brown, how'd you do that?" Elliott came over to my side and brushed some of the goo from my face.

Wagging my tail, I grinned up at him.

"She says that the old Indian who gave her the feather told her how," Seija and Asa relayed for me.

He touched the feather I wore. "It's not covered in slime either. Amazing."

"What's amazing is that we're all still alive. But, I suspect we'd best make sure the folks in the church are okay, and then get out of here before they remember they think you're a witch." Tolbert checked on both Scoot and Asa.

Elliott helped Seija to her feet.

"Zoe, I think your people are safe now," Elliott said.

"Thank you!" She gave us all a very big grin before running toward the church.

Wearily, we followed.

Tolbert pounded on the slimed main door of the church when we arrived. "You're safe now. Best come out."

After a few moments and some frantic whispering inside, the door opened and someone looked out. Not seeing ghosts, he opened the doors wider.

I recognized the man who had thrown our belongings into the fire and growled softly.

"Shh," Elliott said, though he didn't sound mad at me for growling at a person.

The man looked surprised. "Where did the ghosts go?"

"We banished them," Elliott said, voice void of emotion.

He looked around curiously. "And why did you return after you set all the ghosts free."

"Hey, I wasn't the idiot reading the summoning spell. That was you." Elliott pointed, hand shaking with anger. "You summoned those ghosts, after you tried to kill us. You're simply lucky Zoe escaped and begged us to help, otherwise we'd be on a train back home by now."

A woman pushed forward to stand next to the man. None of them exited the church.

"Zoe?"

"Young girl. Cute. Not sure where she ran off too," Tolbert said.

She shared a look with the man before crossing herself. "Zoe has been dead, near ten years. She was our child."

"Huh." Tolbert glanced at Elliott who simply shrugged.

The humans all stared at each other for a moment, before they all stared at Seija.

"She's flickering," the woman gasped.

"Hell of a time for that," Tolbert muttered. His hand dropped to his pistol.

Seija grabbed at a small box on her belt and she stopped flickering. "It's fine. After effect of the ghosts, I'm sure."

The people all stared at each other for a moment longer, and when it became obvious the villagers had nothing else to say, Elliott put his arm around Seija and led her away.

"Guess we're off then." Tolbert nodded and we hurried away from the silent villagers.

"Ungrateful," Elliott muttered.

"Suppose we should tell 'em saltwater gets the slime off?" Tolbert glanced over his shoulder as we walked, probably making sure we weren't being followed.

Elliott snorted. "Let them figure it out on their own. Where are the horses?"

Tolbert whistled and before long their mounts cantered through the town toward us. "Seen worse than that ghost. Not much gets under their skin. Let's head back to town and get cleaned up. Reckon we can catch the train tomorrow."

Elliott helped Seija mount and soon we were headed toward the rail town, and hopefully shortly after, home.

"What do you make of Zoe helping them out?"

Elliott shrugged. "Isn't the first time I've run across a friendly ghost. I guess she didn't want to see her people killed."

"I'm just glad we're all safe. Elliott, you and Brown really are amazing." Seija tilted her head so she could smile at Elliott.

He tightened his arms around her. "Say, how long are you going to be here for? We haven't actually had a moment to really say hello."

Her grin widened. "I can stay as long as I want."

I could smell Elliott's happiness even over the ghost slime and he hugged her, careful of her injury. "Excellent."

Seija's smile matched his.

Asa touched noses with me. "You are amazing, Brown."

Wagging my tail, I brushed against him. "You're not so bad yourself, Asa. I'm glad you came back. Scoot, you did a great job too. I'll make ghost hunting dogs out of both of you."

❖ ❖ ❖

*Several Months Later*

"Seija, you look lovely," De, Tolbert's deputy, said as she finished fixing Seija's long hair.

"Thank you, you look wonderful as well." Seija glanced over her shoulder at De. "Thank you so much for all your help. I never would have managed this on my own."

De smiled. "You're welcome. There's a lot I'm not sure I got right, but Elliott will never notice. All he's going to see is you. It's just too bad you have to wear your disguise."

Seija giggled. "Elliott said that too." She stood and ran her hands down her dress to straighten it.

"I swore I'd never wear a dress again after I left the east, but I guess some things are worth it." The light colored dress contrasted nicely with De's dark skin and hugged her tall, fit frame in a way I knew humans liked.

Woofing, I tried to let them know I approved. Asa was off with Elliott so he couldn't translate for me.

De ruffled my ears. "Hasn't Elliott noticed your weight gain yet?" She addressed me, but Seija gave her my answer.

"We told him she was putting on an extra thick coat for winter and that he hasn't been working her enough. She wants to surprise him. For now he believes us. I think he cut back on her food but I've been sneaking her more."

De laughed and I put my paw up on her hand. "Men are clueless sometimes."

"Yes. And he has been distracted." Seija blushed.

De grinned. "I'm so happy for you Seija Tolbert." She smiled over the last name. We still used the story that Seija was Luke Tolbert's sister. It satisfied everyone well enough.

"He'll be here soon. Are you ready?"

Seija's grin lit up the room.

Hearing Tolbert's footsteps, I perked my ears and glanced at the door. Shortly we heard a quiet tap and De answered.

Tolbert, dressed in his uniform, stood on the other side and smiled. "You all look wonderful." He included me in his glance.

De had brushed my coat until it shone before fixing Seija's hair.

"Thank you, Luke. For everything," Seija said.

"Of course. Ready?"

"Yes." Seija stood.

Tolbert offered her his arm and we all filed out of the room together.

Fall was in full force, the air crisp and clean, the aspens a vibrant yellow—at least according to Elliott. I had yet to figure out what he meant by yellow. I heard my sheep *baaing* and saw a small group in the pasture near the cluster of people.

Tolbert escorted Seija and we followed. She held a small bouquet of fall flowers as did De. They'd even secured a couple of flowers to my collar. I heard a few surprised whispers about a dog walking down the aisle, but anyone who knew Elliott at all wasn't surprised.

Ahead, Elliott and Asa and Scoot waited for us with the priest.

Someone played a tune on a violin.

I could smell Elliott's nervousness from here. I didn't know why he was worried. It wasn't like Seija would change her mind.

We reached the end of the aisle and Tolbert gave Seija's hand to Elliott. They clasped their hands together and stood in front of the priest.

I wanted to go stand by Asa but I knew I was supposed to stay by De, so I did. Asa met my gaze and wagged his tail.

The priest droned on about something which I ignored. Finally he addressed Elliott. "Do you, Elliott, take Seija as your wife..." he continued on for a bit and Elliott said yes and repeated the words the priest told him to repeat. Seija did the same when he addressed her.

"Then I pronounce you man and wife. Congratulations."

They kissed and everyone cheered, and we barked and it was time for the party.

I'd never smelled Elliott so happy. I walked over to him and leaned against his leg. He ruffled my ears.

"Good girl, Brown."

I licked a few tears from his eyes and then he and Seija were whisked away.

Scoot, Asa and I went over by the fence and lay down to watch. Normally I would have worked the crowd for food, but I just wasn't interested.

"Are you hungry?" Asa gave me a concerned look.

253

"No."

"Are you sure? I could get you something."

"I'm fine," I snapped.

"Sorry." He wilted.

Huffing, I relented. "Sorry. I've just never done this before."

Asa wagged his tail, forgiving me.

"When do they come?" Scoot asked.

"Tonight, I think."

"Oh, good, can I come see them soon?"

I considered for a moment. My protective instincts warred with my friendship with Scoot. Friendship won. "Yes, but wait a short time."

"Thanks, Brown!" He wagged his tail excitedly.

The party went on into the night and I grew more uncomfortable. Finally, I got up and headed for the house.

"Are you okay?" Asa got up to follow.

I refrained from snapping a reply and merely grumbled.

He and Scoot followed, though Scoot said goodbye when we passed Tolbert. I circled around to the dog door and squeezed through.

"I called Seija. She's coming. She told Elliott she'd be back in a bit and left him with Tolbert."

"Good. It's time."

"Seija, what are you doing? You vanished hours ago. If you weren't enjoying the party, you could have said so." Elliott looked into the room Seija had prepared for me.

"Elliott, Brown has a surprise for you."

"What? Oh!" His eyes went wide and he stared at the puppies that snuggled against me, drinking their first milk.

254

Wearily, I wagged my tail. Asa sat anxiously next to me, staring at the puppies, obviously not sure what to do.

"I...You knew, didn't you?" Elliott sounded a little annoyed, but mostly amazed.

"She wanted it to be a surprise," Seija said softly, not taking offense at his annoyance.

"Can I come in?" Elliott's tone turned to awe.

"Yes, tell him to pet them so they know his scent right away."

Seija relayed my request and Elliott knelt at my side, carefully petting them.

"Bring the light over here please, Seija."

She did what he asked and I anxiously watched while he inspected my puppies.

"Brown, black and what color is this? It's hard to tell by lamp light." Carefully he lifted the puppy and held him close. "Blue? Brown, he's got antennae." Elliott glanced at Asa and laughed. "I suppose congratulations are in order, Asa."

The Plutonian dog wagged his tail but all of his attention was on the puppy that Elliott held.

"How many do we have?"

"Seven," Seija said. "Only two take after Asa."

Elliott laughed again. "I don't mind the antennae but that is probably just as well. How are you doing?" He put the puppy back in its place and sat on the floor next to me.

"She says she is fine," Seija relayed.

Elliott gently stroked my shoulder. "Good girl, Brown. Congratulations on your puppies."

I licked his hand and lay back down, exhausted.

"I think Asa can let us know if she needs us," Seija said, standing and holding out her hand. "Shall we leave them be for the night?"

When I didn't object, Elliott grinned and let her help him to his feet.

"Good night, both of you," Elliott said before wrapping his arm around Seija.

She laughed when he scooped her off her feet and cradled her in his arms. They kissed and he carried her away.

Asa lay down next to me and licked my cheek. "I told you he would be happy."

Grinning at Asa, I answered. "Yes, but I was still worried." I nuzzled each puppy before settling again. They were all fine.

"I will keep watch while you rest."

"Thank you. I wonder if they will want to herd sheep or fly space ships when they grow up."

Asa woofed. "Probably everything. Any job their people need to do, they'll be the dogs for the job."


The End

# About the Author

Julie has been many things over the last few years, from college student, to bookstore clerk and an over the road trucker. She's worked as a 911 dispatcher and in computer tech support, but through it all she's been a writer and when she's not out riding horses, she can usually be found sitting in front of her computer. She lives in Colorado with her three cats, her vampire-hunting dog, Kira, her Traveler in Training, Triska, and her Irish Sailor. She is the author of many Vampire and Ghost-Hunting Dog stories and the young adult urban fantasy series The Clanless as well as the Tales of the Travelers young adult fantasy series. She's a member of the Horror Writers Association and the Dog Writers of America Association and the editor for Steampunk Trails fiction magazine. You can find out more about her at her website: www.writerjacampbell.com.

# Other Works

Tales of the Travelers
- Sabaska's Tale
- Sabaska's Quest

Doc Vampire Hunting Dog
- The Moths of Miller Place
- Camping Tales

Into the West

Sky Yarns
- Serpent Queen

Clanless Series
- Senior Year Bites
- Summer Break Blues

Appearing in Various Anthologies
Brown Ghost Hunting Dog
- Brown and the Saloon of Doom
- Brown and the End of the Line
- Brown Goes Full Steam Ahead
- Brown and the Sand Dragon
- Brown vs. the Martians
- Brown Takes to the Skies
- Brown and the Lost Dutchman Mine

Various Short Stories
- Darkness Taken - Dragonthology
- The Baron and the Firebird – Happily Ever Afterlife
- The Martian Menace of 1897 – Science Fiction Trails 11
- The Life – Six Guns Straight From Hell (Written as Dakota Brown)
- Doc Vampire Hunting Dog, Sheep Interrupted – These Vampires Don't Sparkle II

To Anna, horses were more than a fascination, they were everything. Luckily, she had the opportunity to spend every summer on her grandmother's horse ranch in Colorado. Life was perfect, until she received the devastating news that her grandmother had been tragically killed. Anna knew she was the only member of her family who could take over the ranch and hopefully find new homes for her grandmother's beloved Arabians.

Anna wasn't alone for long. Her grandmother had hired a local teenage boy to help tend the horses for the summer. Anna didn't stand a chance against Cody's quiet charm and the two rapidly become friends. however, even with the responsibilities of the ranch, Anna quickly discovers the secrets her grandmother had been hiding and a legacy that sends her on an adventure she never thought possible. An adventure in the saddle of a horse that wasn't a horse at all. Sabaska, her grandmother's favorite Arabian, was a Traveler; a magical being that could travel between worlds. With Anna at the reins, they find themselves trapped in a fight against evil with the highest of stakes... Their very survival.

Edited by J.A. Campbell
Published by Science Fiction Trails
The second issue of Steampunk Trails brings a world
of steam and airships and clockwork contraptions within
your grasp. Discover kidnaping schemes foiled, mutinies
thwarted and what happens when the spring has sprung in
a clockwork heart. Fly through the air with smugglers and
pirates and honest captains. Read as legendary feats of
human strength overcome soulless machines, and machines
with souls protect their owners. Discover the true story of
the Great Airship of 1897 and encounter some really short
fiction all about fog machines. O.M. Grey, Peter J. Wacks,
Lyn McConchie, David Boop, Jessica Brawner, Eric Aren,
Jeffery Cook, Katherine Perkins, Liam Hogan, Henry Ram,
and more fill this issue with tales from all over the world
and adventures sure to get your heart racing.

46100530R00148

Made in the USA
San Bernardino, CA
25 February 2017